Angela's ARM

ROLAND ALLNACH

Angela's Arm

Copyright ©2018 Roland Allnach

ISBN 978-0-9967854-4-0 (Print edition)

ISBN 978-0-9967854-5-7 (eBook edition)

Book design by StoriesToTellBooks.com

Tabalt Press
PO Box 354
Kings Park NY 1175

Other books by Roland Allnach

Remnant (2010, sci-fi)

Oddities & Entities (2012, horror and supernatural)

Prism (2014, short stories)

The Digital Now (2015, sci-fi)

The Writer's Primer (2015, non-fiction)

Oddities & Entities 2: Vessels (2016, horror and supernatural)

Award Recognition

Foreword Reviews Book Awards (*Oddities & Entities*)
National Indie Excellence Awards (*Remnant, Oddities & Entities*)
USA Book News Best Book Awards (*Remnant, Oddities & Entities*)
Readers' Favorite Book Awards (*Remnant, Oddities & Entities*)
Pacific Book Review Book Awards (*Oddities & Entities, Prism, The Digital Now*)
Feathered Quill Book Awards (*Remnant, Prism*)
Book Excellence Award (*The Writer's Primer*)

"I found The Digital Now *to be completely enthralling, terrifying, and unique."* Pacific Book Review

"Allnach has a voice that speaks so loud readers lose themselves in the stories...A dazzling collection." Feathered Quill Reviews, for *Prism*

"If you only read one book this year, make it this one." Readers' Favorite, for *Oddities & Entities*

"A nearly perfect gem of sci-fi." Foreword Reviews, for *Remnant*

Angela's ARM

I

‡ ‡ ‡

Angela was first known as a dream, a notion within a name before she was yet to exist in form. When she came to be, she remained a mystery to the world outside her mother's womb, and so too she existed as a mystery to the muffled world of noise that would soon greet her. There she hid, a little fetal ball nestled in a close space of soothing darkness and maternal warmth, her shape, her countenance, and her thoughts nothing more than a budding trinity of potential.

So she grew, and the looming, lurking question of her destiny curled around her much as the selfsame character of query might exist on a blank page.

Nine months. In the span of a life, a mere blink of inconsequence.

Too soon the time came. The soothing darkness contracted about her like a rhythmic, crushing vice to purge her from the serene warmth that had formed her sole impression of existence.

Like so many before her, she greeted the world with a cry, a cry of pain for the rigors of delivery, a cry of anguish for the unknown bliss now lost, a cry of defiance to show the world she was alive, she was present, and she was real.

Yet her cry was not alone, for the first sound she heard was also a cry. It was the cry of those who were her first witnesses, the cry of those who had waited upon her with such hope and elation.

But it was not a cry of those inclinations. No, they looked upon her, and their collective outburst became something quite different.

It was a scream.

‡ ‡ ‡

Reverend Nathan Purdy paced back and forth across the width of his austere sitting room, arms crossed over a slim, leather-bound book clutched to his chest. A long, black suit coat hung from his wide, bony shoulders to enclose the tight constriction of his body. His black pants were held in place by a gun belt around his narrow hips, and the silvery mass of a six-shot revolver existed as little more than a half-seen yet malevolent rumor beneath the trailing length of his coat.

The angles of his harsh face were drawn in sharp relief as he listened to the screams in the next room. Still he paced, jaw clenched, as the cries yielded to the sound of a newborn's squeal.

"She has come to us," he said under his breath, his eyes alight with anticipation. He ceased his pacing and looked across the stark white room to a plain wooden bench. Two young boys, mirrored in image by clothes and their connection as twins, met his stare. "Judah, Jonah, your sister has come to us."

The two boys looked at each other. They were small forms, very young, dressed in black and sitting against a stark white wall. They met Nathan's words with a bewildered gaze.

"Do you see?" Nathan said, staring deep into their eyes in turn. "The vision was true."

They replied with a dutiful nod, their little chins sinking into the folds of their maroon scarves.

The front door to the house swung open and allowed a chill wind to enter before a dour-looking woman leaned into the door to seal it shut. Mena Semenic checked the gathered mass of her dark hair and smoothed the length of her long black dress. "Reverend Purdy," she said with a respectful curtsy. She lifted her chin to stare down her thin nose at the twins. "Have you boys been good?"

They nodded once more as their collective gaze sank to the floor.

"Did you hear the cry?" Nathan said, stepping toward Mena.

"Clear across to my house. No wind could smother that holler."

Nathan clenched a fist and shook it at arm's length. "Because she's strong, Mena. That's her strength you hear, a strength that has earned its right to be heard. Listen! That's not the cry of some weakling wait. The blood in her runs fierce." His eyes bulged as he pronounced each word with conviction.

Mena looked at the closed, white door of the birthing room. "Have you seen the child?"

Nathan glared at her for using the gender-neutral reference. The reference wasn't enough to say she doubted his vision, yet it was enough to needle him. Mena had a way about her, something her husband, Ivan, was too slow to perceive. Nathan regretted not taking her as his own, but he was master of his flock and he had to maintain appearances. Even so, he knew there was no denying his desire for her tenacity.

He tapped a thumb against the leather-clad book clutched to his chest as he wandered among his thoughts. Mena didn't waver under his scrutiny nor flinch at an unexpected cry from the next room. Perhaps, he wondered, behind her stolid gaze she reveled as recipient of his tight focus.

He let a crooked grin play across his lips.

Jonah and Judah kept their gazes on the floor between their dull black boots.

"I will see my daughter now," Nathan said at last. "Tell Ivan to keep watch outside. I need to speak with Doc Connors."

"My blessing to your child." Mena glanced at the twins to be sure they were still staring at their boots before reaching out to Nathan's hand. She gave his fingers a firm squeeze as her thin lips drew up in a faint smile. "And my blessing to you," she added in a whisper before leaving.

He watched her go, his stare lingering on her as she walked across the dried brown turf toward her home. Even with her slender frame, she was unfazed by the cold wind tearing at the length of her black dress.

Nathan took a deep breath as his hand tightened on the book clutched to his chest. Ivan was a fool. A faithful fool, but a fool nonetheless.

‡ ‡ ‡

Nathan tore himself from the window to open the door to the birthing room. Ruth and Rachel, the young twin midwives, jerked to attention at his presence. Despite their subservient demeanor, they failed to conceal the bewildered cast of their eyes. "Reverend," they said in unison.

He raised his book to his shoulder. The sisters retreated to a corner of the room, sank to their knees, and clutched their hands before their closed eyes.

The room was silent but for the low, deep breathing of his wife's exhaustion. Her limbs were still bound by leather straps. Her wrists were red and swollen where they were tied to the iron head rail. The toe pads of her cloven feet poked out beneath the soiled, white birthing sheets covering her flaccid form, but the soft pelt of black fur coating her ankles saved them from injury. Strands of long black hair, the loose curls soaked and matted with sweat, clung to her cheeks and forehead.

The child rested at her side, bundled in a white swaddling cloth.

Nathan moved to the bed. Before inspecting the now quiet babe, he rested a hand over his wife's head and muttered beneath his breath. His words were indecipherable, but his voice summoned the return of her conscious mind. Her eyelids parted to reveal the featureless black orbs of her gaze.

"It's what you saw," she whispered, her voice weak. "It's a girl."

He laid a finger over her parched lips. "Rest now, my sweet Calliope." He leaned over to press his lips to her forehead before moving back to regard the baby. With his book still clutched to his chest, he used his free hand to undo the swaddling cloth, fold by fold. The child bucked as cool air hit her skin, and two tiny feet kicked free. They had ten toes and were normal by all appearance.

Rachel's head lifted. "Reverend, I have to warn you . . ."

"Be silent," he ordered, pointing at her with a stiff finger as his scrutiny held on the baby.

Rachel shifted on her knees before squeezing her eyes shut. "Forgive me."

He ignored her, withdrawing his hand to pull at the last of the swaddling cloth. The child's legs kicked in vain to recapture the warmth of the blanket, but it was not her legs that held his attention.

No, it was her arm, her one arm, for she had no left arm of which to speak, and her right arm defied the mundane human form.

It was no typical limb; instead, it coiled at her side like a pale snake, devoid of angular joints. The sinewy length of flesh ended with an enlarged hand possessing six long fingers spaced at even intervals about the palm. Exposed to the October chill permeating the house, the arm wriggled, thrashed, and then moved with an apparent mind of its own. It slithered across the newborn's plump, pink flesh to grab the loose ends of the blanket and pull them closed.

The child calmed in the warmth of its body. The hand lifted. Though it appeared to hang loose at a wrist it did not possess, it swung to and fro as if it searched for something more.

Nathan watched, intrigued.

The fingers closed, the hand holding for a moment before turning its knotted fingers toward Nathan. His breath seeped from his lungs in anticipation. The moment his body's warmth hit the hand, its fingers snapped open to reveal the palm.

Nathan recoiled, unable to restrain his body's instinct.

A single green eye stared at him from the center of the palm, its large orb fixed on him until the hand snapped shut and darted under the blanket.

Nathan gasped with excitement. "Behold this child," he said, his voice quaking. "Behold this miraculous child. Behold our beloved Angela!"

2

‡ ‡ ‡

Out in the main room, Jonah and Judah peered through the open door. They turned to each other before looking toward the floor once more. So they sat until Ruth and Rachel emerged from the room and closed the door.

"It's a girl," Ruth said, keeping her voice low.

Rachel nodded. "It's just like the Reverend foretold."

The boys exchanged a glance, their faces blank, before looking at the midwives. Their stare did not rest on the faces of the twin sisters.

Ruth sighed and nudged her sister forward. They went to the bench, the boys popping to a stance as the sisters neared. Ruth sat by Jonah, while her twin settled by Judah. Without a word they unbuttoned their heavy gray sweaters, untied the breast flaps of their white cotton shirts, and welcomed the boys into their laps. Eager with hunger, the boys clutched the sisters as their heads sank to suckle.

The sisters let their heads rest against the wall as the boys nestled to them. A thought drifted through the cool air, one they shared in their two-fold twinning, a thought so innate it seemed more a voiceless, indelible impression.

We are one, we are together, and we are forever.

‡ ‡ ‡

Nathan was wrapping Angela in her swaddling cloth when Doc Connors emerged from the back washroom. He was a burly fellow, his rotund mid-section accentuated by the white apron tied over his clothes. With a rumbling humph from his barrel chest, he drew Nathan's gaze away from Angela.

"I know you want to see it," Connors said over the metal basin held in his beefy hands.

Nathan peered into Connors' brown eyes. "Your impression?"

"It's afterbirth," the doctor said with a matter-of-fact tone. "No signs of hemorrhage, the border is intact, color looks good." He shrugged. "But that's just a clinical impression. You can look at it for yourself."

Nathan pointed to the dresser away from the bed. He waited for Connors to set the tray where indicated as he stared at Angela. Only when Connors backed away did Nathan move to the dresser. His eyes narrowed as Connors reached inside his apron to pull a cigar from his vest.

"I won't have you foul her first breaths," Nathan hissed.

Connors glanced at the cigar. He chewed his lower lip before closing his eyes and running the length of the stogie between his bushy mustache and bulbous nose. With a sigh of distinct pleasure, he returned the cigar to his vest and opened a hand to the dresser. "Well then, have your look."

Nathan rolled his shoulders back, lifted his head high, and stared down his nose into the tray. A moment passed, then two. He extended an open hand over the placenta and closed his eyes. Veins bulged between the sinews of his knuckles as his jaw clenched, his other hand squeezing the book to his chest. His lungs swelled with a breath, his face reddening as he held it, held it, and then let it burst forth. He fell back a step as his eyes popped open, glazed and dilated.

Connors studied him. "Well?"

Nathan's face bunched with an involuntary reaction of disgust. "I will love her," he whispered. "And she will only know to love me after she learns to hate me. Yes, hate me she will, hate me as she will hate no other."

Connors pulled at his chin. It was clear he knew better than to make a sarcastic retort to Nathan's grim proclamation. "Do you think we'll have to bury this one?"

Nathan's eyes flashed. "No, you heathen."

"Fine by me." Connors hesitated a moment before nodding. "I've dug enough of your little holes out there."

Nathan ignored him. "Get out. And take the tray with you." He let his gaze settle on Angela's sleeping form. "The sisters need their protein to make good milk."

‡ ‡ ‡

Nathan waited to leave his wife and daughter until he heard the metallic scrape of the tray on the wood floor outside the room. He opened the door to find Ruth and Rachel with their shirts still open, their breasts dangling free, as they huddled on hands and knees with Jonah and Judah around the tray. The boys held back the loose ends of the sisters' sweaters as the midwives jostled heads in their desperate drive to lick the tray clean.

All four were too preoccupied to notice Nathan's presence.

He cleared his throat.

The sisters snapped upright, staring at him in surprise, strings of bloody drool dangling from the thick red smear about their mouths. In the frenzy of their feast, the neat buns of their hair had become disheveled. Several strands were caked to their cheeks. A few longer strands clung to their nipples, still glistening with the boys' saliva. Without a word Ruth pulled Rachel close so they could lick their faces clean.

The boys grunted as they struggled to cover the sisters' breasts.

"You are not to be ashamed of your nature," Nathan said with a stern tone. "But that's no excuse to abase yourselves like craven scavengers. Clean yourselves and tend to my family."

"Yes, Reverend," the girls said in unison. They grabbed the boys by their collars and dragged them to their feet to lead them into the back washroom.

Satisfied, Nathan left the house. Only then did he feel the deep thumps of his heart as it beat within his chest. He was, in that moment, a very satisfied man. He knew what he wanted, and so it came to him with little surprise that he was walking with long, determined strides toward the Semenic house.

The sun had almost set and the day's last light came as a broad yellow slash across the horizon, leaving the house as a dense, featureless black outline. A quick glance over his shoulder revealed the dark dome of night behind him, punctuated by the milky glow of the moon's slender crescent.

His face grew taught.

The rap of a hammer caught his attention. He turned forward to see Ivan's broad shadow emerge from the inky pool of the backlit house. The man was carrying a large board studded with dulled spikes from old railroad ties.

"Pardon me, Rev," Ivan's disembodied voice called out. "But you mind givin' me a hand with these? The stars are out already. Won't be long before them stargrazers come by. Don't want them knockin' in the doors again when they scratch up against the house."

"Then you best maintain your watch tonight."

"Wouldn't mind some company, Rev," Mena's husband said before grunting under the load of another studded board.

Nathan ignored the man with a dismissive, sidelong glance. As he let his long strides carry him to the front steps of the Semenic porch, Ivan dissolved into the shadows behind him.

Inside, Mena looked over her shoulder when the front door creaked open. Nathan stood in the foyer, book clutched to his chest, his gaze locked on Mena where she stood in front of the kitchen washbasin. Slick bubbles of soap slid down her forearms. There wasn't a sound between them other than the dull thuds of Ivan's work.

Mena tipped her head back. "Your child?"

"She sleeps." His long thumb caressed the worn leather of his book.

"And your wife?"

"She sleeps with my daughter."

"Did you examine the afterbirth?"

He took a breath. "It is as I expected it to be."

"And are you satisfied?"

His jaw clenched. "It is as I expected it to be," he said, straining to keep his voice even.

"I see." She raised an eyebrow at another thump from Ivan's labor. "Then that's that." The corner of her mouth lifted. She turned to the basin.

He took another step.

She planted her hands to either side of the basin table. Her reflection stared back at him from the kitchen window.

Once, in what seemed to be a dream from some far distant time, they had found themselves in a precipitous moment between the abyssal allure of temptation and passion. For reasons long kept hidden between them, they had retreated from that ledge, a mutual, figurative, hand-in-hand retreat from something that gaped beneath them in brooding shadow. They had framed the moment of their retreat with a promise, a deal between their aspirations, a sacred vow beneath the lofty portent of their grand ambitions to hold the line between them until the whisper of premonition was at last fulfilled.

So ran Nathan's thoughts in a dash of quicksilver grace, supple and sultry with the images they burned into his mind's eye. He went to her, went to her where she waited by the sink, ever rigid in her discipline. While others found her cold and distant, he found her desires as treasures buried deep within, reserved behind veils of caution and restraint. His journey to her core was a compulsion he found well worth the effort, for he knew full well she looked upon him and saw a creature far too similar to her own nature.

In simple terms, it wasn't a matter of if, only a matter of when.

He had his Angela. Calliope, his wife, had served him well. He had read the afterbirth and embraced the horror it foretold.

The matter was decided. The End Time had begun. Restraint had become a meaningless word.

He went to her with measured steps. No, there would be no mad dash, no frenzied pulling of clothes, no pants or gasps of passion to give away their moment. Just as they hid their nature, so too they would hide their collision in a collusion of deceit and so keep their promise true.

They were firm people of austere emotions. There was no need to speak. He put his book on the kitchen table and leaned against her back. Her eyes slid shut, her knuckles blanched with the vise-like grip of her hands on the edge of the table. He rested his face on her neck and pulled up the length of her black dress.

He opened his eyes only once. Ivan was hammering a board in place. Nathan made a point of matching his thrusts to the bang of Ivan's hammer. It was a despicable act of contempt, supercharged with the decadent rapture of deceit.

He looked at Mena's reflection.

Her eyes remained shut over the black circle of her open mouth.

‡ ‡ ‡

The rap on the Purdy's front door sounded through the house as night assumed its mantle over the land. Among the darkened rooms, the only sign of life was the low rustle of Calliope's breathing as she slept. She was flat on her back, her limbs splayed around her where her husband had left them after undoing her bindings. Across from her birthing bed, Ruth and Rachel had brought in a simple crib Ivan had built years earlier from a set of wood planks. Within its protective depth Angela slept in her swaddling cloth atop several blankets.

Nathan opened the door to the room. Neither Angela nor Calliope stirred, but Angela's arm popped out from the cloth. The long fingers folded back to reveal the glaring orb nestled within its palm.

Nathan stared into the little hand.

The little hand stared back at him.

The room was quiet. A cool wind sighed across the roof.

The hand closed and withdrew.

Nathan lingered, his thumb caressing the binding of his precious book before he took a breath and left the room.

Not a heartbeat had passed after the door clicked shut than the hand emerged once more. The fingers popped open so the eye could stare at the door. After a period of delicate scrutiny, the hand turned to look down upon Angela before working itself free of the swaddling cloth and her body. Pink tendrils of tissue wriggled where its length had merged with her shoulder. The eye looked back and waited until the flesh congealed to form a pointed tail. Only then did Angela's arm move, coiling its body to spring from her crib onto Calliope's bed and then spring once more onto the windowsill. There it perched, stabilized by the pads lining the inside of its fingers.

Its eye roamed. It watched Ivan as he sat on the front porch, a shotgun across his lap as he fiddled with a harmonica. A candle was lit in a room above him, and Angela's arm watched as Mena undressed and changed for bed. It looked toward the now-darkened kitchen window where it had spied on Nathan and Mena rutting against the kitchen washbasin.

Its thoughts were images, just as Nathan's impressions of the afterbirth were images. It didn't know if Nathan sensed its awareness in the same way it could sense his thoughts. To Angela's arm, the question held no meaning. It knew what it knew and held no query regarding the source.

The eye darted away from Mena as the house shook with a thump. Ruth and Rachel had chased Judah and Jonah to the Semenic's home, so it couldn't be the boys' wrestling that jostled the house. No, what the arm saw was something quite different.

Five lumbering beasts sauntered out of the darkness between the Purdy and Semenic houses. Ivan stood on his porch. The beasts resembled long-horn cattle except they were gargantuan in size. Their horns reached a full ten feet to either side of their heads before curling upright, and the furry brown mounds of their shoulders reached to the second story windows of the houses. Featureless black eyes glinted beneath the stars as they moved along, their massive hooves impacting the ground with seismic force. In no rush, complacent in the peculiar way of grazing cattle, the land leviathans came to a halt to look over the two houses. One by one their heads sank to regard the single green eye staring at them from a window of the Purdy house.

The eye blinked.

One of the stargrazers bobbed its massive head before looking at its fellow stargazers. They lingered for several moments before resuming their march.

Angela let out a cry.

The hand turned from the window. Its home was hungry. Ruth and Rachel would be coming into the room. It was time to return.

Angela's arm coiled against her, its tail splitting to attach to her shoulder and merge with her flesh. For Angela it was a thoughtless contentment to once again be whole. She cried to be fed, but her cry lost its lonesome wail.

3

‡ ‡ ‡

Nathan sat on the edge of his bed, peering out the window at the morning sun. From beyond his closed door, he heard the occasional clatter of pots and pans in the downstairs kitchen as Ruth and Rachel prepared a breakfast. Ivan's voice carried from outside as he called orders to Jonah and Judah to help remove the stud boards protecting the two houses.

Nathan was sure Mena was at her basin, working in her own kitchen.

It took a moment before he perceived the smile on his face.

With a grunt he rose from bed, went to the corner of his bedroom, and washed his face. He braced his hands to either side of the basin and stared in the mirror. A silvery bead of water hung from the end of his nose. The angular features of his face sharpened as his skin drew taught.

It was going to be a tricky day.

‡ ‡ ‡

Judah and Jonah were busy with their rakes, smoothing out the imprints of the stargrazers' hooves, when the sound of a horn reached their ears. They turned in the direction of the note and stared for a moment before dropping their rakes and running in opposite directions, Judah to their home in the Semenic house and Jonah to the Purdy home.

In a matter of moments, the porches were astir with activity. Rachel and Ruth came out from the Purdy home and waved for Judah and Jonah to join them. Doc Connors sank into a chair at the far end of the front porch and lit a cigar. Ivan and Mena stood before their front door, Ivan leaning on the railing of his porch, while Mena stood motionless behind him, arms crossed over her black dress. Her eyes darted between Nathan and the source of the horn blast.

Nathan patted a thumb on his book as he settled it to its usual position against his chest. His other hand dangled at his side where his long black coat hid his holstered revolver. He ordered the twins inside with a quick motion of his eyes. Judah poked his head out from behind Rachel to have a look before Ruth waved him toward the door, her other hand keeping a firm grip on Jonah's shoulder.

Nathan waited until the door closed before looking back when he heard another blast of the horn.

Doc Connors chuckled as he tapped some ashes from his cigar. "You'd think the man was afraid something might come out and bite him."

Nathan ignored the insinuation. A visit from Woolly Ben was never a laughing matter. Nathan came down the front steps and waved to the line of twenty horsemen riding abreast as they neared his home. At the middle of their line, in the lead, sat Woolly Ben. In the flesh. Woolly Ben was an oddity of his own, the son of a Chinese immigrant and a statuesque Danish duchess. He stood just shy of six feet in height; his height accentuated the length of his thin face and sunken cheeks beneath the slight taper of his dark eyes. He also kept a sparse mustache and beard, and his black hair hung from beneath the wide brim of a brown hat to sweep over his narrow shoulders.

Nathan knew the man under his real name, Wu Li Benjamin. It was Ivan's sense of ignorant humor that condensed the moniker to Woolly Ben in light of his beard and the length of his hair. Although Ben was known as a rather stoic fellow, he nevertheless took a liking to Ivan's wordplay and the name stuck.

Ben and his escort were in no rush. As they neared, Ben rested his little salutary brass horn across his lap and waved to his side. The riders behind him split off toward the Semenic house, where Ivan moved to help them unload the parcels slung across the backs of their mounts. As the escort peeled away, they revealed an extra horse with an empty saddle, trailing on a short length of rope behind Woolly Ben's mount.

Ben slouched in his saddle with a world-weary gaze. He waited, engaging Nathan in a tense staring match until Nathan tapped his thumb against his book and took a step. Only then did the corner of Ben's mouth lift in an almost imperceptible grin. It held there as Nathan made his way closer, even though Nathan made a point of not lifting his head to maintain the lock of their stare.

"Good to see you," Ben tipped his head and sat up straight.

Nathan crossed his arms over his chest. "How are things outside the Range?"

"No greeting, just business? And here I was kind enough to personally deliver your scheduled provisions." Ben let go a sigh. "I should expect as much."

"If you expected it then you shouldn't be disappointed." Nathan took a breath. "How are things outside the Range?"

"Stable." Ben shrugged then hooked a thumb toward his escort. "A full stock of goods should tell you as much." He sat up straight in his saddle. "You know why I'm here. Did Calli deliver?"

"Her name is Calliope."

"No, her name is Callista. You changed it to Calliope after you brought her out here."

"She left that other name behind."

"Well, she didn't have a whole lot of choice in that, did she?"

"No." Nathan smiled in the face of Ben's disapproval. "No, she didn't."

Ben looked toward the Semenic house. "I see Ivan still does your grunt work. Mena looks as stern as ever. And I see you have those four-fold freaks still running after each other." His gaze fell to Nathan. "How long do you think you can keep this going?"

Nathan held his smile. He knew it was a loaded question, so he held his silence.

Ben glared at Nathan as he called out, "Doc, you ready to go?"

"I'll get my bag," Connors said.

Nathan's eyes closed when he heard the creak of the porch chair as Connors hurried into the house. Without realizing, the fool had betrayed Nathan's deception.

Ben tipped his hat back and swung a spidery leg over his horse to dismount. "Looks like I'll get some answers after all," he said with a know-ing little laugh. "I've been counting days since you came to town to fetch Connors. If you don't need Connors anymore, then Calli must've delivered. And if Calli delivered, there's a baby I want to see." He patted Nathan's shoulder as he walked by. "Congratulations on being a father—again. Nice to know you'll get to keep one instead of burying it."

Nathan fumed, but he held his silence—and his stance—as Ben headed to the house.

After a few minutes Doc Connors ambled by, waved at Nathan, and took the reins of the extra horse tied to Ben's steed. The cigar was still pressed between his lips. Without a doubt the lit cigar had been in the house. As they waited for Woolly Ben, Connors grinned, looked at Nathan, took the cigar from his mouth, and blew out a purposeful ring of smoke.

Nathan's eyes narrowed on the man before he turned away.

After several minutes, Woolly Ben emerged from the house. He stood on the porch, staring into his hat, the creases on his forehead building like waves ready to crash ashore until he rubbed his face. With a shake of his head, he came down the front steps and walked toward Nathan.

"Now you see," Nathan said as Ben passed by to take his mount.

"You know what I want, Nathan," the lanky man replied as he settled into his saddle.

Nathan lifted his chin. "I've seen what's to come."

"I won't be swayed with your prophet diatribe," Ben said with a wave of dismissal. "You know I'm a man of pragmatic concerns, all the way back from when we were boys. I want gold, silver, something, but not carnival freaks. You've had your experiment and your people all on my patience. We made a deal—gold for time. You promised me gold, promised me riches in an area of the country where no one else believes they'll find it. You told me it was your vision, and on the grounds of our long friendship, I decided to invest in that vision. That's our agreement. That's the plan, and that's the way it's going to be." He pointed at Nathan. "I only entertain my patience because of our long history, but that rope only runs so far. Don't force me to do something you will most certainly regret."

"You do what you need to do," Nathan said. "Don't worry about us."

"I'm not the one who has to worry.' Ben pointed to the windows of the birthing room "It's not my child at risk."

"I know."

"Don't forget it," Ben said in warning.

"Do you think I ever could?"

Ben stared at Nathan for several moments, his face blank. "It's a funny thing, to see a reverend's daughter born with a serpent for an arm. What do you read into that?"

"Anything," Nathan said with confidence. "Everything. Alpha to omega."

Ben hummed in thought. "I guess time will tell, won't it?" He lingered a moment longer then turned his horse and waved to his escort. He looked back at Nathan as his mount carried him by one of the massive impressions left by a stargrazer's hoof. "You mind explaining that?"

"I mind," Nathan said and walked back to his house.

"Time's counting, Reverend," Ben called out.

"And I'll be ready," Nathan whispered.

4

✝ ✝ ✝

Seasons passed across the Range in tireless march, in no different a way than the lumbering stargrazers. Angela matured with surprising speed, outgrowing her crib in several months' time. Likewise, Judah and Jonah experienced their own growth spurt, often groaning with the strain on their bones as they shot up to newfound heights. By Angela's second birthday she was tall enough to rest her forehead on Nathan's hip when he stood on the porch and watched Judah and Jonah work the land with Ivan, securing stud plates when the stargrazers grew near, raking smooth the massive hoofprints left in the creatures' wake, disappearing for extended hunting trips, and tending the expansive vegetable garden.

Angela spent her days between Mena and Nathan in the servitude of home schooling. Her young mind matured apace with her physical form. By her third birthday she could read, write, manage simple arithmetic, and found ways to be productive on the Range without constant instruction. She even took to giving orders to Judah and Jonah, the two mute twins nodding and grunting to her direction, provided she graced them with a smile and pecks on their cheeks.

Ruth and Rachel took no offense at the affection she showered upon the boys. After all, the sisters and brothers were betrothed twins. With Judah and Jonah grown to man-size, their day of recognition was not far off.

Angela's father ignored any mention from Calliope regarding a wedding celebration.

‡ ‡ ‡

While Angela found Mena humorless and her father strict, she neverthe-less caught the approval in their gazes when they thought she wasn't looking. Even Ivan, who, even at her young age, she knew was not the fastest think-er, took special interest to show her what he knew about taking care of the houses and garden.

It was her mother, however, who held a special fascination within her budding awareness. To say there was something wild about Calliope seemed both unfair and misinformed. Without a doubt her diminishing capacity for spoken interaction did little to help with those immediate suppositions, but Angela was quick to learn from her father not to make such mistakes. Free of hindsight comparisons that might otherwise amplify facile and false assumptions, Angela accepted—and loved—her mother as she was.

There was one other inescapable factor weighing upon Angela's impres-sions. And that, of course, was her arm.

It was at once both a part of her and its own creature, a twin of more primitive and yet more intuitive intellectual faculties. While Angela learned to write with her one hand, she often found it easier to take a pencil between the toes of her right foot and scrawl large block letters. The spidery fingers of her arm often revolted against her will when she sought to tame and train them for writing. Aunt Mena, ever the disciplinarian, seemed to relish whacking Angela's backside with a wooden spoon for the poor use of her hand, until her father one day caught Mena in mid-swing and grabbed her wrist.

Angela remembered the moment with stark clarity. There they stood, his hand clasped around Mena's wrist, their eyes locked, the spoon all but hum-ming in the air with the energy flowing between them. It was something Angela felt, something she knew without thought, for it reminded her of what she knew in relation to her arm.

There was something else as well that struck her in that moment, a vision too dim to comprehend that crept from her arm's thoughts into her own. What that vision held and what it might mean were two mysteries Angela decided were better left alone. Even though they failed to manifest in con-scious form, her arm tingled with dark portent.

It struck her, because fear was something new to her. The Range was her home, and everyone around her seemed possessed with an innate concern for her welfare. At the same time they never let her forget that she was part of their societal group and had to be a productive member. She saw and felt nothing but harmony in their social construct, so there was no reason for her to know fear.

One occasion changed that perception. Although the singular sight of her father and Mena locked like wind and rain troubled her, it paled in comparison to something that both thrilled and terrified her. It was the idea of invaders—Outsiders—coming onto the Range. Her young mind had never questioned the idea of other people, of people outside the Range, so the concept of meeting someone new set her curiosity ablaze. At the same time, the idea that people could come upon their homes with ill intent, that people who had no care for her welfare might grab her, congealed her blood to cold tar.

‡ ‡ ‡

One afternoon her mother came to the houses at a full gallop. It was an early return from her usual rounds on the Range. In a matter of moments her father and Ivan grabbed their lever-action repeating rifles, shotguns and ammo belts, and sped off on their horses. Mena, Ruth, and Rachel brought Judah and Jonah into the Purdy house with Calliope.

Angela raced up to her room. From her window she watched her father and Ivan disappear over the mound of a hill.

Long after they were out of sight, she sat at her window, transfixed. In some way it seemed a familiar moment.

In the hours of her wait, her trepidation grew to a suffocating constriction in her chest. At long last her father and Ivan returned at a casual saunter. Her father's face was its usual impassive mask, but Ivan bore a broad smile to match the two sets of extra saddlebags thrown over his horse. Angela raced downstairs to slap her arm around them in turn when they dismounted.

For all her joyous relief, the reunion was short-lived. Ivan scooped her up in one of his powerful arms and kissed her cheek, laughing all the while. When she went to her father, though, he welcomed her embrace, gave her a perfunctory pat on the head, and pushed her back with a gentle yet forceful arm as he called for Ruth and Rachel.

The twin sisters came around the back of the house, already on their horses. Mena ordered Angela back onto the porch, where Judah and Jonah paced anxiously at the departure of the sisters.

It was source for a new concern until Angela caught the sisters' eyes and found a wild, predatory gleam lurking in their gaze.

She wasn't sure why, but it drove her tightly into the protective fold of Mena's arms.

Her father and Ivan returned with the sisters after the sun had set. It was a rare thing for any of them to be out on the Range in the dark; her father had a strict rule forbidding nocturnal forays. Too dangerous, he said. A stargrazer, docile as the leviathan could be, was yet a fearsome force of Nature when panicked.

Big things are best left to themselves, her father had taught her.

The next morning the sisters slept late. While Mena made breakfast, the foreign saddlebags were emptied by Judah and Jonah and added to the provision stores. As to the night and what happened on the Range, not a word was spoken.

Big things are best left to themselves.

‡ ‡ ‡

The more Angela grew, the more she found her relation to her arm maturing in its own way. Some mornings she would wake to find her arm missing, only for it to slink back with some dead rodent in its grasp. Angela wasn't one for butchery, but she found either Judah or Jonah happy to provide that service. While they took care of her arm's catch, she would suckle from Rachel or Ruth and then eat her little prize.

Satisfied, her arm would coil about her with delight and wait to absorb the nutrients she digested. Although her arm was her own and a servile creature to her will, she also found it had its own sensibility, its own primitive intuitions, and a curiosity all its own. Some days she would let her arm go and then chase after it in the lands about her house. More than once, cresting a hill upon which her arm had halted, she found a lumbering mass of the stargrazers on the other side of the hill.

Just as her arm would stop and stare at the beasts, so too would the stargrazers stop and stare at her arm. Angela wondered if it was a mutual interest in the disparity of size or perhaps a mutual interest among unique creatures. Either way, when she walked up from behind the hill and came into the stargrazers' sight, they would stare at her, bob their heads, and then walk off.

She asked Ivan once where the beasts went at night. He said there was a small lake straight south from the houses where the animals rested their hefty masses in the comfort of water. Floating, he said, gave their tree trunk-like limbs a rest from their weight. There they would sleep, hidden from all but the stars that looked down upon them.

It painted a peaceful picture.

She wondered if there would ever be a night when she could slip away to sit with them at their hidden lake.

‡ ‡ ‡

There were many things Angela could do in her little world. Aunt Mena and her father had their demands during the day to teach whatever she was ready to learn, but her life wasn't all tasks. On days when she was set free from the usual routine, she ran with her mother out on the Range. It was impossible to keep pace, given Calliope's prancing legs, yet her mother would grunt with delight at the time they spent together and run circles around her if she fell behind.

Though her mother had lost all but a few rudimentary exercises of speech, she welcomed any opportunity to play with Angela. Her mother's favorite game was hide-and-seek, although it was more Calliope running over a hill, circling Angela's position, and then charging her from behind. She would scoop her daughter in her arms, crush her in a tight embrace, and adorn Angela's brown hair with sprigs of wild flowers.

When the afternoon sun wasn't too hot, her mother would crouch so that Angela could climb atop her back. It was a special treat, because in those times her mother would let loose the full speed of her legs. Angela's arm would coil around her mother's neck like a lasso, tight enough to keep Angela secure but not too tight to choke. The grasses of the Range would speed by as the wind pulled at Angela's short curls. Her joy seemed to spur her mother to even greater speeds, so fast that sometimes she outran Ivan's horse at full gallop.

In Angela's bedroom over the birthing room, she kept track of the seasons on her wall, using the thick pencil Ivan had given her. While it seemed Judah and Jonah could grow in visible jumps from one dawn to dusk, she found she grew at a more balanced rate. It drew little curiosity from her, as she knew no different. Her world was the Range, her life consisted of the few people of her relations, and even though she had learned much in her short time, she did not yet know enough to ask the larger questions lurking around her.

Until, that is, the morning she sat on the floor, took the pencil between the toes of her right foot, and marked off the end of her third summer.

Just as she did this, her father came to her room and stood in the doorway, his precious book held tightly to his chest. "Get dressed. We're going for a ride."

Her arm shot out from her bed and melded to her shoulder. "Where?"

His eyes narrowed on her until he decided to answer. "Thetis Springs."

5

‡ ‡ ‡

Father and daughter rode out from the houses and headed across the Range at no particular rush, as Nathan preferred to ride with his reins in one hand while he clutched his book in his other hand. Angela had donned the poncho Ruth and Rachel had made for her. The poncho, a long heavy garment with wide, interlaced rows of blue and white threads, along with her brown canvas pants, sleeveless white shirts, and black boots, formed the only clothing she possessed other than two plain black dresses, one for everyday wear and the other clean and pristine for dinners.

She liked the poncho, as it allowed her arm to move about without any obstruction. Even in a saddle her arm seemed to know when to hold on tightly so she wouldn't fall and when it could rest. It was a comfortable agreement, made more so by a soft leather glove, the palm cushioned to protect her hand's sovereign eye.

As usual her father held his silence while they rode. She didn't mind. He wasn't one to talk much, and when he did he was often straight to the matter at hand. What with him and Mena, her mother's steady loss of language, the mute exchange of glances with Judah and Jonah, and the rare talks with Ruth and Rachel, the only real chance she had for pointless talk was with Ivan. Her father made no effort to hide his opinion that Ivan wasn't too smart, and she often caught Mena's strained patience at some of Ivan's statements.

Be quiet; be dutiful. It was one of her father's dictates.

Smart or stupid, Angela didn't care. Ivan was good to her. When she had some free time, he even took her up in the milking basket he had made for the stargrazers. It was fun, swinging under the belly of a massive beast, and one day Ivan was happy to explain the process. He slung one of the udder's giant teats over his shoulder and fed it into an odd contraption strapped over his chest. It consisted of several rolling pins—taken from Mena's kitchen—tied to a band of leather wound over a small drum. He pushed the length of the teat between the rollers and a plate of wood wrapped in quilted cloth and then turned a crank attached to the drum. The device rotated, each rolling pin in turn coming down to press the teat and drive milk from its nipple.

She saw him use his invention several times before her curiosity gained enough momentum to let her ask about its nature. "You made that, all on your own?"

"Well, not quite," Ivan said between grunts as he worked the milking machine. "See, when I made it, I thought it lit up from my own head, but the Rev and Mena told me different. They said the idea came first from some fella named Perry Stalks or somethin' like that." He shrugged as milk squirted into the pail at his feet. "I don't know. Don't care, neither. My milker works just fine, if it's all the same."

She looked into the pail. The only milk she ever knew came from suckling Ruth and Rachel. "What does it taste like?"

"Go ahead and try some. Might as well. You'll be off the sisters' milk soon enough as it is. This is different, but it ain't like regular cow milk."

She looked up from the pail. "How do you mean?"

Ivan tipped his head to the massive body of the stargrazer over their heads. "Well, these gals are something different than regular cows. You wouldn't know, but out from the Range, only bulls get long horns. But our gals got horns like no bull would ever know. I guess it's from them wishin' to be left alone from the butchers' knives that took all their sisters." He reached up to pat the beast's belly. "That's all right by me. They're good girls, and that's all that counts in my care."

Angela glanced at the stargrazer's belly, for the first time contemplating the irresistible might of the animal's bulk. "I guess it would be bad if they got angry."

Ivan laughed. "Well, you know what they say about makin' the female types angry." He laughed again when he saw the confusion on Angela's face. "Guess Mena didn't teach you that one. It goes along the lines that hell got no fury like a woman's scorn."

Angela's arm shrank against her chest. Her hand popped open so its eye could glance at the body in whose shadow they hung. The eye turned to Angela before closing.

Ivan tipped his chin to her hand. "Got a mind of its own, don't it?"

"It's my arm," she said without a thought otherwise. "Does anything make them mad?"

"Our girls? I know they got a likin' for you, that's for sure," he said with a wink. He shrugged. "Other than that, and far as I know, nothin' but the smell of beef gets 'em riled up. Guess they know it's from one of their own that gave it up on the butcher's block. That's why we don't eat beef out on the Range. Nothin' but pork and chickens for us. But our gals don't mind the milkin', which is good." He pointed to the pail. "Go on, try some. Like I said, it's different than the sisters' milk. Mena uses it for makin' our cheese and butter."

Angela leaned into the pail and lapped up a taste. Fresh from the star-grazer, it was still warm like the sisters' milk, yet it was thick with fat. She stood and wiped her mouth on the back of her hand. "That's peculiar."

Ivan squeezed out another load of milk. "Pah-culiar good, or pah-culiar bad?"

"I don't know." She spat over the side of the milking basket. "I like the sisters' milk better."

Ivan grinned. "Well, if I had to be suckin' titties to get milk, I'd be drinkin' all day."

Angela didn't understand what was so funny. She laughed to be polite, given that Ivan had brought her up to the milking basket slung under the stargrazer. Even so, there was something about the joke she found odd.

Odd enough, she felt, that she decided to keep it to herself.

The following night over dinner Angela asked her father about Perry Stalks. There was never any talk about people off the Range other than Woolly Ben.

Her father stiffened. "What's this name? And why do you inquire?"

She explained her prior day with Ivan. "He said the man's name was Perry Stalks."

"Ivan's a fool," her father said with a sigh. "He meant to say peristaltic. It's a type of mechanical pump."

Angela's face fell. "Oh. I'll have to tell him tomorrow."

Nathan rested a hand on his book. "Don't bother. He'll just forget again."

She looked up from her plate. "Father, is there anyone else on the Range beside us?"

He stared at her for several moments. "The Eddingtons. They arrange for our provisions. Carl and Sarah Eddington, to be precise. And they have a son, Kyle."

Her arm dropped her fork, shook off the glove, and turned its eye to Nathan. Angela glared at her hand until it looked at her, closed its eye, and took up the fork once more. Only then did Angela turn back to her father. "Forgive me. I don't know why that happened."

"No matter," Nathan said and relaxed in his chair. He ignored Calli, seated at the other end of the table, and the fact that she was eating with her bare hands. "Is there anything else you'd like to ask me tonight?"

Angela thought for a moment. "May I meet these people?"

"One day." Nathan closed his eyes and let go a deep breath. "Yes, one day."

One day came sooner than she had expected. The conversation took place the night before he told her they were going for their ride.

‡ ‡ ‡

Out on the Range trees grew in far-flung stretches, with one grove just over the hill behind the Semenic house. It was fortunate that Angela's father spotted a tree just after noontime so they could stop in the shade and have lunch. They shared a waterskin, half a loaf of Mena's hearty grain bread, and several strips of jerked meat from Ivan's hunting. When they were done they sat with their backs to the tree and took some time to digest their meal.

Angela sipped her water. She was alone with her father. It was the only time he seemed willing to entertain her questions with any measure of depth. It was also the only time he let her call him Daddy instead of the much more formal Father. She understood. When they were home Father seemed to fit the way he walked, like he had a broom pole up his keester.

At least that was the way Ivan likened the description.

She smiled to hide her laughter. "Daddy, what's Fetus Springs?"

"No, not Fetus Springs. It's called Thetis Springs." He shook his head. "You're spending too much time with Ivan."

Her smile dissolved to a frown. "I like Ivan. Why don't you?"

"I have little patience for his stupidity."

"Aunt Mena said he's ignorant, not stupid."

Her father turned to her. "Do you remember the difference?"

"Ignorance is when you don't know enough to know different. Stupid is when you can't know enough to know different."

Nathan rubbed a thumb on the cover of his book. "Well said. Ivan is both."

"If you and Aunt Mena think he's stupid, why is he still on the Range?"

"You see how much work Ivan does for us. We live in an order, Angela. I'm sure you can see that." He pointed to the ants crawling over the bark between them. "See, even the lowliest creatures understand the necessity of hierarchy. There are workers, there are dependents, and there are masters. They all need each other. Hierarchies fail when these disparate parties forget they depend upon each other for survival. The workers work. The dependents support. The masters define purpose and direction."

Angela felt her arm tighten as she digested her father's words. "What am I?"

"You are the shape of the future."

She turned to him. "What does that mean?"

"All things pass, my child. Change is relentless." He dropped his hat on his head and stood. "We should go. You will understand these things in time."

She walked with him to their mounts. "Are these things just about us? What about Woolly Ben and these Eddington people?"

"You will understand in time," he repeated. He settled in his saddle and waved for her to mount.

‡ ‡ ‡

It was late afternoon when they arrived at an outcrop of sandy rock protruding from the back of a high hill. The spot was far past any place she had ever wandered, even when she rode atop her mother's shoulders and enjoyed Calliope's fleet feet at full gallop. She looked about to note her landmarks the way Mena, her father, and Ivan had taught her so that she would never get lost in the expanse of the Range.

A glance at the sun and her shadow gave her direction. Mountains far to the west. Rolling hills east and north. North led home.

South led to wider lands, treeless and empty. It seemed an uninviting stretch.

"Daddy, are we still on the Range?"

"Yes." He pointed ahead. "See the change in the land southward? The Range goes on for days of riding until it reaches our natural border."

"How would I know?"

"It's unmistakable." He looked at her. "It's a wide, rapid river with treacherous currents lurking beneath its placid surface. It keeps us safe. It keeps the Range our own."

She turned to either side. "No one comes here? How could we even know?"

"The Range once belonged to other people."

"What happened to them?"

"Woolly Ben and I drove them out, never to return. The Eddingtons helped." He tipped his head. "For the Eddingtons' assistance we entrusted them with guarding the eastern edge of the Range. They work the land so we can afford our provisions. They manage those transactions with Woolly Ben's people."

"With people outside the Range?"

"Yes, with people outside the Range."

"And the Eddingtons keep everyone else out?"

"Outsiders don't belong with us."

She remembered that strange day when her father and Ivan had ridden out with their guns. "Because of the hierarchy?"

He smiled upon her. It was a rare acknowledgment of open approval. "Yes, because they would upset our hierarchy. There is another reason, one of perhaps greater importance."

"Is it this place? Thetis Springs?"

"Yes. It's only for us." He closed his eyes for a moment. "Now, follow me."

6

‡ ‡ ‡

Angela and her father left their horses to chomp the grass as they went on foot around the outcrop. What confronted them left Angela agape. The outcrop, she came to see, was not a simple mass of rock stripped bare by Nature. What she saw looked more like the remnants of some violent act, much like she saw when Ivan plowed over the garden. Instead of fresh furrows of dirt, though, she could tell from the hard cake of the ground and the smooth slopes of its furrows that whatever transpired had happened many, many seasons in the past.

A broad trench ran straight away from the outcrop, its depth diminishing with distance in its southern reach. The outcrop was a mass of rock, stripped at the end of the deep trench where it collided with the hill. And a collision it seemed, for what she saw at the base of the trench was a mass of tortured, fractured, broken bedrock on a scale she had never witnessed. What drew her curiosity—indeed, her fascination—was the opening of a cavern into the hillside at the bottom of the trench.

She looked back to her father. He clutched his book to his chest and tipped his head for her to continue. Without a heartbeat's delay she clambered down the rough slope to the bottom of the trench and picked her away across the strewn boulders to stand at the mouth of the cavern. It towered over her head, and she could see that it had once been large enough to span the full width of the trench. Time and the weakened rock had conspired to collapse part of the cavern's mouth, leaving only a high, triangular gash into the darkness beyond.

She waited until her father came to her side. "Are we going in?"

"The springs are inside." He pointed to the shadows. "Once we're inside, your eyes will adjust. Don't worry about the darkness."

She spun, hesitated a moment, but then went into the cavern. After a few paces into the darkness, sheltered from the sun's warmth, the air was quite cooler. The air was also still, which she found odd, having always heard the ceaseless wind on the Range since her first memories. It fueled her fascination, so she pressed on, slowing as the shadows thickened and she had to take greater care not to trip over the loose rocks scattered about the floor. On it went, straight into the Earth. Farther from the cavern's mouth she was able to discern the consistent shape of the cavern, its length a smooth round bore at a consistent angle of descent. In several places the roof, at least fourfold her height over her head, had cracked and dropped debris in some bygone, forgotten time.

She stopped when she saw nothing but oil-black darkness ahead of her. "Daddy?"

His voice reached from behind her. "Continue."

Her arm trembled against her side. She fell back a step, then steadied her nerves, anchored her curiosity, and pressed on. It was hard to keep an idea of time between her careful steps and her mounting anxiety. Before long, though, it seemed that the darkness ahead diminished. She wasn't sure until she looked at the rocks at her feet and saw their back faces illuminated with a faint yet distinct light, while their sides, pointed to the cavern mouth, were left black. Looking past her shoulder, the cavern mouth was a tiny triangle of light far behind her father's shadow.

His voice drifted to her once more. "Continue. The light will guide you."

She pressed on. Soon she heard the tinkle of water, and she knew for sure they were far underground. One time she had helped Ivan and her father dig a well. Ivan had built a frame over the ground with a center stay hole through which he fed a spiral bit of metal and attached segments of pipe. Up and down they worked the bit as a team of horses turned the shaft in its center stay. They had kept at it until water at last bubbled up around the pipe.

The light grew as she moved on, becoming a milky twilight like that of the full moon. So too the sound of running water grew louder. Then with little warning the cavern swept out around her in a vast subterranean chamber. The bore continued its descent straight into the water, which formed a vast pool filling the chamber. Off to her right the water flowed with foamy turbulence into a black fissure of rock. Overhead, water dripped from random seams in the roof and fell to the water below, teasing its surface with little ringlets.

What caught her attention, though, was the water in the pool. Not only was it crystal clear, but she could tell it was deep, deeper than she could imagine or even guess, despite the fact that the water was the source of the weird twilight around her. She stared transfixed until her eyes adjusted to tell her something quite different. Down in the water, nestled on some shelf of rough rock, was the true source of light: a large, shattered metallic vessel that yet gleamed with life in its apparent ruin.

She spun and looked back along the cavern's length before turning back to the vessel. It lay in a straight line with the bore. Then it hit her; no matter its believability, no matter its fantastical nature, no matter its defiance of all reasoning she could summon, the ruined vessel was somehow responsible for the trench and the bore, and had found its final rest at the bottom of the cavern in a vast pool of groundwater. It was as if that tortured metallic pile of debris had hit the ground like some giant bullet—a bullet of indescribable speed and force—blasting its way to such depth.

Her mouth hung open, her jaw slack with wonder. She turned to her father.

He smiled and opened a hand to the pool. "Now you see."

‡ ‡ ‡

Angela stared at her father. "I don't understand."

"We can't explain everything in the world," Nathan said with a dreamy tone. "The irony of an enlightened mind is the ability to accept something beyond explanation on the indisputable veracity of its existence. And so, on this reasoning, we have Thetis Springs."

She looked at the waters. "This is ours? This is why nobody comes on the Range?"

"We keep it ours. It's why we don't allow anyone on the Range." He walked to one side and settled on a boulder. "The time has come for your baptism. Remove your clothes."

She stared at him.

"You won't be hurt." He held her stare. "None of us ever were."

Her arm coiled about her chest. It was a protective reflex. She followed her arm's intuition and fell back a step. "Everyone's been in the water?"

"Everyone except you. Now it's your turn."

When she failed to move, he took a breath, a breath that swelled his chest and was a sure sign of his growing impatience. "This is what defines us, Angela. We were once explorers looking for gold on the Range. A fierce storm came upon us. This cavern was the only shelter we could find."

Her throat went dry. "We?"

"Yes, we. Me, your mother, Aunt Mena, Ivan, and the five head of cattle we brought with us. In our curiosity we delved into the cavern, found the pool, and filled our waterskins." His hand constricted on his book. "It was a defining moment."

Her eyes narrowed in thought. "Five head of cattle. The five stargrazers?"

"Yes."

She looked at her arm. "Is this why I'm different?"

"We're all different. Some of us in ways we cannot see with the naked eye."

Her gaze darted back to her father. "My mother is different, different like I'm different. But you, Aunt Mena, Ivan . . . how are you different?"

Nathan's angular features settled into a stern mask. "I told you. We're different in ways that cannot be seen. Now, do as I bid. Disrobe and go into the water."

"What's it going to do to me?"

"That's up to you. It may change you. It might make you more of what you are."

She turned her body away from the water to protect her arm. "I don't want to change."

"Time will tell." He tipped his head. "Yes, time will tell."

She looked at the glowing vessel. "How many times do I have to go in?"

"Once. Never more than once, ever, in your whole life." His lips pressed together in a tight thin line. "There were two other men with us. They went in twice."

She kept her gaze on the water. "What happened to them?"

"They died horrible deaths."

"What did the water do to you?"

He smiled. "Go in, and then I will tell you." He studied her. "I love you, my dear child. I would never ask you to do something that would hurt you."

She felt her eyes drawn to his unblinking stare. Her arm pulled her poncho and shirt over her head and let them fall beside her. Next her suspenders were unbuttoned, her arm spiraling around her to work her pants down until they drooped over her boots. Still staring at her father, she sat on a rock and let her arm push off her boots and drag her pants free of her feet.

She stood and walked to the water's edge, her gaze still locked with that of her father. "

"Daddy?"

"Yes?"

"I trust you." She stepped in the water.

The rock ledge was steep and slick. Before she could steady her balance, before she could step back, her feet slipped from beneath her. The water enveloped her as her head went under, her bottom hitting the hard rock with a jolt of pain. She thrashed to right herself, but the rock ledge offered no traction and her struggles left her sliding deeper into the pool. Panic spurred her to cry out, only for water to gush into her mouth. By some stroke of luck, a combined kick of her legs drove her head above the surface long enough for her to cough and draw a saving breath. Her arm fled her, only to slam into her back as its length wriggled with desperation to keep her afloat.

Her father was shouting at her, his voice echoing in the cave.

"Calm yourself! Let the waters support you."

"Daddy . . ."

Calm yourself, calm yourself.

Let the waters support you, support you.

"Listen to my voice. Listen to its truth!"

"Daddy, please, help me!"

Calm yourself.

Daddy.

Listen to my voice. Listen to its truth, its truth.

Her thrashing eased. Her arm kept her afloat. She closed her eyes and listened to the echoes of her splashing. Her father was right. She had to relax, and so she did. Whether it was anxiety, trepidation, or faith that prevented her drowning, she had no care to discern among the calm that flowed through her as she floated on her back. Her arm took turns melding with her shoulder and wriggling against her back to support her until the serenity of buoyancy silenced her thoughts.

"Listen to the echoes," her father's voice spoke to her. "Listen to them as I once did. In the echoes the past and future overlap."

The water warmed around her. She could feel the warmth rising from the depths.

Listen to the echoes. In the echoes the past and future overlap.

The warmth was emanating from the glowing vessel beneath her.

The past and future overlap.

Her eyes popped open to the roof above her.

Past and future overlap, overlap.

A drop of water fell and hit squarely on her forehead.

She blinked. She looked at her arm. Its eye stared back at her.

Her strength fled in the bliss of the waters. It seemed she could stay there forever, adrift forever, dreaming until the end of her life, the end of Time itself, until all the world dissolved around her and there was nothing left but one glowing green eye and soothing echoes of prophecy.

The echo changed.

Come back, come back.

Her arm deserted her once more, thumped into her spine, and wriggled to drive her toward the water's edge. Feverish, flaccid, her body was useless. Her arm returned and then stretched its length to coil around her father's waiting hand. With his feet braced he dragged her from the waters to lay naked on the cavern floor.

She looked at him. "Daddy?"

He cradled her face in his hands. "Yes, I'm here."

"What's happening to me?" she said, her voice little more than a whisper.

"You're becoming your future. Your past came in, but only your future will leave."

She turned her face to his palm and struggled to form words. "What did it do to you?"

"I see things. Like the echo, I see how the past and future blur together. I see how they are one. I see how they can only be one."

He rested her head on the cavern floor, stood over her, and spread his long arms to either side, his book clutched tightly in his right hand. "I have seen your future, Angela Purdy, and know it to be true."

She stared up at him. He seemed larger than life, towering over her.

"You will change all that we know, my precious one. You will set our path in time, and in so doing you will summon ruin upon us all. Before it is done, you will learn to hate me and love me in the same breath, and in hating me the justice of ruin shall be levied against us. And what glorious ruin it shall be!"

Her dilated eyes widened upon him.

And what a glorious ruin it shall be, glorious ruin it shall be!

Her heart fluttered. Her arm dropped limp at her side, and she knew no more.

7

‡ ‡ ‡

Angela woke with a start to find the stars above her. After a frenzied moment of her arm swarming over her, she realized she was dressed and set out on her blanket roll beneath the night sky. An extra blanket was draped over her body. She sat up and found her father seated across from her, his face lit with eerie reverse shadows from the small fire crackling between them.

"I had to let you dry before I could dress you," he said. "The water. I can't touch the water." He held up his hand to show her the blistered flesh on his palm. "Just the dampness from pulling you out did this to me."

She stared at him. "Never go in twice," she thought aloud.

He nodded. "Yes, never go in twice."

"Why do you call it Thetis Springs?"

"Thetis was the mother of the mythical hero Achilles. She was a water spirit. She dipped Achilles in holy water and made him invulnerable, except for his ankle, where she held him." Nathan stuck out his pointer finger and jabbed the back of his ankle. "Achilles died from an arrow wound to that very spot. Do you understand?"

She nodded, her gaze falling to her arm. "The water gives, but it doesn't give everything." Her mind cleared around a sudden question. She looked at her father. "You said the water changed everyone. It gave you foresight. It gave my mother her legs. What about Aunt Mena and Ivan?"

Nathan poked the fire with his boot. "My childhood was steeped in apocalyptic Bible sermons. I wanted answers to the mysteries of the world. When I went into the water, I gained the power of foresight. Your mother was born with clubfeet. She learned to walk, but she was never able to run. It was the one thing she dreamed of doing. The water transformed her legs. Ivan suffered from asthma. He came out here for the clear air, but he remained sickly. He wanted nothing more than the health of his body. Now he never tires, and he can heal from the most horrendous wounds."

Angela waited as her father fell silent. "What about Aunt Mena?"

His jaw clenched, accentuating the angular protrusions of his cheekbones. "Aunt Mena was told she could never have children. In these lands no man can consider a sterile woman for a wife, no matter how much he might love her." He stared at the fire for several moments before his gaze returned to Angela. "All Mena desired was to be fertile. Ruth and Rachel grew out of her back. Judah and Jonah grew from her shoulders. She suffered greatly for them to live."

Angela nodded as her thoughts churned. "What about the stargrazers? Why did they get so big?"

"I bought them from a cattle farm outside town. Somewhere in their dim little brains, they must remember their sisters going to slaughter, and I imagine that sense of hurt sits not far from something so inherent to a cow's existence, and that is to be big."

"So the water gives what you want from it?"

"Perhaps." He was silent for a moment. "The stargrazers are just animals. They responded in a way an animal might respond to a threat, in ways that they know. And so they grew to their massive proportions. Though they're females, they grew horns dwarfing those of any bull they might encounter. In a life where might is right, their might is unique. Likewise, their anger is not to be tested."

"Ivan told me they don't like the smell of beef. That's why we don't eat it on the Range."

Nathan tipped his head. "Well, I must give credit where credit is due. Ivan is correct on that point." He took a breath. "Now. Does nothing else beg your curiosity?"

There was one question that still lingered in the air.

Angela had to know. "All of you—even the stargrazers—changed after you went into the water. I was different before I went into the water."

Nathan smiled. "Yes."

"Why?"

"Because you are the child of three forces of Nature—me, your mother, and the water that already transformed us. You were not yet baptized in its depths, but its glow already lit you with potential." He raised a hand to his temple and extended two fingers. "I saw it before you were born."

Angela settled back on her bedroll. The stars floated across the black dome of night. Despite her father's claims, she only knew herself as a single girl adrift in a mysterious world. Her father chose to look into those mysteries and call them prophecies. She rolled onto her side, put her back to him, and let her arm snake around to pull the blanket over her huddled form.

Her arm seemed intent to shelter her from something unseen. What its primitive instincts failed to recognize nevertheless stared back at her with stark clarity.

She closed her eyes. There would be no restful sleep.

She knew her father was hiding things from her.

Worse, her arm told her his words were steeped in lies.

‡ ‡ ‡

She woke early. Before her mind cleared she realized her arm was missing.

Her father stared down his nose at her as she bolted upright, her gaze darting about.

"It's here," he said. He patted her head as he walked by her toward their little fire. "Your arm has been busy," he said, showing her two skinned carcasses before thrusting each onto a cooking stake and holding them over the fire.

She looked up at her father, not paying her arm any attention as it snaked under her poncho and melded with her shoulder. The moment it was with her all thoughts disappeared behind a singular, towering sense of hunger.

Her father turned the stakes to cook the carcasses evenly. "Prairie dogs," he said without looking at her. "Not much meat, but these two were a good size."

"I didn't know I was so hungry."

"You knew on a different level." He glanced at her over his shoulder.

"How do you feel this morning?"

Her hand popped out from beneath her poncho and opened its eye. She stared at herself for several moments before looking up to her father. "I told you. I'm hungry."

"Have you ever thought to give it a name?"

"Did you give your arms names?" she said at once. Before she could be surprised by her spontaneous retort, she heard her voice once more. "My arm doesn't need a name. It's mine. I'm Angela, and my arm is Angela's arm."

He offered no response to her brazen attitude. Instead, he turned to her with one of the cooking stakes. When she took it, he sat and sniffed his own meal. "Indeed," he said.

"Are we going home today?"

"No. We're going to the Eddingtons."

"I want to go home."

"We will." Nathan took a bite of steaming flesh. "After we see the Eddingtons."

She stared at the rigid, lean form of her prairie dog. "Why did you take Ruth and Rachel out that night after you and Ivan rode off?"

He studied her for a moment. "Eat your breakfast," he said.

The morning breeze rustled the short curls of her hair. She looked into the rising sun and took a big bite of meat.

‡ ‡ ‡

It was early afternoon when they crested a hill and found the Eddingtons' house. There wasn't much surprise, as the creaky height of a windmill had caught Angela's eyes long beforehand. She looked at her father while their horses sauntered down the backside of the hill and across the brown, autumnal fields surrounding the house. It was a well built dwelling, its exterior boards weathered to a wintry gray as if to match the coming cold.

A man with a pail came out the back door, obviously headed toward the pen where two cows patiently waited. Nathan raised an arm in greeting and the man stopped and shielded his eyes with a hand from the bright sun before waving a reply.

Angela looked at her father. "I guess that's Carl Eddington, the father?"

"A fine man," Nathan said with a nod. "And he has a fine woman in Sarah."

"Then I guess their boy is double fine."

Nathan gave her a glance before looking back toward the house.

Angela said nothing more. For all the fire she felt to meet someone new, she had awakened that morning with a sour disposition that quenched all her social motivations. She couldn't care less for the Eddingtons or their stupid son. None of them had been in the springs, so what could they possibly know about her, much less her arm? No, she was alone in the world, alone with her father and the people she already knew, alone with all of them beneath her father's deceptions.

She turned to him. "Why are we seeing these people?"

"They're like Outsiders, but they help us. It's important you see them."

"I don't want to talk to anybody today."

"That's your arm talking, so I will forgive your insolence," her father said with a sharp tone. "It's less than a day since your baptism. Your body and mind will need time to adjust. For now, be silent, be respectful, and remember your manners."

Angela frowned. Her arm trembled as she tightened her grip on the reins. She could tell it wanted to bolt, to go off and hunt on its own, but she wouldn't let it. If she had to sit and stew, her arm would have to join her in the stewpot.

She looked toward the house when she heard Carl Eddington call his wife's name. After a few moments a woman emerged from the back door. She wore a long blue dress with a white apron, but what caught Angela's attention was the woman's flaxen hair, its length pulled back in a long braid that swayed across the small of her back in the passing breeze. The woman smiled, and Angela decided at once that Sarah had a warm, kind smile. It reminded her of the way Ivan smiled when she helped him with his chores.

Angela turned to her father. "What's with her hair?"

"Blonde," he said without looking at her. "Not everyone has dark hair."

"She looks strange with hair that color."

"Don't stare. It's rude. And remember what I told you. Part of why you're here is to observe and learn from what you see." He turned to her. "Strange is only a matter of perspective. Not everyone is like us. In fact, no one is like us."

She lowered her head. "Judge not lest you be judged."

"Very good. Now remember your manners during dinner."

They trotted the rest of the way to the house. Carl came off his back porch to take the reins of their horses. Sarah moved to help Angela, but Angela made a point to swing a leg over her saddle and hop to the ground before she would have to accept any aid. Dismounted, she could appreciate the woman's slender height. Not quite as tall as Nathan, and just a wink under Carl's height, but a tall woman nonetheless.

Angela was barely up to the woman's chest. She had to look up to meet Sarah's welcoming eyes and say her hello.

Sarah tipped her head. "And hello to you, too. What might your name be?"

"Angela Purdy, ma'am." She let her arm snake out from under her poncho. With her custom leather glove and the way she kept her sixth finger curled under the fifth, her hand looked no different than any other hand.

"Please, call me by name." Sarah smiled upon her. "And there's no need to shake hands, Miss Angela. Your father and I are cousins. We're all family here."

Without delay Sarah moved forward and embraced Angela. A sudden panic raced through Angela as she worried the woman would be able to tell that she only had her one arm. Back home she never thought of such a thing. Confronted with two strangers, with their two arms and two legs, lit a glaring awareness as to just how different she was with her one, independent arm.

To her relief, though, Sarah didn't make a single start of surprise as Angela's empty left shoulder was closed in the fold of Sarah's elbow.

The woman leaned back, cupped Angela's face in her hands, and smiled once more. "Nathan," she said without looking at him. "Why didn't you tell me you had such a pretty daughter?"

"Leave the man at peace," Carl said with a sigh. "It's a long ride across the Range between us and them. Enjoy the visit while we can."

"It is indeed a long ride," Nathan said as he let Carl take the saddlebags from the horses. "Time gets lost in the distance."

"Now there's an understatement," Sarah said with a little laugh before looking back at Angela. "You wouldn't care to tell me how long you've been a secret, would you?"

Angela blinked. She had the sudden sense that honesty would not be rewarded. "I've seen a few seasons. I don't keep count."

"Ah, the carelessness of youth," Sarah said in a singsong as she fixed a pointed stare on Nathan. "Are you so careless keeping track of my niece?"

"Twelve," he said and took his hat from his head. "If you must know, she's twelve."

Angela glanced at her father. The ease of his lie sowed its conviction.

"Well, now, forty-eight seasons, and about an inch for every one of them." Sarah let her gaze roll down Angela's height. She laughed and caressed Angela's cheek with the back of her hand before hooking her husband's arm. "Let's go inside. Carl has some chores to settle, and I'm cooking a chicken for dinner. Kyle's in the office, going over our books. I'll call him out so he can say hello."

Nathan glanced at Carl. "You handed the accounting to your boy?"

Carl grinned and tipped his head. "He's a young man, Rev. He ought to know a man's responsibility. And a man can't know a bigger responsibility than the duty to manage his affairs—business, family, and otherwise. I'm sure you can't take any offense to that, can you?"

Nathan folded his arm to clutch his book to his chest. "No, none at all."

8

‡ ‡ ‡

The house was filled with the delightful aroma of basted chicken, even with the fresh air blowing in from the open front windows. Sarah led them through the back door into the pantry, through the kitchen, and extended her arm for them to proceed onward to the spacious sitting room. Carl walked past them and pointed up the stairs hidden behind the partition wall separating the kitchen from the sitting room. The stairs creaked as the man ascended with their saddlebags slung over his shoulder.

Angela looked at her father, but he showed no concern. His calm was a clear sign that he was well acquainted with lodging at the Eddington house.

"Kyle," Sarah called from the kitchen over the squeak of the cast iron stove as she checked the chicken. "Kyle, put down your pencil and come out of that office. We have company. Reverend Purdy and his daughter, Angela."

Angela didn't realize her eyes had drooped shut as she took in the enticing smell of the chicken until she heard a distinct clop at her side. She blinked and looked over her shoulder to where the back of the sitting room held a closed door in the middle of its wall. The sound repeated two more times before the handle of the door turned with a click.

Angela's arm tightened against her. The clop came in the rhythm of a stride.

Was Kyle like her mother? Had her father lied about something of such import?

Could he lie about something of such import?

Trepidation clamped her breath in her chest, only for her breath to seep free as the door swung open to reveal a tall, young man. His body was somewhat askew as he leaned on a cane with his right arm. Despite the baggy length of his pants, there was no hiding the tortured, withered reality of his right leg or the fact that his right foot dangled in his shoe with the shortened length of the afflicted limb.

He cleared his throat.

Her gaze popped up to meet his eyes. She had been staring.

"Forgive me," she said, her voice creaking on her tightened breath.

Kyle smiled, a smile he had without doubt inherited from his mother, for it held the same disarming warmth. He shuffled forward, his cane clopping on the wood floorboards until it came down with a gentle shoop on the room's wide carpet. There was a visible easing of his countenance to be free of the accompanying sound.

He extended his arm to shake Nathan's hand. "Good to see you, Reverend." He let go of Nathan as he looked down on Angela. "And this, I assume from my mother's introduction, is your daughter, Angela?"

Angela swallowed as she tried to remember how her father had taught her to address a young man. It was a stern lesson from their Sunday dinners, when everyone on the Range sat at the Purdy table. Mena had once taken a spoon to her backside for forgetting to use the proper title for Judah and Jonah as young men.

She cleared her throat. "Pleased to meet you, Master Kyle."

"Master?" he said with a little laugh. He shifted his weight for a moment before settling on his cane once more. "Now, Miss Angela, how about we make an agreement right now—begging your father's permission," he said with a dutiful nod to Nathan. "Let's dispense with all the proprieties. We're all friends here, family to a degree through my mother and your father, so how about we just keep it to Angela and Kyle?"

Nathan headed for a chair. "You have my approval," he said as he passed between them. He settled into a cushioned armchair with a spontaneous sigh of satisfaction. "Yes, indeed, you have my approval. Kyle, you're a fine young man." He closed his eyes. "Now, would you be so fine as to fetch your godfather a glass of water?"

Kyle shifted his weight.

Angela gawked at her father before she could suppress the reaction. Awkward at once, she looked back at Kyle when she heard the first shoop of his cane on the carpet. She put a finger on his arm as she passed him toward the kitchen, but Kyle settled a firm hand on her shoulder. The strength of his grip surprised her, his fingers clamping into her shoulder as if he were a much larger man. Then again, she realized all his years using a cane had likely fostered an unusual degree of strength in his arms.

She looked up to meet his gaze. He gave a quick shake of his head. "He asked me," he whispered. He showed her his warm smile and proceeded to the kitchen.

At the first clop on the wood-slat floor, Sarah emerged from the walkway and handed her son a glass. Kyle nodded in gratitude and made his way past Angela to set the glass on the small table beside Nathan's chair. Angela's father showed no greater acknowledgment than to raise the finger of his right hand where it rested over his book, cradled to his right hip.

Kyle turned and made his way back to Angela. By the time he reached her, she didn't know which way to look or what to do to look occupied. She was left in the sitting room of a strange house, among strange people. If the abandonment of all things familiar and comfortable was what it meant to be with Outsiders, then she decided she'd be just fine on the front porch of her house with the empty expanse of the Range staring back at her.

"I think he's about to nap," Kyle whispered and indicated Nathan with a dart of his eyes.

Angela glanced at her father. Her arm coiled with wariness, her hand clutching the expanse of her poncho to draw it close about her narrow frame, her eyes on the view through the front windows.

Kyle leaned a bit to catch her gaze. "You can sit outside if you want," he said, his voice still low. "Or I can show you our library. It's in the office, so we won't disturb the Reverend. Would you like to see our books?"

Angela's eyes snapped onto Kyle.

He smiled. "Books it is," he said with a tip of his head and shuffled toward the office. He looked over his shoulder when he stood in the doorway, an expectant cast in his eyes.

She fidgeted for a moment, but she knew what she wanted. Without further delay she scurried past Kyle into the office and waited for him to close the door. "I only have a few books," she said at once. "They're all from my Aunt Mena. She wrote them. My father said they have everything I could ever need to know."

Kyle's head bobbed at her claim, his eyes narrowing in thought. "Everything? In just a few books? Hmm. I'd like to see those one day." He put his free hand on the corner of his desk before pointing his cane at the shelves on the opposite wall. "It's not a big collection, but I do like to think it covers the basics. Please, have a look. You can read whatever you want."

She took one step, then a second, to stand before the books. They consisted of the same thick, leather-clad and canvas-clad volumes she knew from the few books in her house. Unlike those tomes, though, Kyle's books had their titles and different names displayed in shiny gold letters. Her arm emerged to take a book from the shelf. It was tough to balance the weight in her one hand and flip it open, but she managed it with some effort.

To her surprise the books were not handwritten like Mena's volumes. Instead, the pages were filled with small block text and vivid drawings. She didn't read a single word until she flipped a wad of pages and recoiled at the intricate detail of a vivisected horse.

She spun toward Kyle. "What is this? Who would do this?"

Kyle made his way to stand just behind her shoulder. "Oh, that's a book on anatomy." He met her gaze when she gave him an opaque stare. "Anatomy, it's the study of the way living things are put together. It's to help learn how living things work by understanding what's inside them. The actual science of how living things work is called physiology."

She frowned. "I think you could learn a whole lot more by leaving them in one piece and seeing what they do."

He seemed to find some humor in that. "I guess you do have a point in that."

Angela blinked in surprise when her hand slapped the book shut.

"Perhaps we'll put that one away," Kyle said. He took the book from her and slid it with care back into its place. He moved his cane and hopped over one step. "Here, take a look at this one. I'd like to know what you think." He settled his shoulder against the bookshelf, pulled out a volume, and opened it before setting it into her waiting hand.

Her face bunched up. "What kind of words are these?"

"They're French. Parlez-vous Francaise?"

"What?" She shook her head. "I don't understand what you're saying."

"Because I said it in French. I asked if you spoke French. It's another language."

"I don't understand," she said once more with another shake of her head. "Why learn a whole bunch of different words to say something between people when we already have words that work just fine?"

He shrugged. "Not all people use the same words."

"You think I'm stupid," she said, annoyed with his calm demeanor. "It's not nice to think people are stupid. My father and Mena say Ivan is stupid. He might not know the same things they know, but I know he treats me like I'm the best thing in the world to him."

Kyle stared at her in surprise before he caught himself. "I'm sorry. I didn't mean to offend you. Let's try this a different way. My parents have told me about your Aunt Mena. I haven't met her, but I hear she's very smart. She's a former schoolmaster, in fact. I have met Ivan and yes, I agree with you, he's a good man. So. How about you tell me something you've read in one of the books Aunt Mena wrote for you, and I'll show you something similar I have here."

She hesitated. "You don't think I'm stupid?"

"No. In fact, I think you're quite insightful for your age."

"What do you mean by that?"

He held up a hand. "Well, there are three kinds of ways of knowing things in the world." He raised a finger. "First is most obvious, and that's reading a book. Scholarly knowledge." He raised another finger. "Second is wisdom, learning things by doing things. Let's call that working knowledge." He raised a third finger. "Last but by no means least is insight. That's when you see through things you may not know to see them in a way they weren't intended to be seen."

"I know about that. You're talking about the moral of a story."

He smiled upon her. "Precisely. It takes a different kind of intelligence to see something that isn't staring you straight in the face." He gave her a quizzical look. "Angela, may I ask your age?"

She stiffened as she went blank for a moment. "Twelve?" Her throat dried around the lie. "I'm twelve. That's what my father told me."

He held his smile. "In that case, you're a very clever twelve-year-old." He turned away from her. "Come here, please. I think I have something that might sit well with the curiosity of a clever youngster."

She walked around him. "You talk like you're older than you are."

"That's because I live in these books. I don't have much choice, you see," he said with a rap of his cane on the floor. "Now, where is it . . . ah! Here. Let's open it on the desk. It's a heavy book."

She followed him to his desk. The thump of the book when he set it down surprised her with the idea of its weight. It was larger than the other books, she noticed, and much thicker. She watched as he took a breath, licked the tip of his thumb, and opened the book. Pages fanned beneath his hand too fast for her to make out anything until he stopped short and pressed his hand to the book's binding to keep it open. "Welcome to the world, Angela."

She looked down as he tapped a finger on the page. "It's a map," she thought aloud, remembering the drawing in one of her books. Mena's handiwork was crude in comparison, crude and simple in ways Angela had never known until she stared into Kyle's book. Her mouth dropped in wonder as the abstract borders of her world swept out in her imagination to unseen and unperceived distances.

The impression upon her was so great that she forgot Kyle stood beside her, even as she let her mind devour every detail of the map around his hand. Without a thought she clamped the edge of her glove between her teeth and pulled her hand free, desperate to trace the drawings of mountains, rivers, and lakes with the delicate skin of her fingertips. Her six fingers spread out to their spidery length until she bumped against his thumb, and then she remembered.

Her hand shot under the seclusion of her poncho. She struggled to swallow before giving him a furtive sidelong glance.

The glove dangled from her teeth.

He didn't flinch. Instead, he said the only word she wanted to hear, and in just the way she wanted to hear it said, without a trace of anything but acceptance and acknowledgment, plain and simple, straight and honest.

He tapped his cane as his only explanation. "Angela," he said, his voice soft, and gave her a gentle pat on her shoulder.

She looked back to the map. She glanced at him, twice, and reached two conclusions. First, she had nothing to worry about in the Eddington house.

Second, she enjoyed his attention.

Her hand emerged from the poncho. Without a thought she let the glove drop from between her teeth and into the palm of her hand. Her hand closed and withdrew to the poncho.

Not once did he look down.

It was a comforting moment. She returned his smile.

9

‡ ‡ ‡

Angela lay in bed that night, staring at the ceiling. Her father slept in the bed next to her, across the doorway of the guest room they shared. Moonlight shone through the one window on the wall opposite the door. Her clothes were in a neat little stack on the bench beneath the window, with her father's clothes at the other end of the bench.

The bed was comfortable. She knew there shouldn't be any reason not to sleep. It had been a long day's ride, dinner had been delicious, her belly was full, and she had lingered in the sitting room until she couldn't keep her eyes open.

She had asked to look at Kyle's book of maps before going to bed, but her father would have none of it and told her to turn in straightaway. Disappointed, she had dragged her tired body upstairs, washed her face in the basin at the end of the upstairs hall, and flopped into bed. To her surprise her father followed soon after. There were a few sounds of the Eddingtons cleaning up their kitchen before those noises also ended with the creak of the stairs and the closing of another door.

She listened as best she could, but she never heard the clop of Kyle's cane on the stairs.

Of course not. He can't climb the stairs.

It was strange for her to see him with such a body, its stark limitations failing to serve him as it should. She was different, and there were times when she figured a second hand could be helpful, but in all her other times she knew her arm could do things beyond anything two typical arms could offer.

Kyle, by contrast, knew only constraints from his malformed leg. He wasn't just different; he was frail.

She wasn't sure why, but that one idea woke a fierce compulsion in her.

It was the compulsion to protect him.

‡ ‡ ‡

Despite her many thoughts and worries that she'd be staring at the ceiling all night, she nevertheless fell into a deep sleep. Her father had to call her once, twice, and then yank the blanket off her huddled body to get her moving. The source of her lassitude was a mystery in those first waking moments of her day. It hadn't been too late a night; she had stayed up later on prior nights. She thought perhaps it was the sum of things from the day . . . until a different thought crept into her awareness.

The water.

Those two words lingered behind her eyes as she sat at breakfast with her father and the Eddingtons. Her thoughts of the mysterious underground pool were haunted by three words more unsettling than she could've imagined.

It's changing me.

The thought hit her in stark contrast to the forgetful comfort she knew of sitting at breakfast without her glove. After her talk yesterday with Kyle, she felt reassured that there was nothing to fear about showing her arm in the Eddington house. Although she had her nagging certainties that her father had lied to her about many things she couldn't define, she felt a distinct clarity of truth regarding his statements that the Eddingtons understood life on the Range. There was nothing of note about Sarah and Carl, and she figured that worked just fine for them to go among Outsiders and secure the provisions needed to keep the Range going.

Sitting at the table, listening to her father's usual metered statements and the casual talk of the Eddingtons, reminded her that there was a sense of familiarity to the idea of people from her world visiting the Eddingtons. The practice wasn't new; it was tried and true. It had the sense of a routine, and she knew enough to know that routines were like seasons, coming and going in their cycles with the comfort of predictability.

Change, by its very nature, was a force to upset predictability.

She opened her mouth as her arm gave her a bite of heavy grain bread slathered with rich butter.

‡ ‡ ‡

Sarah cleared away the breakfast plates and brought out a glass cake dish. "I know it might not seem right to have something sweet with the smell of bacon still over the table, but I'd hate to see these tea cakes go to waste."

Carl's face lit with a broad smile as he lifted the cover of the cake plate. "Oh no, I won't have that under my roof," he said with mock severity.

Sarah poked him with a stiff finger. "Mind your manners. Guests first."

Nathan turned to Angela. "Tea cakes are the sweet cookies your mother taught Ruth and Rachel to make."

Angela's eyes lit with glee as she surveyed the yellow, shallow dome shapes of the cookies. "I wish Aunt Mena would let the sisters make them more often."

Nathan was unfazed by her comment. "No reward without its demand." He took a breath under the pressure of her blatant expectation. "You ate your breakfast. You can have some tea cakes. Three. You can have three."

"Not yet." Carl looked at his wife. "Aren't we missing something?"

Sarah rolled her eyes, stood, and fetched a small sifter from the pantry. "I'll agree they're better with some confectioner's sugar."

"Allow me," Kyle said. He took the sifter from his mother and shook it to give the cakes a light dusting of powdery white sugar. When he was done he looked at Angela, only to find her mouth hanging in silent disappointment. He took the sifter once more, shook it, and continued to shake it until her lips curled in a grin of delight. He laughed as he set the sifter on the table and put three cookies on Angela's plate. "There you go. Reverend, interested?"

Nathan drummed his fingers on his book where it rested on his thigh. "No, I've had quite enough for now." He looked at Carl. "Were you planning on going to town today?"

Carl grinned. "Well now, Rev, that sounds like you're about to make plans for me to go to town today. You got a list of goods?"

"A few items," Nathan said.

Sarah settled in her chair. "Pressing, I imagine, if you rode all the way out here."

Nathan opened his mouth and then closed it, caught in a rare speechless moment. Instead, he glanced at his empty mug and raised an eyebrow at Sarah. "If you wouldn't mind."

"No," she said with a sigh. "I enjoy getting up after I just sat down." She went to the stove, grabbed a dishrag, and brought the still-steaming coffee pot to the table. After filling Nathan's cup she set the pot in the middle of the table on the trailing end of the rag. "You could show Carl your list. We might have extra stock here. You can take that, and then we'll go another day to replace it."

Carl pushed the sugar bowl toward Nathan. "Unless you have other things on your list."

Nathan took a breath and held it for a moment.

Carl opened a hand. "Woolly Ben's been asking about things on the Range." He tipped his chin toward Angela. "He's been asking about your daughter's welfare."

Angela looked at her father. "You're going to see Woolly Ben?"

He took his hand from his book and waved for her to stay calm. "A visit to an old acquaintance is none of your concern," he said with a glare at Carl. "For now you can eat your cakes in the sitting room. Perhaps Kyle can show you more of his precious books while I talk with his parents. Please close the door to his office so you don't disturb us."

Angela didn't need to think twice to know it was his way of telling her to leave at once. Her arm took hold of her plate with its remaining pair of tea cakes and held it close as she left the table. The clop of Kyle's cane followed behind her. She went around the corner of the partition wall, past the stairs, into the office, and settled in one of the chairs by Kyle's desk. Morning sunshine lit the room with a yellow glow and made the specks of dust floating in the air glint. The gold text on his books jumped out as if to summon her to their many secrets.

Kyle closed the door then sat in a chair beside her rather than behind his desk. "Do you want to look at the maps?"

She shoved a cake into her mouth. She reveled in its fluffy sweetness for just a moment before turning toward Kyle. "I'm sorry. Do you want some? I haven't touched the last one."

"I can have one later." He was still for a moment before pushing up with his cane and moving to the bookcase. "I can show you where France is located on a map of the world. Did you ever see a map of the world?"

She watched as he tucked the atlas under his arm. "Is France where they speak French?"

"That's right." He settled the heavy book on the desk.

"Why would I want to go someplace where they use a different word for everything?" She shrugged. "I'd have to learn all those words. I don't want to learn new words for everything. I want to learn what's around me."

He shifted in his chair and flipped through the pages. "Then we'll go back to the map of the Range. We'll start there."

She looked at the bookcase, imagining the conversation on the other side of the wall. "Have you ever met Woolly Ben? I've only heard mention of him. I've never seen him. Does he have a big beard?"

"No," Kyle said, a glint of amusement in his eyes. He eased back in his chair, leaving the atlas open to the map of the Range. "His real name is Wu Li Ben. My parents told me they worked with Ben and your father to secure the Range. After that they parted paths. My parents built this house, Ben went back to town, and your father moved out on the Range with everyone else."

Angela nodded as she chewed. "How long ago was that?"

"I'm eighteen," Kyle said as he gazed at the ceiling in thought. "I think my parents were in the house for two years before they had me, so I guess it's at least twenty years."

"Have you met this man?"

"A few times." Kyle sighed. "I don't care for him. He's very patronizing." He opened a hand when Angela shot him a glance. "It means he acts like we're only here because he lets us live here. But this is our land."

"I know."

"Begging your pardon, but I don't think you do. Ben's from town."

"Town is different. I know that. My father told me about that."

"It's more than town being different. Outsiders, they live a different way than us. We trust each other. We trust in each other." He shook his head.

"There's a reason we don't have Outsiders on the Range."

"I remember." She waved her fork in the air. "My father told me your parents helped him and Ivan drive out the people who used to live here."

Kyle's face fell.

Her thoughts clicked. "Wait. Woolly Ben's not on the Range. What was his part?"

Kyle shifted in his seat. "Angela, this may not be my place to say, but there's something you need to understand. If your father hasn't told you already, I'm sure he'll tell you later, so I won't be out of bounds to tell you now."

Angela felt her stomach tighten. "Tell me what?"

Kyle propped an elbow on the arm of his chair and leaned toward her. "I went through the same questions with my parents."

"What did they tell you?"

"The first time they told me the same simple things your father told you. The second time I asked, they told me the truth." He took a breath. "People in town are different. Your father and my father have both told me the townspeople are nothing but whores, drunkards, thieves, and murderers. What they don't smash they steal, and those they don't exploit they kill. Anything with four legs they send to the butchers to be chopped to pieces. That's what's waiting in town. That's why my parents helped your father and Ivan chase the people who once lived here toward the river to the south. They weren't townspeople, the ones who lived here, but they traded with the townspeople. In your father's eyes that made them just as bad."

Angela shook her head. "What about us? We trade with the townspeople."

"But we stay away from them. We stay away to stay pure."

The knot in her stomach grew a little tighter as suspicions crept up her arm. She forced a swallow. "Why don't the people who used to live here try to come back?"

Kyle stared at her for several moments. "Woolly Ben and his posse killed every last one of them." He frowned. "That's the due Outsiders afford their fellows."

She dropped her fork. Her arm withdrew under her poncho to coil against her.

"Forgive me. I didn't mean to upset you." Kyle shrugged and looked out the windows, squinting against the glaring sunlight. "My goodness, what a beautiful morning."

10

‡ ‡ ‡

Nathan kept his horse at a trot as he rode to town with Carl. He rested a hand on the revolver strapped against his thigh and glanced at the lever-action repeating rifle Carl had tucked beneath the saddle of his mount. Nathan had a sawed-off double barrel slapping against his ribs, cushioned only by his precious book where it rested in a special pocket of his vest.

The Eddington house and its veil of pastoral tranquility was already far behind.

He had mixed feelings about leaving Angela in Sarah's care. The moment he considered that emotion, though, he understood how it was misplaced. He was more concerned about Angela spending time with Kyle. Sarah's son was a respectful young man, dutiful, and showed every indication that he knew his place. The apparent age difference between Kyle and Angela would provide a certain barrier, even if it were an inconsequential thing to Angela. It was different for Kyle, who would only look at her as a girl of twelve years or so and then keep a corresponding distance of propriety that a young man should keep from a pre-adolescent girl. The fact that they were distant cousins was of no consequence. Cousins married as a matter of course out on the plains. People married within social circles, and social circles were most often composed of relations of some sort or other.

No, it wasn't any of those things that bothered Nathan. Only one thing bothered him, and that was the boy's confounded sense of curiosity and misplaced confidence in the knowledge he gleaned from those damned books his parents brought from town. For Nathan, the Range was not only a secure barrier of physical isolation but also one of mental and ideological isolation. It had to be, or the life he foresaw would have met its doom long ago.

Yet for all those misgivings swirling in his head, he remembered what he had foreseen for Angela and knew the inevitability awaiting everyone in his life.

Regardless, he had to ride to town. He had to see Woolly Ben.

He had his prophecy, but he knew it was yet to come.

He wasn't riding for fulfillment. He was riding to buy time.

‡ ‡ ‡

Angela was staring at the atlas when Kyle returned to the office with a cup of coffee.

"Still studying the same map?"

She looked up, impressed that he didn't spill a drop as he hobbled along on his cane. The clop hadn't registered among her thoughts. "You're good at balancing things."

His eyes narrowed for a moment. "I had to adapt. I guess you've made your own adjustments, if we're going to talk about those kinds of things." He shifted in his chair, grimacing as his weight came on his bad hip for a moment.

"It's that sore?"

He sighed as he eased in his chair. "Yes. The way my hip is malformed I can't tolerate any weight on it, whether I'm sitting or standing. Sometimes, it hurts even to rest on my side in bed. And anything that might jostle me, like riding a horse or wagon, well, let's just say it's perhaps the least pleasant thing I might ever consider." He stared at his foot for a moment before his gaze settled on her hand. "How about you?"

She flexed her six fingers. "I'm short one arm but I've got an extra finger. Besides, I've learned to be good with my toes."

His eyebrows rose in sudden interest as he sipped his coffee. "Would you mind showing me what you can do?"

She smiled, welcoming a bloom of pride for his appreciation of something she took for her everyday life. Then again, she remembered how she was impressed that he didn't spill any coffee. They were, she decided, two people sharing how they lived in a world designed for bodies different than their own.

With a smile she took the atlas and set it on the floor. She sat, wiggled her toes, and balanced on her backside as she flipped through the pages. Until that moment it hadn't occurred to her that she had left herself barefoot, just as she did in her own house.

"That's impressive," he said with a nod. "Very good."

"Not as good as your mom's tea cakes," she said with a little laugh.

Before she thought of anything else, her arm separated, sped around her, spiraled up the side of the chair to take the plate from the table, and brought it to her side.

Kyle's jaw dropped.

"See," she said without looking at him. "I can even use a fork." With that she wrapped her toes around the utensil to pick up the last piece of cake on her plate. "My hips are loose, and my arm can bend any way it wants."

Her arm reared up on its coiled length, fanned open the six fingers to expose the palm, and opened its single large eye upon Kyle.

She giggled, her head turned away, as she perceived her arm's sight of him agape in his chair. "You should see yourself. Be careful or a fly might land in your mouth."

He said nothing.

She looked over her shoulder, and for no particular reason she could figure, she kept her unblinking gaze on him while she let her arm give him a wink.

His mouth closed with the same speed as if he were hoisting a bucket of stones. For several moments he sat still before returning to his senses. "Angela," he said, his voice cracking. He sat up straight and cleared his throat to try again. "Angela, that's extraordinary."

"It's just my arm," she said and looked back to the atlas. Her head bobbed to either side. The hand twisted to regard Angela, her back turned, before settling once more on Kyle. The large green eye did not blink.

"Does it think for itself?"

"Not always." She shrugged. "I don't know to describe it. Sometimes I see things." She pointed at the map with a big toe. "I didn't realize the river to the south was so big."

Kyle rubbed his chin. "I guess it's akin to a telepathic link."

She glanced at him over her shoulder. "Is that another one of those French words?"

"What? Oh, no . . . no, it's a way to communicate mind to mind. It's just a theory."

She looked back to the atlas. "Well, people can say or guess what they want. I know what I know and that's that."

Kyle grinned. "And there's no arguing with logic like that."

She ducked her head to tap her temple with a big toe. "Thinking without knowing." She gave him a smile. "Insight, right?"

He steadied his body by propping an elbow on the arm of his chair. "Yes," he said with a nod of appreciation. "Insightful it is."

She beamed with delight and looked back at the map. Her gaze fell on the depiction of the Range. It was easy to spot the things she knew: the Purdy and Semenic homes, the wide fields, the rolling perimeter hills, the southern river, the Eddington house, on and on. Her world, everything she had seen, everything that seemed so large and endless around her, was just a little slice of a far-reaching land.

There were, however, two things the map did not contain. First was the omission of the lake where the stargrazers took their rest. Second, and for all she stared and studied, there was no denying the omission that whispered so many things to her suspicions.

The map was blank where it should've indicated the cave that led to Thetis Springs.

She tapped the map with her toe as she let her arm wander around the office to distract Kyle. He was smart, there was no hiding from the fact that she liked him, and the Eddingtons were part of the Range, but she understood that even though they weren't Outsiders, they weren't quite insiders either.

A little grin played across her lips. Insightful, indeed.

‡ ‡ ‡

The town of Deepwick greeted Nathan and Carl with a distinct and pervasive odor.

It had been a matter of poor planning to put the butchers at the far end of town, in the head of the prevailing winds that carried across the lands. Under normal situations perhaps it wouldn't have made any difference, but Deepwick was different. Although not much meat was butchered in the windowless barn other than what the residents could consume, the adjacent cattle pen was a holding spot for herds on their way to distant railheads. The reek of feces was inescapable, often mixing with the odor of entrails left for consumption in crematory heaps. Between those tendrils of revulsion lurked a different odor: the acrid stench of tannery baths kept in an open shed beside the butchers' barn.

Smell was not the only affront Deepwick sent as a greeting, for there was also a sound, a desperate, wailing pleat of mothers separated from their calves. Their primal agony was too much to be drowned out by the dissolute merriment of Deepwick's human inhabitants.

Nathan's jaw clenched as he rode with Carl down the middle of the town's parched central avenue. Baggage and postal carriages passed by, their wooden wheels kicking up enough dust from the roadbed to mask some of the sights. It wasn't necessary to see everything. Nathan knew well enough what hid behind those buff-colored plumes, and he was content to let his vision be clouded. He didn't need to see the drunks slumped by the raised wood-plank sidewalks running along the store fronts, he didn't need to see the whores with their tight corsets and the upward thrust of their powdered cleavages, and he had no interest in seeing the ghost-eyed derelicts sitting outside the opium den at the opposite end of town from the butchers.

He looked to his right as he passed the black wood frame of the den on his left. Set back from the avenue was the town's church, gleaming with its whitewashed clapboards under the noonday sun. The bell tower rose just shy of thirty feet from its base and held a polished, gleaming trio of bells in various sizes. Beside the church, and so behind the town's supply stores, sat the schoolhouse, and behind the schoolhouse, raised up on a small slope, was a grand two-story house distinguished by a white colonnade.

It was Purdy Mansion, the home of his family. The house had been rebuilt several times over the years, yet in one shape or another, members of his extended clan had been born, raised, and sometimes died within those walls.

His immediate family and his cousin Sarah were the only ones of Purdy blood to live outside the home.

He looked to his left once he was past the opium den. Set back a good distance from the road was another grand house, the Van Delebois estate. It was the home of Woolly Ben's mother. Once the grand palace of a European duchess, Ben had transformed it to one of mock propriety where he conducted the sanitized transactions of his various unsavory business interests.

Carl waved to get Nathan's attention. "Want to visit the folks?"

"I have nothing to say to them." Nathan pointed to Ben's house. "Let's see to our business and be on our way."

"Just saying they might take an interest in seeing the wayward son."

Nathan lowered the rim of his black hat. "They abandoned their convictions and chose to preach redemption in the midst of squalor and sin. They chose to profit from sin through the town's tax revenues."

Carl laughed. "Don't mind me saying, Rev, but that's the same money you used to purchase the Range, if I'm not mistaken."

Nathan's jaw clenched. "I did not raise that wealth, but it was my due. The Range has cleansed that money of its filth." He glared at Carl. "And as far as my relations are concerned, I lay no claim to them. If they wish to pretend condemnation holds no sway over the land, then I choose not to think of them as kin."

Carl tipped his head. "You are indeed a hard man, Rev."

"It's an unforgiving world. I see no need to extend forgiveness if none is to be afforded."

"Did you write that in your book?"

"My book is none of your concern." Nathan rolled his shoulders. "Stay outside with the horses. I won't be long."

Carl pulled free his repeating rifle when some of the men lounging on the covered porch of Ben's house fixed pointed glares upon him and Nathan. He settled the butt of the stock on his thigh so there was no missing the gun by the length of its barrel.

Nathan dismounted. "Don't pick a fight."

"Looking to stop one before the fuse gets lit," Carl said, his gaze panning across the porch. "I'll be waiting for you, Rev."

Nathan tossed his reins to Carl and faced the house. When he was a boy, the house had been an inviting place. It was for the better, he decided, that after this visit, he would never see the place again.

‡ ‡ ‡

Angela was behind the Eddington house, helping Sarah throw out some chickenfeed, when she spotted a welcome surprise come over the hill from the Range. Forgetting Kyle where he stood behind her in the shade of the house, she shouted to Ivan by name and ran off to meet him as his horse sauntered down the hill.

She threw herself against him and let her arm wrap tightly across his broad back. Ivan let out a hearty laugh as he returned an embrace of equal vigor. She leaned back and looked up to him. "I didn't know you were coming! Why are you here? Are we going back?"

Ivan patted a meaty hand on her head. "Well, aren't you just full of questions?" He waved to Sarah and Kyle before putting an arm around her. "And look at you, you already grew up some on just one little ride from home. You been drinkin' somethin' special?"

Her head snapped toward him. Before she said anything, he winked. She nodded once as she caught his inference. He didn't have to say anything for her to understand he was talking about Thetis Springs. No matter what her father and Mena said, she liked to believe that Ivan wasn't stupid.

"So what you been doin' out here?"

"Kyle showed me his books. I've been looking at maps."

"Maps?" Ivan shook his head as he brought his horse toward the water trough. He kept a hand on Angela's shoulder as he embraced Sarah and then Kyle with his other arm. "Let me tell you somethin' about maps. Maps are for people who don't know where they been and can't figure where they're goin'. Then there's us kind, who set down in one place and don't need to go nowhere else." He smiled and looked at Kyle. "Ain't that right?"

Kyle hesitated. "Oh, I understand what you mean, but sometimes it's good to know what's around you."

"I got my eyes for that. I want to see the world around me, not look at some pictures in a book." Ivan tipped his chin to Kyle's cane. "No offense, but me growin' up sick all the time and you stuck on that cane, I guess makes us kind of the same."

Kyle looked down at his cane. "Not quite. I'll always be on my cane."

"Hmm. Guess you got me on that." Ivan patted Kyle's shoulder. "Sorry. Didn't mean to make offense. Just talkin' about what was in my head, is all."

Kyle shifted his weight and looked at Sarah. "I'm going inside to sit down."

Sarah rested a hand on his cheek and nodded. "I'll finish out here."

Angela watched Kyle hobble into the house. She waited for the door to close before turning to Ivan. "Why'd you say that to him? He's so nice. You hurt his feelings."

"Think so?" Ivan's eyes narrowed in thought as he rubbed his forehead. "Maybe you're right. I guess I'll have to make amends."

Sarah waved it off. "That's not necessary."

"No, it is," said Angela, surprising both of them. She pointed to the back door. "I'll take care of your horse. You go say sorry to Kyle."

Ivan stared at her for a moment before giving her a dutiful nod and heading inside.

She turned and stopped short under Sarah's stare. "What?"

"For a young lady, you're awfully headstrong," Sarah said. "That's good. I see the Purdy in you."

Angela smiled but then blinked in surprise as she remembered her father. She spun, only to find Ivan behind her as he returned from the house.

"I asked my forgiveness," Ivan said, his head hanging.

"That's good." She rested her hand on his chest. "Why'd you ride out here?"

Ivan pointed to the distance beyond the house. "The Rev told me to wait one day and then come on out. Told me to meet you here while he went to town with Carl. Told me to come fetch him if he wasn't back by dark."

Her hand withdrew. "Just you?"

"Just me." Ivan gave her a wink. "I'm tougher than I look."

II

‡ ‡ ‡

Nathan stood still in the spacious parlor of Ben's house. For all that the atmosphere of the house had changed, it nevertheless retained its ostentatious image of privilege. Textured wallpaper still adorned the room, and wide chairs covered in maroon velvet could still welcome visitors. A large oak desk, stained dark brown, dominated the wall across from the fireplace, right where Ben's father had once conducted his own various businesses. In those times Ben's mother would retire to the library to read her books and perhaps pretend she had married a man whose reality lived up to the illusion of a respectable entrepreneur.

Nathan had found Ben's mother to be a most curious creature, a rebellious duchess, her regal height accentuated by a mass of long blond hair gathered atop her head. There were times when he had been a boy that her cold blue eyes would settle on him, stare through him, and see things he could not fathom. Then again, by the time he was twelve, whatever thoughts were in her mind had suffocated beneath the same pall of opium that would soon take her life.

Nathan glanced to where he had once hid when he and Ben played robber and lawman. He had always taken the role of lawman. It seemed a natural inclination after all the beatings he took from his parents.

His back stiffened. Old thoughts. They belonged to another life.

Ben emerged from the back walkway joining the parlor to the kitchen. He was barefoot, an unbuttoned white shirt hanging over his lean frame and the waist of his black pants. A woman followed behind him. She was dressed in a long black skirt, her black hair pulled up in a disheveled mass atop her head, her neck adorned by a pearl choker, its black lace border accentuating the pearls' silvery sheen. Her torso was clad in a black corset similar to the ones worn by the whores in town. What set her corset apart, though, was that it left her breasts exposed.

Ben swirled a fancy crystal in his hand before sipping the red wine it contained. He opened a hand for Nathan to sit before settling into the chair behind his desk. The woman stood behind him. The moment Ben was still she went to work massaging his shoulders.

"It's nice to know you still remember me," Ben said and sipped some more wine.

Nathan cleared his throat as he rolled his shoulders.

Ben hooked a thumb. "Does she bother you? She relaxes me." He stared at Nathan. "At least some of the time."

"No, she doesn't bother me." Nathan took out his book and held it against his chest. "It's been some time since I had to talk business on your grounds."

Ben tipped his head towards the gunbelt half-hidden by Nathan's long coat. "It's rude to bring loaded guns into a man's house."

"Town is dangerous. It's for what's outside, not for you."

"And that's a lie." Ben laughed. "Now that's rude, Reverend, to say such a thing to a friend you've known all your life. A friend, I'll remind you, who still has twenty hired guns in his employ right here in town. Deputized as well, since I made my payments to Marshall Lowery to keep his nose out of my business here and elsewhere."

"Still importing your slaves?"

"Laborers," Ben said and pointed at Nathan. "Not slaves. No such things as slaves in this Union, not for years now. Before that war was fought and won my father started bringing his countrymen here all the way from China. They agreed to the journey. Now they dig this country's mines and build its railroads to earn back what they owe me. With interest, of course."

"And the whores?"

Ben rested his head against the woman's breasts. "All under contract with their families." He gave Nathan a tired look. "You know all these things.

Why ask?"

"Two old friends talking business." "I see your business is going well."

"You're asking about what you already know I do to gauge how much you can stall me." Ben studied Nathan. "I killed a lot of redskins for you."

"That was your decision. I only asked you to remove them."

"And what did you think that meant? Those people weren't going to leave by the will of any man. The only way they'd relinquish the land was to be buried in it. I knew that, you knew that, no matter how much you wish to think otherwise." Ben looked at his wine as he swirled the delicate crystal goblet. "Now. The gold. We had a deal. Gold in return for my services."

"We're prospecting."

"So you haven't found it yet," Ben said with a shake of his head. "How many years has it been?"

Nathan took a deep breath. "I bought the Range. It's my land."

"And I did the dirty work so you could prospect for gold. Don't forget, Reverend, no matter what you say or believe, you promised me something when we first rode out on those lands. Gold, plain and simple, nothing more, nothing less."

"It's a great deal of land to prospect."

"Stop with the excuses." Ben pointed over his shoulder. "Even she knows you're full of shit, and she doesn't understand a single goddamn word we're saying." He stroked his beard as he studied Nathan. "I've given you more time than anyone can expect. I only did that because of our history. No matter what you think of yourself, no matter what you think of me, we're one and the same. We're the same kind of arrow, just flying in different directions. Now you can sit and steam about that all you want in your soup of righteous indignation, but that's the way it is and that's the way it's been. Remember, you paid me to get Mena free from her proprietor. She might dress like a nun, but you and I both know her innocence left town a long time ago."

Nathan frowned. "We found our purity out on the Range. We left our old lives behind."

Ben's eyes narrowed. "But we both know you found something altogether different out there. Not gold, but something else."

"We are one with our land."

"That's what the redskins said."

Nathan closed his eyes for a moment. "We digress. As I was saying, we're going to prospect in the northwest."

"How long?"

"We both know I can't tell you that. The land is a closed book until we start work."

Ben stared at the ceiling as his jaw clenched.

The woman behind him looked down at the tension on his face. She stroked his hair to smooth it back before resting her hands over his eyes and putting her lips to his ear. Her dark, blank gaze bored into Nathan as she whispered.

Ben grinned. "She says you remind her of her father before the bastard sold her. She says I should castrate you to sever you from the poison of your pride." He took one of her hands, kissed it, and opened his eyes to look at Nathan. "Let's put out all the cards. Deepwick is a dying town. We don't have a railhead, and we won't be getting one. There's only a fraction of the herding traffic we once had. Towns like Abilene and Dodge City have taken the lead. Both our families rely on people for business. We just cater to opposite ends of the spectrum of human needs."

Nathan stiffened. "Our families are nothing alike."

"No, they're exactly alike, because without people, neither your kind nor my kind have any business." Ben sighed and looked out his windows. "I have tried to keep this place alive. I bring in exotic women, not your typical whores. I set up the opium den. I bought my own deputies and bribe whomever I need so it all runs, and it's still not enough. Yes, Time's drawing down on this place." He shrugged and turned to Nathan. "I need something to keep Deepwick alive, Nathan, or everyone will move on and all this will be forgotten. I can set up shop somewhere else, but it won't be the same."

Nathan met the stare of the woman rubbing Ben's shoulders. Her eyes were opaque with the hardness of her life. "Perhaps it's better that Deepwick fails."

Ben took a breath. "You have one year. After that, If you don't come back here and tell me there's gold, I'll ride out with my men. I'll lease out your freak-show wife and daughter to one of the traveling circuses that I supply with exotic animals. Do you understand me?"

Nathan didn't flinch. "Two years. You know the size of the area."

Ben leaned forward in his chair and rested his elbows on the edge of his desk. "If you were anyone else, Nathan, I'd be listening to her instead of you." His eyes darted to his private concubine. "Two years," he repeated. "Mark your calendar because I'll be out there two years to the day."

"Two years to the day." Nathan stood. "Good to see you, Ben. He tipped his hat to the woman. "Good day, mademoiselle."

She muttered something Nathan failed to understand, but her disdain fell with inconsequence upon his wall of superiority. To him her vitriol was just savage words in a savage's tongue, nothing more than self-spawned recriminations from a fallen woman. Who was she, with her plump little breasts hanging in open sight, her body a soiled plaything for a few grubby coins, to cast judgment upon him?

"Two years," Ben said to Nathan's back. "Don't make me ride out there."

"You won't be disappointed," Nathan said.

He waited until he was out the front door to let his satisfaction play out in a wide smile.

‡ ‡ ‡

Angela walked into the Eddington's kitchen in the late afternoon, hot and tired from helping Sarah with the day's chores and the preparation of the evening meal. Earlier, there had been a short discussion between Sarah and Ivan that started with Ivan saying he was hungry and Sarah commenting that they had more chickens than they needed. The discussion had ended when Ivan reached over the wire mesh of the coup, grabbed a plump bird, and snapped its neck.

At home Ivan had taught Angela how to butcher chickens, pigs, and pretty much anything else that walked the earth and had meat on its bones, but she nevertheless found little interest in the shredding of a living thing.

When she had watched Ivan do his work, her arm had coiled tightly against her side until she thought it would burrow through her ribs. Her arm's reaction wasn't much of a mystery to her; it could come and go at will, and watching a creature go through the irreversible process of dismemberment struck her and her arm with a gruesome sense of finality.

She found a washbasin inside the back door to the kitchen, a rag hanging over its edge. Her eyes closed as she rested against the basin table and bowed her head to let her arm do the work. It separated from her, slid around the basin to hook its tail in one of the large handles, and then used that anchorage to grab the rag, soak it in the cool water, and plop the dripping cloth on the back of her neck. She all but gasped at the welcome coolness of the water as it ran over her head, through the short curls of her hair, around her cheeks, and dripped from her nose and chin. After another dousing, her hand crushed the rag in the vise-like enclosure of its six fingers, let go of the handle to swing its tail back up to rejoin her shoulder, and then wiped her face and head.

Once that was done, her arm gave the rag a good shake and slapped it over the side of the basin to dry. Her fingers spread wide, the eye in her palm gave her its sight, and Angela turned to find Kyle watching her.

"Your arm," he said, his voice soft. "It really is remarkable."

She closed its eye and wiped some moisture from her forehead. "I told you. It's me."

He looked down at his leg. "I envy you," he whispered.

"What?"

"Oh, nothing." He shook his head then looked at her with his welcoming smile. "I'm sorry. I didn't mean to stare. I thought, now that you're inside, you might want to look at some more books."

She reached into a pocket, took out her glove, and held its hem between her teeth as she worked her fingers into the glove's confines. The clarity of his loneliness hit her in that moment. He might be a young man, but he was also crippled, an isolated boy hungry for company. The realization intensified her motivation to protect him.

She knew she liked him. The urge to protect him imparted a sense of power upon her; something she understood might be the handiwork of the water's effect. Either way, after only two short days, she felt he fulfilled needs in her she'd never known existed.

His head sank in her moments of silence. He turned to move away.

"Wait," she said at once. "I'm sorry. I was just thinking. Yes, I'd like to look at more books. I mean, after my father gets back, it'll be dark, and then I think we're leaving in the morning." She looked around the kitchen, taking it in before turning to him. "Let's look at books."

He watched as she ran her hand over her head. "Are you worried about your father?"

Her hand fell to her side. "Well, I certainly don't like the part about Ivan having to ride into town to bring him back. Aren't you worried about your father?"

"Of course, but I'm a little older, so maybe I worry in a different way."

"I'm not a baby."

"I didn't say you were. Oh, you seem older than your years, I'll give you that." He put a hand on her shoulder. "So. What do you want to look at?"

"Nothing with animals and things pulled apart."

He grinned. "Okay, we'll leave anatomy on the shelf." He stopped short, leaned on his cane by the doorway to his office, and raised a finger. "Say, I have a large Bible, footnoted with historical references, drawings, and maps. I can tell you like maps, so you might like to look at that. It's probably a lot different than your father's little edition."

She gave him a quizzical look. "What do you mean?"

He tipped his head. "Your father's book—the book he keeps with him, that he holds to his chest, that never leaves his side. I figured a reverend would keep his personal Bible close at hand."

She stared at him. She didn't know what to say.

He read through her silence in a heartbeat. "It is a Bible, isn't it?"

She looked into the office, to the shelves of books. "I . . . I don't know. I never thought about it. He's mentioned the Bible. He talks about God and Providence, the Chosen and the Condemned, salvation and damnation." She thought for a moment. "But I don't ever remember him looking in his book or any other book when he talks about those things."

Kyle studied her for several moments before waving it off. "No matter. It's his personal book. It's none of our business." He knocked the end of his cane on the floor to summon a change in the conversation. "So. What do you want to look at?"

She gave him a sidelong glance. "Show me your Bible."

‡ ‡ ‡

Nathan sat atop his horse, holding the reins to Carl's mount. He was outside one of the town's provision stores, waiting for Carl to fill the short list of materials they could transport in their saddlebags.

He looked down either end of the avenue as the sun set to the west. Long rays of light scattered in the dust kicked up from wheels and hooves. Music spilled from the swinging half-doors of the various saloons. Several of Ben's hired guns wandered down from Ben's house to take their posts on the porches outside the saloons, brothels, and even the opium den. Each man kept the shiny, pointed wheel of his deputy's badge on open display.

Some of them grinned when they caught Nathan's emotionless gaze.

It was his practiced façade, but a façade it was, for the disgust he felt for the town rose up his throat from the acid gurgling in his stomach. If he could he'd summon every drop of caustic vomit he could muster, let it dissolve his very bones if need be, and let it erupt over the heathen creatures around him. He imagined their screams as the flesh ran from their skeletons, as their corrupted bodies boiled away to leave their staggering, twisted souls as translucent gray shadows in the evening light.

He snorted and spat to his side. How wrong his parents were those years ago when they made their efforts to sway him to the idea of salvation and redemption. It was a vile act of hypocrisy for his family to preach such things when all he knew in the Purdy mansion was intimidation and predation. At the same time, he often wondered if they chose such a course in their sermons because of the rot they hid beneath their clean clothes.

Either way, when he came of age, he took his portion of the family finances, bought the Range, bought Mena from her proprietor so that he'd never have to share her again and left the town behind. If his parents were still alive, he'd wish to challenge them, to gut their conviction as he spread his arms to the town's despicable reality.

Mena was the only one he tried to save, and even there, deceit had undermined his aspirations. In her past she had been a schoolteacher married to a respectable man. When her infertility came to light, her husband cast her out—cast her out as an embarrassment—and used his contacts to prevent her from securing a teaching post. Farther she wandered, and more desperate she grew, until she arrived at Deepwick and faced the option of ill repute or starvation. She made her choice, and though she no longer wanted for sustenance, she starved in a more profound way.

And so she buried the secret of her infertility beneath the humiliation of subjugation. There it lurked, hidden as deep within her as the barrenness itself, even when Nathan whispered his intention to set her free. She kept the secret of her infertility until after he secured the transaction. Delirious with the euphoria of emancipation, she at last revealed her truth when he said he wanted to make her his wife. Among her tears and shame, he hit her once, a single slap, an eruption of hurt that forever derailed them from the lives they had once known and the future they had believed they would share. His will refused any idea of a sterile marriage. Yet for all the irrefutable energy of that conviction, he lusted for her all the more as the years passed.

The only salvation was his vision, the precious sight of his prophetic gift. He foresaw having her in the glorious end of all he knew, the explosive release of an apocalyptic foresight.

"Well, look here, if it isn't Reverend Purdy," a familiar voice called.

Nathan blinked. He retreated from his reverie to see Doc Connors strolling toward him, a cigar in his mouth and a fancy vest enclosing his rotund frame. "Good day to you."

Connors puffed his cigar before pointing it at Carl's mount. "Rode in for some goods? Who's with you?"

"A few supplies, yes." Nathan rested a hand on his long coat, over the bulge of his holstered revolver. "I rode in with Carl Eddington."

"Good man, he's a good man," Connors said and puffed his cigar. "Say, how's that girl of yours? She's coming along okay?"

"She's just fine. A glimpse of perfection, I would say."

"Glad to hear, especially for a cripple with one arm, and a malformed one at that. I guess she'll adapt, just like that lame Eddington boy." Connors glanced over his shoulder at a shout from inside one of the saloons. "How about the missus?"

"Also well."

Connors stepped closer. "I heard Woolly Ben gave you two years."

Nathan glared at the man. "I see news travels fast."

Connors pulled out his pocket watch, flicked it open with a thick thumb, and grimaced as he looked at the clock face. With a shake of his head, he snapped shut the timepiece, slid it back into his pocket, and blew a smoke ring toward Nathan. "You enjoy your time, Reverend. What time you have left, that is." He laughed before turning toward one of the saloons.

Nathan said nothing as he watched Connors walk away. The man went up the steps onto a patio, put his arm around a powdered woman with an emerald green dress and black corset, and whispered something in her ear. She yelped, laughed with the empty, manic cackle of a dissolute existence, and slapped his chest. Connors ogled her as she lingered in the fold of his arm before leading him inside.

A cool wind blew down the avenue, dragging the malevolent stench of feces, burning offal, and mud. Nathan turned to the east to see night creep up from the horizon.

"The darkness nears," he thought aloud.

And when it comes only hellfire shall pierce its veil.

12

‡ ‡ ‡

Angela looked up from Kyle's Bible when she heard Ivan's shout from the front porch. She stood, forgetting her spot on the floor in front of the massive tome. Its open page showed a map of the Holy Lands and the frantic dispersal of the Judean Tribes. In a somewhat similar way, she hurried from the study.

At least she wondered if that was Kyle's impression. He was sitting in a chair so he could point out the map's details with his cane. In her wake he pushed up to a stance. The clops of his cane were lost to her as she made her way out of the office.

For all her sudden rush at Ivan's shout, she found herself hesitating as she stood by the house's front door. She stared out to see her father and Carl trotting toward the house, their shapes almost lost in the darkening night. A strange knot of anxiety tightened in her chest as her father neared—anxiety for leaving Kyle and the Eddington house, anxiety for returning to the isolation of the Range and, perhaps worst of all, anxiety as to how and when she should put her father to task for his lies of omission.

There was one more target for her anxiety.

She wished Kyle hadn't asked her about her father's book. Now that her father drew close she was stung by the desire to find out what hid in the worn little volume he kept so close.

Curiosity, she learned, was a restless companion.

‡ ‡ ‡

The tension at the table was palpable after Carl asked Nathan to say a blessing.

Nathan stood and extended an open hand over the roasted chicken as he clutched his book to his chest with his other hand. "Dominance to the devout, primacy to the pure, and may ruin fall upon the weak and corrupt."

There wasn't much said by anyone after those words. Dinner was a quiet affair.

Nathan ordered Angela to bed after Sarah cleared the table. She trudged upstairs, disappointed that her plea to look at more of Kyle's books had been met with a flat denial. Uncomfortable under Nathan's austere stare, Kyle shifted on his cane until he seemed to think better of things to do and retired to his office.

Alone in the guest room, Angela shed her clothes for her nightshirt, sat on the edge of her mattress, and stared at her father's empty bed. He was downstairs, talking with Carl and Ivan, their voices audible but hushed so that she couldn't discern anything that was said.

She had asked once during dinner if things had gone well in town. Carl had been about to offer an answer when Nathan glared him to silence and changed the topic. Deflated, frustrated, she had eaten her chicken and potatoes without asking again.

Her father had scolded her when he caught her playing with the bones of the denuded chicken wing on her plate. "Animals play with the dead, not people," he had said, reminding her of the way he often spoke down to her mother.

Her father was a difficult man.

When Sarah brought out the tea cakes, he ordered Angela's plate be taken away as punishment for playing with her food.

She changed her opinion. Her father wasn't difficult; he was cruel.

Before she went up to bed, Ivan called her into the kitchen and told her to help Sarah put away the dishes. When she rounded the corner, he ushered her toward the back door and tipped his chin toward the washbasin.

He had left a plate with three tea cakes piled under a generous layer of confectioner's sugar. It was hard not to cry, not just out of gratitude but for the fact that Ivan was so kind to her while her father only called him stupid.

He put a finger to his lips for her to be quiet, grinned, and kissed the top of her head.

When she ate the cakes, they tasted better than she remembered. Spite, she realized, could be an intoxicating confection.

She would have liked to talk more with Kyle. He was kind, the way Ivan was kind to her, and the way her mother was kind to her. They welcomed her. They smiled on her. She was at ease with them.

Sitting there, alone in the dark in a bedroom far from home, she was struck by a new conviction, one that hit her out of the shadows with as much violence as a horse's kick.

One day she was going to have it out with her father. Somehow, in some way, she knew only one of them would walk away from that confrontation.

‡ ‡ ‡

She rose early from a fitful sleep. Her father followed soon behind her. The sun was just cracking the horizon when they went outside to throw their saddlebags over their mounts. Ivan came down, stretching his arms high as he yawned.

When Sarah offered to put on a pot of coffee to fend off the morning chill, Nathan refused. "We have to go," he said. "We've consumed enough of your hospitality." He turned to Ivan. "Get on your mount. Find Calliope and tell her to be more watchful while she runs her perimeter."

Carl came out from the kitchen. Kyle followed a few moments later.

"Can we interest you in some breakfast, Rev?" Carl asked.

Nathan clambered atop his horse and shook his head. "No. I wish to depart. We need to be back at our homes. There is much work to do." He glanced at Angela. "Yes, much work."

Her head sank. With nothing else to say or do, she went to Sarah and Carl, embraced them, and thanked them for their hospitality. When she came to Kyle, she hesitated, stared into his eyes, and then threw herself against him, her shoulders bunching up when he put an arm around her.

When she stepped back from him, conscious at once that she might have betrayed a sentiment she wished to keep secret, she noticed the black hat Kyle held in his hand. It was a low hat with a flat top and a broad, stiff brim. A long chinstrap dangled from the cap liner.

Ivan pointed. "Hey, there, Kyle. I remember bringin' that back for you a while ago."

"And now it's for Angela," Kyle said and settled it on her head. "A caballero hat to keep your head cool and the sun off your face."

Her eyes rolled up as she settled her hand atop the hat to push it down on her head. It was a little big, but she still had some growing ahead of her. She looked at Kyle and smiled, even as she felt ready to cry. "Thank you."

"My pleasure," he said. "I'll look forward to your next visit."

Nathan brought his horse around and stopped between Angela and the Eddingtons. "Time to leave," he said, his voice flat.

She lowered her head to hide her sniffle.

‡ ‡ ‡

It was nearing noon before a word was exchanged. She worried that if she said one word, let go one breath, she would sob and cry to go back to the Eddingtons. Her pride refused to give her father the leverage of even a single teardrop of emotion.

His voice came to her ears. Its sound sickened her.

"Take off that hat."

She answered without any conscious thought. "No."

He stopped his horse. His hand clenched to a fist around his reins.

Her throat went dry. "I like this hat. It was a gift." She kept her head down, afraid her father's gaze would skewer her where she sat. "It does what Kyle promised. It keeps my head cool. It keeps the sun out of my eyes."

Her father said nothing.

She lifted her chin and stared ahead. Their home was beyond sight, some intangible distance from where they had stopped. She thought of Kyle's maps.

She summoned every scrap of courage she could manage, sat up straight, stilled her arm so that it wouldn't fly from her side, and spurred her horse. The beast came around to block her father's mount. After a few metered breaths, she found the will to meet her father eye to eye.

"Why haven't you taken Kyle to the springs?"

"He doesn't need the water."

"He's in pain." She shook her head, confounded by her father's deadpan stare. "The water could fix him. Why does he have to suffer?"

"The water isn't for him. It's only for us."

Her body tightened as she wrestled to loose the words she craved to say. Her perceived injustice for Kyle's condition was all she required to surmount her ingrained patriarchal respect. "Is that why you've been lying about things?" Her voice cracked. "Is that why you've been lying to me?"

He took a deep breath. "I knew this day would come."

Her heart pounded. The gate had opened. There was no point or reason in holding her tongue. "Why have you been lying?"

Her accusation drew no visible response from her father's frozen features. Instead, he pointed off to his side, toward town. "To protect you from the truth, you foolish ingrate." His voice slithered with restrained fury even as it struck with the lethal speed of an angered rattlesnake. "You wish to know the truth, do you? You wish to throw away the protection I've provided?"

She blinked to remember her determination. "No—yes, if it means you tell me the truth, yes, I want to know!"

He spurred his mount to come up beside her. He sat straight in his saddle to glare down his nose at her, his stare withering her resolve in a heartbeat. Before she could utter a word, his hand whipped out in a wild backhanded slap. Her world flashed white in a simultaneous instant of disbelief that he might assault her. Stunned, she swayed, her hat flew loose, and her arm popped free. The world spun away as she flopped senseless from her saddle and crashed to the ground in a confused heap, the black caballero hat offering itself as a meager cushion when her head smacked against the hard turf.

Her father hopped from his saddle and seized the neck of her blue and white poncho to jerk her to a prone position. His other hand shot out to his side to catch the length of her arm as it launched toward him, his grip clamping beneath the hand as her arm's length swung to entrap his arm in a stubborn but feeble coil.

"Do you feel this? Do you see what it means to be powerless?" He shook her until her eyes focused. "This is the moment of your awakening. You dare criticize me? You dare challenge me? Do you know what innocence is? Innocence is nothing but benign ignorance. Insolence is the price paid for ignorance realized, and resentment is the price paid for innocence spent!" He threw her to the ground and slapped her once more. "Now, beg my forgiveness, beg my mercy to take you back as my child or else grovel as a wench for Woolly Ben. Tell me your choice!"

She cowered at his feet, defenseless without her arm. Blood dribbled from her lower lip.

He grabbed her poncho once more, heaved, and let her flop on her side. When she tried to right herself, he sped toward her and stomped his boots on either side of her chest, pinning her to the ground beneath her poncho. Her feet flailed, to no use, and she went still.

"You hate me in this moment," he hissed. "Don't pretend to hide it. I see it in your eyes, plain as day and hotter than the sun, even as your pathetic tears seep across the filth on your face. Is this all you are, a hopeless cripple, or are you more?"

"Daddy, please—"

"Silence!" His chest heaved as he caught his breath. "This, this, right now, this is the savagery of the outside world. You accuse me of deceit? You shall repent for conceit. I hid this savagery from you because I love you. You are my child, a miraculous creature unknown and unseen to the blighted world surrounding us. But this, this you experience now, this is what that world has in wait for you, for me, for everyone you love."

He leaned over, grabbed her hair, and shook her head until she thrashed in defense. Her efforts faded to futility, even as her jaw clenched and she glared at him with an incendiary stare.

"That's it," he whispered. "Feel it. Feel this. Know this. This is what Outsiders will give you. Hate me in this moment. Embrace the disgust you feel, revel in the hurt that drives your pointless resistance, and learn that this—only this—is the reality of the world."

Her fingers trembled as her arm wriggled in his unbreakable clutch. With nothing else to do, nothing else left to her, she spat at him. The muddy, bloody glob of saliva came apart as a weak spray of dark flecks that peppered the black sleeve of his coat.

He shoved her head into the dirt and let go of her hair. With a slow, deliberate straightening of his back, he enforced his state of superiority to glare down at her once more. "Think of me what you will but know that there is one irrefutable difference between me and the world outside. It is this one act I do now, and nothing else."

He stepped away to set her free. She kicked at the ground to drive herself back.

"I let you go because I love you," he said, his voice returning to its typical restrained monotone. "You are my precious daughter. I love you, so I grant you this gift of mercy."

He climbed into his saddle, pulled her arm free, and tossed it onto her chest. Keeping his gaze on her, he reached toward her saddle, snatched her waterskin, and dropped it beside her.

"Outsiders show no such mercy. Their only reprieve is death." His face fell to a worn mask. "This is what I hid from you. Now you know it in a way no words can impart. The pure and the corrupt cannot share the Earth in harmony. They are not meant to share the Earth in harmony. The land can only suffer the presence of one of these factions. The wicked are complacent that those who are just will fail to defend themselves. The wicked believe the just will fail to do whatever they need to do to prevail in the timeless struggle of good and evil."

Her arm joined her shoulder. The moment it was secure she braced her hand and popped to her feet. "If you ever hit me again . . ."

"What?" He scoffed. "What would you do?"

She was powerless against him, but it didn't matter. The water was changing her. She could feel it, knew it as a certainty somewhere deep down, deep down in a dark place that was yet lit with a hidden, glowing light. Her father had overpowered her and her arm. They had to be stronger. She knew then what she wanted from the water's change. She didn't want to be different, she wanted to be more; she wanted to be an amplification of her current embodiment so that no one could challenge her supremacy.

She spat the blood from her mouth. "If you ever hit me again, I'll kill you."

For a moment the words hung between them, became locked between them in the same way she remembered her father and Mena locked over Mena's hand waiting to strike her. And then, to her surprise, to her dismay, to her deepest feral rage, he smiled upon her.

"Now you know what it means to be my child," he said, holding his smile a moment longer before it faded. "Remember it. We two, and only we two, have the strength to be wicked in our justice and just in our wickedness."

She stared at him. She wasn't sure what to say, so she said nothing.

Her father gave her a single nod to end the matter. "Now. Woolly Ben plans to destroy us, so we must plan to destroy him first. We have less than two years to prepare."

He nudged his horse, gave the reins a slight tug, and trotted away.

13

‡ ‡ ‡

The hurt transformed over time, and Angela came to see the heart of her father's cruel lesson. For weeks after returning home, she despised him, hated the very sight of him, cursed his every breath, and prayed every night for his death, even as the bitter tears of that hypocritical plea eked from the clamped folds of her eyelids. When the wisdom of the hate began to have its sway, she at first resented him all the more. He was her father. Austere, unforgiving, strict, she nevertheless, in all her prior days, had been imbued with the unerring impression of his love for her.

Such a belief changed after that day on the trail. He said he loved her, but she came to the belief that he loved her only for her capacity to serve his vision. If she was of no use to him, if she dared defy his prophetic vision, she was certain he'd cast her aside, if not destroy her outright. All she had to do was look at the contempt with which he treated poor Ivan and the cold shoulder of disdain he turned to her mother's declining condition.

Yes, all those things worked their way through her sensibilities as she lay in bed at night and stared at the blank white ceiling over her head. Their true source, and their true conviction, she knew came from something far different, from something guarded deep within her, a deduction so simple she called upon all the greater forces lurking unseen beneath her existence to keep its source hidden from her father's withering stare.

Sometimes, she would even soothe the coiled fury within her by letting the source manifest as a simple chain of words to stifle her troubles. No sooner had they first come to her than she found them truncated to one single word, the one word that stabilized the world of her thoughts, and let it seep through her mind with every tidal flow of air in her lungs.

She drifted away then, drifted away to a different place, a place alight with the golden rays of dawn and the glint of dust floating on the lazy currents of her living breath. Her head turned, she looked over her shoulder, smiled, and the word at once formed with intangible effort and momentous relief.

It was more than a word, though. It was a name.

Kyle.

‡ ‡ ‡

For all that her heart ached to return to the Eddington house, her father's unforgettable assault scarred her in a way she could only fathom in the tender slice of wisdom she knew in her short life. Embittered by the beating he inflicted, the hurt within rebelled with caustic condemnations whenever she recalled her parting with Kyle and the foolishness she displayed by throwing herself against him. It was something a child would do, she decided, something a stupid little girl would do, something a girl who knew nothing about the world around her would think she could do without betraying herself as a complete fool.

No, even though a natural curiosity within her longed to sit with Kyle and revel in the attention he seemed all too willing to lavish upon her, she found a different compulsion stirring within her. It resided with his disability, in the very frailty of his physical existence. She was growing tall and strong, fast like her mother, and her mind was sharp. No, what she believed compelled her was an urge to supplant his frailty by buoying his body in the way he had sought to buoy her mind.

He could teach her all the wondrous secrets in his books, and in return she could protect him. If there was one thing she came to know after returning beaten and bloody from her ride to the Eddington house, it was the fact that the water of Thetis Springs was indeed transforming her from a powerless girl into a Force of Nature.

‡ ‡ ‡

She woke one morning to a warm spring day, the commotion from the kitchen beneath her room catching her attention. Her arm, perched by her window as had become its habit, turned its eye to her the moment she stirred and shot across the room in one modest spring of its length. In a blur of flesh, it sped around her and joined her shoulder, drawing a sigh of relief from her before she met the day with a yawn.

Judah and Jonah were waiting in the foyer. They were seated, silent in their mute obedience, but they were boys no longer. No, like Angela, they had grown tall and strong, and their loose black coats hid the banded musculature heaped upon their imposing frames. She had always thought Ivan a strong fellow, but he paled beside the might of his sons. Though they did not share all of their father's remarkable constitution, they displayed an ability to heal any wounds they sustained in the exercise of their brawn.

Angela caressed their cheeks as she passed, smiling in greeting. The twins responded by bowing their heads and pressing their faces in turn to the palm of her hand. It wasn't the pointed glare of desire they cast upon their betrotheds, Ruth and Rachel, but more akin to the filial devotion she showed her mother.

The scene she found in the kitchen lit her with excitement. Mena was busy collecting dishes. She glanced at Angela and pointed to a single dish piled with scrambled eggs and some strips of smoked pork that had been left on the table. Angela's arm trembled with hunger, but her attention was drawn elsewhere. On the other side of the table, her father sat with Ivan, the two men busy loading rounds into their repeating rifles. Ivan smiled and waved to her; her father settled an icy gaze on her and pointed for her to sit.

She grabbed a fork and let her arm shovel a glistening pile of eggs into her waiting mouth. Careless for the offense of speaking while eating, she tipped her head to the guns and voiced a single word.

"Outsiders?"

Ivan nodded. Before he could speak, her father silenced him with an upraised hand. "Three men. Your mother spotted them on her morning run."

She coughed and willed her arm at ease as she almost choked on another pile of eggs. "You're riding out with Ivan?" she asked as Mena set a cup of milk by her plate.

Her father held her in his stare. "That's all you want to ask?"

"Are they Woolly Ben's men?" she asked as her arm brought the milk to her lips.

"Don't know right off," Ivan said. He rested his rifle across his lap. "Could be, might not be. Guess we'll find out the hard way."

Her father said nothing.

She met his stare. "Judah and Jonah are going to protect the homes?"

"No one can get past my boys," Ivan said with a nod.

"Our boys," Mena corrected without looking at her husband.

Ivan took a breath and flipped open a double-barrel shotgun.

Angela ignored everyone. For a moment the world faded to just her and her father. She knew what she would say before she heard her voice. When she spoke it wasn't a question, it was a statement.

"I'm riding with you."

Her father propped the butt of his rifle on his thigh. After a few moments of pregnant silence, he consented with a single nod. There was nothing else to say. They both understood the change. Her days of asking permission ended without a word of note.

She looked down to find her arm waiting, a few strips of pork stuck on the tines of her fork. Her mouth opened and she let her arm stuff the savory strips of meat between her teeth. Without hurry, without sense of any authority over her, she ignored everyone around her while she finished her meal. She said nothing, just marched up to her room after she handed her plate off to Rachel when the twin maidservant appeared at her side.

Ascending the stairs allowed her a moment of reflection. It wasn't so much the physical act of ascension that struck her but more so the symbolic notion of her ascension. Twenty months had passed since she had ridden away from the Eddington house and Kyle had receded to the hallowed ground of her treasured memories. Much had changed since then, also in symbolic ways. That day she left Kyle, so sure of her position that she challenged her father, she had soon found herself a young girl sprawled bloody on the ground, pinned under his feet, helpless as he slapped her into submission.

She was, by outward appearance, now a full-grown woman. Her eyes had assumed a hardness she had learned that day her father beat her, and her arm had grown long and strong, imbued with the secret power of Thetis Springs. Her days had not been idle in preparation for Woolly Ben's deadline.

No, she was no longer an ignorant girl. She was a woman not to be trifled with.

She dressed, slipping into the same clothes she had worn to the Eddingtons. Ruth and Rachel had added material to her pants to accommodate the rapidity of her maturation, while Ivan had made her a new set of boots from hides Carl Eddington brought out to the Range. Her blue and white poncho now hung to her hips rather than her knees, allowing her arm to launch from her shoulder.

Despite Mena's objections, Angela had let her hair grow down to her shoulders. It wasn't a bother. She had her caballero hat. It fit her just fine now.

She came downstairs to join her father and Ivan. They had their guns. She had her arm. Mena stood by the sink, serious as ever, although her lips couldn't be pressed into a tighter line of austerity if she tried. Ruth and Rachel were in the foyer, sitting with Jonah and Judah as they ate. No one spoke, and no blessing was uttered.

Angela followed her father and Ivan out the front door.

Her mother waited outside. Months earlier, Angela's father had decreed Calliope had become too feral to live in the house and had banished her to the stable with the other horses. A rough brown shirt served as her only clothing. Dense brown hair, slick as a horse's coat, covered the rest of her body.

Calliope's head snapped up, her large eyes as they rested on Angela growing ever larger when it was clear Angela was to join the sortie. A series of plaintive grunts welled up in Calliope's throat as she stomped a hoof in the dirt.

Angela stopped on the last step to meet her mother's gaze. "I'm ready. Don't worry."

Her mother stomped her hoof once more. The corners of her eyes grew moist with dismay. She reached out to cradle her daughter's face. Her hands had become clumsy and all but useless, her fingers curled tightly and half fused into hooves.

"I'm ready," Angela said once more.

Her mother sniffled. She trembled, drew a breath, and struggled to speak. "Love," she said. Satisfied, she nodded. "Love."

It sickened Angela to see her mother so devolved. The day Nathan had banished Calliope from the house a terrible argument had ensued. Her father had withdrawn behind his usual resolute mask of indifference, while Angela had screamed and tried to block the door. Her mother had bucked and whinnied but offered little resistance as Nathan yanked at the guide rope tied around her neck. When Angela grabbed for the rope, Mena had thrown herself against Angela and held her down, a carving knife to her throat. Angela's arm had coiled, ready to strike, and held back only when Calliope had cried out in protest.

The matter was decided. She embraced Angela, nodded to Nathan, and let him lead her out to the stable. That had been several months ago.

Now Angela stared at her mother. "Love," she whispered.

Calliope bobbed her head as tears streaked her face.

"Enough," Nathan said and pulled at his wife's guide rope. He unwound the loose end from the porch rail, loosened the knot to work the rope over her head, and slapped her back to send her speeding away.

He gave Angela a stern glare before pointing to the horses. "We have to ride."

Angela held her silence. As with many things, there was nothing to say. After the horrible night of her mother's banishment, she told Ivan she hated her father and Mena. Ivan, in his good nature, tried to allay her anger. It was a price Calliope had accepted long ago. They had all gone into the water of Thetis Springs, but she had stayed in far longer than anyone else, had stayed in until her skin broke out in a rash.

"Rev told us back then," Ivan had explained. "Greed got its own price to pay. I know she's your ma and all, but she stayed in them waters when the rest of us got our fill and got out. Said she didn't care none, said it felt too good to get out. Rev told her not to stay, but he couldn't go back in, even burned his feet when she wouldn't come out at first, but she was stubborn and stayed in until she knew she couldn't stay no longer."

Angela climbed into her saddle. She loved Ivan, so it pained her to realize he could indeed be a fool.

14

‡ ‡ ‡

They rode at a full gallop to keep pace with Calliope. Angela's blood surged in anticipation to confront the intruding Outsiders and repel them from the Range. Even though she had her differences with her father, her fill with Mena's demands, and ached to see Kyle again, when push came to shove, the Range was her world to understand and suffer its demands. She didn't take from Outsiders, and she refused to let them take from her— on that she understood her father in full.

It was late morning when they rounded a grove of trees. Calliope signaled for them to stop before speeding off on her own. They stayed in their saddles and gave their mounts a chance to catch their breaths. In short order, though, Calliope charged back to them, her nostrils flared with the exertion of her run.

She pointed and grunted, then scratched at the ground to draw a simple map when it was clear they didn't understand. Nathan glanced down for several moments before waving for them to dismount. Calliope continued to stomp at her map until Nathan grabbed her wrist and swept the map clear with his boot. Once he had her stilled, he looked at Ivan and Angela and pointed them in opposite directions. Ivan pulled his rifle from his horse before tossing Nathan his own rifle. He nodded to Nathan, turned, and scurried off.

"You," Nathan said to Calliope. "You stay here. Angela, make your way through the trees to come from the left. I'll follow on the middle. Don't let your arm go until you hear us open fire."

Angela stroked her mother's head and ran into the woods.

‡ ‡ ‡

It didn't take long for Angela to spy the Outsiders' camp. They were still having breakfast, betraying their whereabouts with the smoke from their smoldering fire. She sank low to stay out of sight and dodged from tree to tree until she was as close as she could get without being seen.

Three men were sitting by the fire: one on a stump, two others on a fallen trunk. They were rough looking men, unshaven, with worn clothes. She couldn't hear what they were saying, but they were saying something to each other, as she made out an occasional hoot of laughter. They had set up two tents consisting of simple canvas throws supported by a central rope tied off to two metal stakes hammered into the ground. For just an overnight camp, they had made quite a mess of bags and tools scattered about.

Five horses were tied off to the trees to Angela's left. They looked like sturdy beasts, good additions for the stable.

At least Angela assumed that was her father's plan.

Her assumption vanished in cracks of gunfire from her father and Ivan. Two of the horses screeched and dropped. Blood erupted from the eye socket of a third mount before it toppled without a sound.

The men threw their cups aside and jumped from their seats.

Angela turned, braced her legs, and let her arm coil against her side. In the next instant it sprang from her, streaking like an arrow with the strength of its launch. The remaining two horses bucked and jerked at their ropes, making difficult targets. Several rifle shots cracked through the morning air to bring them down.

Angela paid no heed. Her arm landed, coiled as it rolled over, and shot forward again. Its fingers, exposed and the tips having grown hard as nails, grabbed hold of one man's neck. The rest of her arm slapped around the man's body, trapping his arms. Helpless, hopeless, his scream of surprise was cut short as her hand snapped shut and ripped out his throat.

Blood erupted from his neck. He dropped to his knees and was dead before his face slapped on the ground.

One of the other men unloaded with a double-barrel shotgun, firing blind in his panic. Shot ripped into the foliage off to Angela's right. She ducked; her arm lunged. With the fingers pressed together, her arm hit the man's belly with the ferocity of a giant crossbow bolt, tearing into his guts and driving him to the ground.

The third man scrambled in terror as blood from his fellow peppered his face. He dodged from one side to the other, not knowing where to run, until three rifle shots ripped through his chest in quick succession. Arms outstretched, he spun in a delirious pirouette and crashed onto his back.

Angela's arm didn't waste any time. It wrestled its way out of its victim's corpse, wriggling along its length to shake off the clinging loops of his intestines. With a rapid reptilian serpentine, it slid through the messy camp and made its way to one tent and then the other, fanning open its fingers so that Angela could share its sight and confirm that the tents were empty.

Satisfied, she stood from cover when she saw Ivan and her father emerge from their firing points behind several bushes. They kept their rifles raised and ready, both of them jabbing pointed fingers at her to stay in cover. She hesitated until she heard a rustle and dropped back. When she turned to the sound, she saw her mother charge past her into the camp and draw to a halt by the dead horses.

Angela ignored the order to mind her safety. She had to move. The wail of dismay from her mother was too sickening to ignore. Despite her devotion to her mother, despite hating her father for forcing Calliope out of the house, she understood in that moment that her mother had indeed changed. Nevertheless, her mother's wails of agony woke deep memories. Whatever Calliope had become, she was still the one who had held Angela when she was young, who had shared her bed when the harsh winter winds chilled the house, and who in times so recent had let Angela ride upon her shoulders.

She went to her mother. Her arm snaked between the two tents, its eye surveying the contents as Ivan and Nathan drew near. The sights were of little consequence to Angela until her arm swung back for one last look.

Four bedrolls.

Three men.

Where . . .

A rifle shot cracked from the woods. Ivan wheezed. Nathan let out a shout and fired blind. Angela's arm sprang from the tent. As Angela spun to place the source of the shot, her mother slammed into her.

A report sounded. Nathan and Ivan let off several return shots. Angela hit the ground, stunned as her mother's weight piled atop her slender frame and drove the air from her lungs.

There was a scream from the woods. Angela's sight flashed to see a man slumped against a tree, quaking hands clutched to hold together the shredded remains of his face. Ivan came into sight, leveled his rifle to the man's forehead, and blew his brains out.

Angela struggled beneath her mother's weight, her boots digging into the grass as she tried to get free. Her mother stayed with her, seeming to refuse to let her go, until she at last slid off to lay sprawled on the ground. Angela fought to breathe as her lungs burned for air. Her head snapped to the side, only for her to gasp in horror.

Her mother was still. Blood foamed on her lips.

"Mommy?"

Calliope's breath rattled in her chest. Her gaze shifted to rest upon her daughter.

Angela rolled over and rose up on her knees. "Mommy . . . no, please, please . . ."

Her arm bounded to her side.

Calliope stared at her. "Love," she whispered.

The moment Angela's arm melded to her shoulder she shook the gore from her hand and stroked her mother's hair. "No, don't leave me. Please."

For the first time in a long time, her mother smiled. She smiled, and then she died.

‡ ‡ ‡

Angela sat by her mother, despondent, careless of time, her arm retracted as a protective coil against her chest. She stared at her mother's blank eyes. For as long as she could remember, her mother's eyes had lost their whites, making it impossible for some to discern her irises and so the direction of her gaze. For Angela, it was never a mystery. When she was near her mother, she knew her mother was always keeping watch over her. Angela was her darling daughter, her precious little girl, and the last link to a semblance of normality lost in her equine transformation.

Calliope had died with her eyes open. Angela came to see that dead eyes lost the bright sheen of living eyes. Her mother's gaze had always seemed like two focused drops of oil, black as night but alive with a reflective gleam.

In death her unblinking gaze had faded to twin lumps of charcoal.

Soon after the scrape with the Outsiders, Ivan came to Angela, squeezed her shoulder, and leaned over to embrace her.

"Sorry she's gone," he whispered. "I remember how much I loved my ma. I know it was both the same and different for you and sweet Calliope. We'll make sure she's laid to rest in proper fashion." He rubbed her back with his meaty hand. "Now look, I don't mean to be cold and all, but there's things need to be done, and there's no gettin' away with that. I got to get my girls so we can clean up. You can come if you want."

It was the only time since her mother's death that she looked away. "I'm not leaving."

"If that's what you want." Ivan stood. "The Rev will be here with you."

She blinked as her mother's death replayed in her head. She remembered that Ivan had been hurt. "What about you? You were shot, weren't you?"

Ivan waved it off. "That? It ain't nothin' worth a fret." He showed her the hole in his pant leg where a bullet had torn through. He widened the hole with his fingers so she could see his leg. The flesh seemed to bubble, like the way batter bubbled, a slow mound, collapse, and then resurgence, each time adding more tissue to the cavity the bullet had torn through his leg.

Her eyes darted to his.

He smiled. "See? I told you I was tougher th'n any might know. You don't need to worry none 'bout me. You got enough worryin' on your plate, so put your energies where you best need 'em."

He patted her shoulder once more, gave her a nod, and left her to ride for the houses.

Her father was busy searching the tents. Only when he was done did he come to stand over Calliope's body, his arm folded to rest his rifle on his shoulder. "Now you know the threat we face."

Angela's arm coiled tighter. She refused to look at her father. "They weren't near our homes. If we had let them pass through, my mother would still be alive."

"But they wouldn't pass through," he said with a shake of his head.

"They'd call for more. That's the mistake the redskins made from the first time white men came across the ocean. There is no deal with Outsiders. If they're not destroyed at once, they'll congregate, multiply, and take everything for their own."

"My mother's dead."

"Woolly Ben won't care. Neither will anyone else."

She closed her eyes for a moment. "Do you care?"

His unflinching stare awaited her. "Your mother was an invaluable scout. Without her we won't know what's happening outside what we can see."

"Is that all you have to say for her?"

He pointed to the unseen distance where Thetis Springs hid in its tunnel. "She took more than her proper due from the water. Her greed sowed her doom. If it didn't happen today, it would be another day." He shook his head once more. "Look at her. Look what she became. There wasn't much human left in her."

"She died protecting me."

He opened a hand to Calliope's body. "Then you best thank her. You got the last of what good was left in her."

15

‡ ‡ ‡

The afternoon waned as they waited for Ivan to return with Ruth and Rachel for the clean-up Angela had once longed to see. Although she could taste the prospect of having that sought-after mystery revealed, she was much more inclined to sit listless and stare at her mother's corpse.

Her father had busied himself poking through the Outsiders' saddlebags and dragging the men from the camp. Once they were clear he stripped them and piled their clothes with the rest of their belongings. With this done he sat by the cold ashes of their morning campfire and chewed on a piece of jerked pork.

"Are you going to sit there all day?"

Angela refused to look at him. "I'll sit here as long as I need."

"She has to be buried. No matter how much you loved her, the flies and vermin will come for her just the same. To them she's nothing more than a nutritious pile of rotting flesh."

Angela's arm begged to rip out his throat, but she held it still beneath her poncho. "I'll bury her with Ivan's help."

"I'm her husband. You're her daughter. She's ours to bury."

She fixed a hard stare on him. "You called her an animal and banished her from the house." She shook her head and turned back to her mother. "No. I don't want you touching her. I'll ask Ivan."

"If you insist." He stood. "It's a task that suits him well."

She kept her head still but glanced past her shoulder to see him turn his back and walk away.

‡ ‡ ‡

It was almost evening by the time Ivan returned with his daughters. Nathan went to Ivan at once. Angela couldn't make out the words in her father's heated exchange, but she heard accusations that Ivan had dawdled, that he should have hurried the sisters, that he knew how dangerous it was for the Outsiders to lay out before being cleaned up, and on and on.

Ivan lowered his head and nodded several times. Not once did he meet Nathan eye to eye. When it was done Nathan stormed off, jabbing a pointed finger at Calliope's corpse. Ivan looked over, saddened at the sight of Angela still sitting vigil by her mother's body.

He walked to her but her attention was already fixed on the sisters.

The twins, always so fussy about the propriety of their appearance and demeanor, demonstrated a behavior Angela had never before witnessed. They walked around the row of Outsiders' bodies, left naked on the grass, before retreating several steps. They then disrobed, helping each other with their clothes, making sure to fold their garments in neat stacks several paces from the bodies. Once they were naked they tended to their hair, making sure the long brown lengths were pinned, piled up, and then wrapped securely with strips of old washcloth. They looked at Angela, noting her wide-eyed gaze of surprise, but they offered her nothing.

Ivan put a hand on Angela's shoulder. "Come on now, let's get to it. There ain't nothin' you wanna be watchin' there anyway. They got a job to do, and we best let them get to it." He waited for her to turn to him before handing her a small shovel. "I know you got your one arm and all, but, well, seein' as you find a way to do everythin' else just fine, I figure you can help me dig just fine for your ma's sake."

At last she stood. Her knees popped from having sat for so long. "Thank you for helping me, Ivan."

"The Rev could've helped you start," Ivan said and drove his shovel into the ground.

"I wanted to do it with you, not him."

Ivan glanced to where Nathan had taken watch, rifle on his shoulder, away from the camp. "It's a fine compliment, and I thank you for thinkin' of me for helpin' you do this, but I don't want to be gettin' in the way of nothin' between you and the Rev."

"Don't worry." Angela watched as he pulled up a blade full of dirt. "I wanted to do this with you because I know you loved her." She forced a fragile smile. "And I know you love me."

"Well, that I do. That I certainly do," he said with a tip of his head. He bobbed to either side before pointing to the ground. "Make an outline, long and narrow."

"Will do." She stomped on the shovel's boot ledge to drive the blade into the ground. With her arm coiled around the haft of the shovel, she found she could work the tool just fine. Once again Ivan proved he had more smarts than he was given credit.

The sound that came from the shovel surprised her. It was a sound that had the drier crunch of the ground but held a new, wetter edge, more as if she was tearing the dirt. She looked at Ivan, but he made an obvious effort to keep his head down.

She knew that sound. She had heard it before. It was the final squeal of mortality that emanated when Ivan butchered one of the Range's pigs.

And then it hit her.

Ruth and Rachel.

Ruth and Rachel and the bodies of the Outsiders.

Clean-up.

She straightened, steeling her nerves before looking over her shoulder. What she saw froze her where she stood. Were it not for the emotional evisceration of her mother's death, her eyes would have rolled out of her head in shock.

There was no recognizing the sisters as the quiet, doleful, dutiful twins she had always known. Instead, she saw two voracious demons, naked but for the splotches of bloody fluids spattered across their skin. Their eyes had turned red—all but the pinpoint black dots of their pupils—and had distended to burning orbs that seemed ready to burst from their faces. Squeals of delight sounded from their throats as they tore into the four bodies left for them, their fingernails revealed as long retractable claws that ripped through flesh and sinew as if it were nothing more than cream-filled pastry.

In the midst of that festival of evisceration, their mouths hung ever wider, the flesh of their cheeks giving way beneath their jawbones to leave them in a state of disjointed hunger, no different than a snake ready to consume its prey.

Ivan rammed his shovel into the ground and threw aside a pile of dark soil.

Rachel grabbed a man's head, denuded his scalp with a single rip of her claws, and clamped her distended teeth into the man's skull. Her eyes narrowed with the tension building in her jaw until the skull cracked and collapsed, squashing its contents in a dark red wash of curdled brains.

Angela staggered back.

Her father stood a safe distance from the sisters, his rifle at rest over his shoulder as he watched them work. He looked no different than if he were watching Mena butter his bread.

Ruth tore open a rib cage. She howled, trembled with feverish delight, and rammed her head into the opened body cavity to gobble its contents.

The sisters were voracious cannibals.

She had suckled at their breasts.

Angela dashed to a tree, doubled over, and retched until the vomit burst from her lips. After several heaves, her stomach was empty, but the madness of what she witnessed lingered in her mind's eye. Her father, Ivan, her mother; everything vanished from her concerns. The sounds of the twins ravishing the corpses continued in its disgusting symphony of wet rips, pops, and crackling bones. Her arm quivered against her, overwhelmed by the horror of the butchery. She had killed, she had focused her arm to help dispatch the Outsiders in violent ways, but those acts were of necessity, of defense, of seeking to maintain the safety of the Range. What was happening behind her was beyond description, beyond belief, beyond anything conceived in any nightmare, for it was a living nightmare, a living hell, a living incarnation of her father's most vehement apocalyptic discourses.

Ivan came to her side. "Get on your way. Go on. I'll see to your ma. I know it's tough to see my girls in the raw."

Angela's head snapped toward him. "They're monsters!"

Ivan shook his head. "No more than the rest of us. They're just a different sort of strange. They're still the sisters we love and that love us back, that love you back."

Angela's arm shot out to shove Ivan away. It didn't hurt him, but there was no hiding the emotional wound of her sudden rejection. He was her dear gentle Ivan. In the moment he needed her understanding the most, in the first moment he ever asked for her understanding, she rejected him.

He retreated a step, the hurt clear in his eyes.

She gasped. It was insane. It was too much to bear.

There was nothing left to do but run, and run she did. With the speed of her mother's legacy, she flew from the despicable scene, found her horse, all but leapt into the saddle, and rammed her heels into the animal's flanks to spur its charge.

Off she went, vanishing into the unknowing depths of the Range.

She sobbed. She screamed. The wind pulled her hat from her head and left it slapping her back as the long chinstrap tugged at her neck.

Against her thirst, against her shock, she rode without relent. She had no choice. She had far to go, and daylight was wasting.

‡ ‡ ‡

She stopped once to give her mount a chance to catch its wind. What water she had she poured down its throat, took the saddle once more, and rode on. The sky darkened behind her, and it seemed the oily veil of night itself gave chase, driving her to ride all the harder. One by one the stars revealed themselves in her wake, their pinpoint twinkles pale beneath the gleaming three-quarter moon dominating the black dome above her. It wasn't much light, but it was enough for her to see.

At last she spotted the top of the Eddington's windmill and she urged her horse over the crest of one last hill to reveal their house. She let her horse slow to a trot, the animal panting and staggering with exhaustion. The sounds carried across the quiet night. She fought to keep upright against her own exhaustion, her bloodshot gaze locked on the back door.

It eased open. There was no mistaking the fat barrel of the shotgun that poked out. "Who's there?" a voice from the darkness demanded.

She remembered the voice. It was Carl.

Her throat was so dry she croaked. She struggled to summon some saliva, licked her lips, swallowed, and called out. "It's Angela. Angela Purdy."

Carl leaned out the door, sweeping the landscape with his shotgun before lowering the barrel. "Where's the Reverend?"

"It's just me." She sobbed. "Please! Help me. I don't know where else to go."

Carl moved toward her with caution, his head swinging to either side to survey the darkness. A moment later Sarah came out, but she darted back inside before returning with a lantern, which she held high.

Angela's eyes narrowed against the sudden glare, causing them to blur with tears as Carl's shadow raced toward her. When she blinked, she at last understood why she had ridden with such haste, and her sanity crept back to her conscious mind to remember what had driven her to choose the Eddington house for her refuge.

Kyle stood behind his mother, leaning on his cane with one hand, his other hand raised to shield his eyes from the lantern's glare.

His jaw dropped when he made out Angela's image. "Angela?" He squeezed his eyes shut for a moment. "Is . . . is that really you?"

Her arm sprang from her side, shot across the grass, wound itself around his cane, and up his arm. The fingers spread wide, and the single luminous eye opened upon him.

Her lungs emptied with a deep sigh of relief. What strength remained in her seeped out with her breath, and her heart eased its frantic pound.

She stared. Tears left glistening trails on her dust-caked cheeks.

"Kyle?"

Without another word she slumped in her saddle. Unconscious, unstrung, she fell into Carl's arms.

16

‡ ‡ ‡

The smell of biscuits and eggs dragged her mind from sleep. Before she stirred a single muscle, her arm slithered under the sheet of her bed, under her nightshirt, and joined her shoulder. It curled around, pulled the sheet down to her waist, and nudged her cheeks until she shook her head and muttered that she was awake.

She sat up with a groan, her legs and bottom sore from the long ride. After several blinks, her memory sparked to recognize the room around her. It was the guest bedroom of the Eddington house, the same room where she had slept with her father on her previous visit. She closed her eyes and let her imagination glide down the stairs, work a slow circle in the sitting room to sweep over the walkway to the kitchen, the front door and covered porch, and last to the door to Kyle's office.

She rolled her shoulders and let her eyelids recede. The bedroom was still around her. It wasn't a dream. She was in fact in the Eddingtons' house.

Her heart bucked.

If the Eddington house was real, then there was no denying the nightmare she had witnessed the day before, and no denying that her mother was dead.

She heard the creak of stairs, followed by a knock on the door before it opened. Sarah stood there, her blonde hair pulled back to hang in a long tail between her shoulders. For some reason Angela half expected the flaxen length to lift of its own accord and stare back at her.

No, that's me.

Sarah cleared her throat. "Good morning. Breakfast is ready, if you're hungry."

"Thank you." Angela arose slowly, her legs shaky.

Sarah put an arm around Angela's waist to steady her. There was no mistaking the query in her gaze.

Angela leaned into her for a moment and then said softly, "I know I have some explaining to do. May I do it while I eat?"

"Of course." Sarah smiled. "Why else would I come get you?" She grabbed the banister and helped Angela down the stairs. "We're all quite concerned. And surprised, I have to tell you. You've done quite a bit of growing since last we saw you."

Angela's gaze darted to Sarah. Her hand clutched the nightshirt against her breasts.

Sarah shushed her before she could speak. "After Carl brought you upstairs, I washed and changed you. Only me, no one else. If you want to confirm this pledge, ask your arm. It kept watch over us the whole time. I just couldn't let you sleep in filth." Sarah turned her focus to the stairs. "The way you've changed since your last visit, well, it's remarkable."

Angela felt her cheeks warm as she blushed. "I'm a fast grower."

Sarah hummed in thought. "That was the first thing Kyle said this morning."

‡ ‡ ‡

They let her eat in peace, making an effort not to stare at her for too long. For her part she resisted the urge to meet their gazes, wary as to what she might discover. She figured an expectant benevolence in Sarah. From Carl she figured there'd be something more pressing, perhaps a strained impatience for her to answer at least a dozen questions regarding her lone appearance in the middle of the night.

Most worrisome and yet most welcome was what she might find on Kyle's face. She expected him to be studying her; she'd be disappointed if there was nothing less than some form of analytical curiosity. But she prayed for much more.

When Angela choked on a piece of biscuit, Sarah pushed a glass of milk toward her. Angela nodded her gratitude, took the drink, and let it wash down her throat. It reminded her of the way she poured water down the throat of her mount.

"My horse . . . is it hurt?"

"No," Carl said. "It needs some rest, but it'll be fine. Speaking of the poor beast, do you mind telling us why you put it through such a rigor?"

Angela closed her eyes as her hand shoved the last of the eggs into her mouth. A moment later the napkin brushed her lips. Satisfied, her hand withdrew under her shirt.

Her eyes popped open. "Where are my clothes?"

Sarah put a hand on her back. "I washed them this morning."

Carl hooked a thumb over his shoulder. "They're outside to dry."

"Angela," Kyle said, at last drawing her gaze to him. He raised an eyebrow in expectation. It was clear, though, that he hadn't slept. "We're all worried sick."

"I know. I'm sorry. Thank you for taking me in," she said with a nod, darting glances to Carl and Sarah. "Outsiders came on the Range early yesterday morning. My mother spotted them. I rode out with my father and Ivan."

Sarah looked at Kyle. "Would you mind giving us a few minutes?"

Carl settled a hand on Kyle's arm to still his son. "No. He's not a child."

"I know about the sisters," Kyle said to his mother.

Sarah turned to her husband. "I thought we agreed . . ."

"Like I said, he's not a child," Carl repeated. "I told him three years ago, after the last time Outsiders came in." He lifted his hand from Kyle's arm and opened it to Angela. "How many?"

"We rode out to their camp. We saw three men. We, we killed them," she said, ducking her head to hide from Kyle. "But there was a fourth man we didn't see. He was going to shoot me." She sucked in a shaky breath. "My mother knocked me away. She, she's dead."

Carl and Kyle sat straight, unmoving, but Sarah moved at once, standing and cradling Angela's head to her belly. She leaned over, kissed the top of Angela's head, and held her as the girl wept. "We're so sorry. We're so very sorry."

Carl only waited a moment. "Was anyone else hurt?"

Angela nodded against Sarah. "Ivan was shot."

Carl blew out a breath. "One shot won't stop him." He was silent for several moments. "Were you there for . . . oh God, you were, weren't you?"

Kyle looked at his father. "Is it what you told me?"

Sarah closed her eyes. "The clean-up."

Angela leaned away from Sarah. "I saw it. Ruth and Rachel. I never, ever, want to see that again." She sniffled, her hand darting up to wipe away her tears. "I didn't stay to bury my mother. I left Ivan to do it. He tried to be nice to me, nice the way he always is, and I shoved him away. I couldn't look at him. I couldn't look at my father. I couldn't look at Ruth and Rachel while they, they, ripped those men to pieces and ate them. And I don't want to go back home. There's nothing there but Mena. My mother's dead. Judah and Jonah can't take her place. No one can." She slumped against Sarah. "I have no home. I have no place to go. I'm lost."

"Nonsense," Sarah said. "You'll always have a home here. You're family."

Carl rapped his knuckles on the table to get Angela's attention. "Does your father know you're out here?"

She closed her eyes. "I don't know. He saw me ride off. He didn't stop me."

"He's going to be worried about you."

"He doesn't care about me. He banished my mother from the house, did you know that?" She took control of her arm to jab a finger to her side. "He called her an animal. He said she was no good to stay in the house with people. She died to save me. She's an animal, but Ruth and Rachel can sleep under our roof?"

Carl frowned. "They have their job."

Angela glared at him. "Have you seen them? Have you? They're demons!"

"Yes, I've seen them." Carl took a breath. "They're just different in a different way."

It was the same thing Ivan had said to her. She slapped her hand over face.

"Angela," Kyle said, his voice soft. "I know what you're thinking."

She parted two fingers to glare at him.

"You're not like them. You're not a monster." He gave her a tender smile. "You're our Angela, and we'll never turn our back to you."

‡ ‡ ‡

Sarah and Carl were discussing things in the kitchen, so Angela went out front and sat in one of the porch chairs. The familiar clop of Kyle's cane reached her ears before she heard the squeak of the door's hinges. Unsure what to say, she shifted in her chair, stabbed by a sudden and profound sense of guilt. She was devastated by her mother's death, yet all she pictured in her mind, and all she yearned for in that moment, was for Kyle to put his arms around her.

Her mind flashed with the image of their last parting, when she had thrown herself against him.

"Can I get you anything?" Kyle said.

"No, thank you." Her gaze darted about the porch boards before flicking up to his waiting countenance. "That's very kind."

"I'm sorry about your mother." He looked toward the distant hills. "You really surprised us last night. We didn't know what to think."

"I'm sorry I disturbed your sleep."

He planted his cane and turned back to her. "Don't be silly. The loss of one night's sleep has no meaning in comparison to the loss of your mother."

She looked up to him. There was no hiding the consternation in his eyes, despite his sympathy. Not that she doubted his sincerity, but she had the clear feeling he didn't know what to think of her distinct maturation since they last met, much less a way to ask about such a glaring reality.

She decided there was nothing else but to call it out. "Kyle, I know I've changed."

He pressed his lips together in thought. "Forgive me. You lost your mother. You shouldn't have to worry about anything else." He lowered his head and turned for the door.

She reached out and took his wrist. "I'm still me."

"I don't doubt that," he said with a little laugh. "I remember a girl of twelve years who had the insight of someone significantly older. Now I see someone who should be a girl shy of fourteen but seems a woman in her full growth." He stared at her for a moment before frowning and resting his free hand over hers. After a tip of his head, he patted her hand and met her gaze. "It's not important. No matter what, you're too young to have lost your mother. For that, you have my deepest sympathy."

She wasn't aware she lingered in his stare until she felt her arm coiling up to his elbow. With a start she dropped her gaze and recalled her arm to her side. The hand turned and glared back at her, but she regained control with a glare of her own and shut the eye.

Kyle stared in wonder.

She forced a smile. "Thank you for understanding. May I have a few minutes?"

"Of course." He swung the door, shifted his weight and, in one practiced move, propelled his body into the house.

She watched as the door shut. Alone, she looked into the distance and came to the simple conclusion that she did indeed have a place to call home.

‡ ‡ ‡

It wasn't long after Kyle left her that she saw Carl ride off over the hill. She lingered for several moments before easing back in her chair. The empty, rolling land filled her sight with its gentle green swells of vibrant growth. Somewhere out there, somewhere not far away, the land yielded to the town and its Outsider denizens. All her life, all she knew was condemnation for those people and the dark labels to match their lies, savagery, and immorality. It was a vicious trinity to set them apart from the Range and the people who filled the world she knew.

But what did she know? Her father had banished her mother. Yes, Calliope had spent too much time in the miraculous water, but did she not pay a heavy price? She may have lost her human refinements of speech and appearance, but her humanity ran true and showed in her sacrifice. In the context of Angela's experience and the life of communal support she knew on the Range, she could think of no greater measure of humanity than self-sacrifice. And savagery? Had she not witnessed a form of bestial savagery beyond belief, beyond anything her father spoke of in his sermons?

No, she had seen immorality. She had seen savagery.

The only remaining leg of the trinity of condemnation was that of lies. She had challenged her father once and he had responded by beating her. Despite the emotional scars of that day, she came to understand that he had, in his own way, lied to protect her. She had indeed disrespected him with contempt born of her ignorance. At the same time, he still kept the truth of his precious little book. Was secrecy not a lie of omission? If there was nothing of harm in the book, then why not share it with her, his precious daughter? He had taught her that lies of omission held equal guilt with bold-faced lies. The very act of concealment necessitated the judgment of guilt.

They were his words, after all.

She blinked.

She hadn't thought of the book since that day he beat her for challenging him. In the time that followed, it often registered in her awareness, but the idea of confronting him had faded to inconsequence. She matured, her arm became a deadly weapon, she grew to a position of ascendance over both sets of twins; no, there had been many other things to crowd out the interest in his stupid little book.

And yet, after all that time, it had reasserted its presence in her thoughts.

It only took her a moment to understand why.

Kyle.

She stood. The long white nightshirt swayed about her ankles in the breeze. She was bare beneath its length. Her skin tingled with the cool air.

If her father could be pardoned for the secret of his book, she saw no reason not to be pardoned for a secret of her own. If nothing else, she could forget about the loss of her mother for a few moments. If her intuition held true, she might be able to restore the solace ripped from her spirit with Calliope's death.

She walked inside. The kitchen door was open. Sarah was just outside, fetching water from the well. The door to Kyle's office was closed. Her arm raced from her shoulder, grabbed the knob, braced its tail to the wall, and used it as an anchor to fling the door open.

Kyle looked up as she walked into the office. She didn't look down as her arm coiled its tail about her ankle to push the door closed. From there it sped across the floor in a slick serpentine, the hand turning to Kyle once to show its eye. It went from window to window, pulling the drapes to block the windows and sunlight. With everything done, Angela's arm bounded to her side, shot up the inside of the nightshirt, and wriggled against her side. It snaked out and hung loose, appearing no different than any other arm.

She took a breath and looked at Kyle. His expression of wonder came to her as a welcome endearment.

"Have you added any new books?" she asked.

"What?" He took a moment to regain his senses. "Oh, no, not since you left. Nothing has changed, though. You're welcome to look at anything you want."

She moved to the bookcases. "Do you still have the book with all the animals in pieces?"

"The anatomy book. Yes, if you're ready to look at that, it's still here."

"No, I don't want to see it. I wanted to know where to avoid it."

He pushed up on his cane. "I still have the big book of maps. It's in the same place."

She rested her hand on the volume, ready to take it from the shelf, when she reconsidered. "Do you mind that I closed the curtains?"

"No. I understand if you don't want so much brightness."

"Why?"

"Because you're grieving," he said with a shrug. "Because you're sad. When I was younger I used to stay in here and close the curtains."

She turned to him. "Why would you do that?"

"Sometimes I got mad." He glanced down at his leg "Sometimes I got sad. Many times I felt both those things." He looked back to her. "Mind you, my parents never told me to limit myself. They raised me with the understanding that the only limits in my life are the ones I accept. It's a noble lesson, but there's no denying that in fact I do have clearly defined limits." He looked around the office. "When I was younger, sometimes I hated this place, seeing it only as a prison and my leg as my chain. Then I found I could live in all the worlds and wonders I could find in my books, and this place transformed to a sanctuary."

She stared at him.

He rubbed his forehead. "I'm sorry. All I'm doing is talking about myself."

She looked into her palm. Its eye opened to stare back at her. She lowered her hand and found Kyle's waiting gaze. "I think you were talking about both of us. Until yesterday I didn't know enough to understand anything you just said." She frowned. "Is that insight?"

"No, that's wisdom." His face fell. "Insight can be instinctual. Wisdom is earned."

"Too bad you can't give it back when you see what it takes to get it."

"Maybe that's the true lesson of wisdom." He opened his hand. "It takes insight to realize what you said."

"How about that." She walked along the windows, letting her fingers run over the curtains. When she came to the middle of a window, her fingers parted the draperies for a moment, allowing a slash of golden light to illuminate her face. The closer she drew to Kyle, the more she realized he was leaning back. By the time she stood before him, she thought he might fall over.

His jaw clenched. "You've grown quite tall," he said, his voice nothing more than a whisper. "We see eye to eye now."

She fought to still herself. "I know what you want to ask, so go ahead."

He forced a swallow, his throat emitting a dry cluck. "How old are you?"

"Does that matter?"

He squeezed his eyes shut. "I . . . I need to understand."

"Then keep your eyes closed and listen." She took a breath. "I could tell you I was three years old when we first met, but you won't believe that because I now look full grown. I could tell you I aged a thousand years in one afternoon yesterday, but you know that couldn't be. So I'll only tell you this, because it's the only thing I understand now and the only truth I can figure of it." She paused to put her thoughts together. Then it came to her, and it was a far simpler—yet much more complex—thought than she would previously have believed she could summon.

"Kyle. Look at me." She waited for his eyes to open. "I'm younger than I look and far older than I seem."

"You defy everything I know," he said with a shake of his head, "and yet there you stand."

"Not there, but here." She followed his gaze as he tried to turn his head away. "With you."

She could see he was nervous. If it wasn't for the emotional stupor of her mother's death propelling her to the surreal comfort of dissociation, she knew she too would have been paralyzed with anxious anticipation. On any other day she wouldn't have ventured into his office, much less stand so close to him. The strangeness of the moment, so long desired and now occupied in such proximity to the tragedy of losing her mother, left her fractured from any normal sense of her life. In that unexpected void, standing by him seemed the only way to find some truth in the shattered mess of her world. So many nights she had dreamed of him, so many nights she had wanted to run away to him, and now she had.

Now she was with him.

There was nothing behind her. Anything might be ahead of her.

Reservation lost its last hold.

She lifted her arm. His gaze darted to her hand. Instead of running, instead of recoiling, he closed his eyes. Her hand trembled. It only took a heartbeat for her to realize it was rebelling against her will to touch him. If not for her current state of mind, she might have heeded her arm's intuition and backed away, but she would have none of its doubts. She took a breath, asserted her will, and watched her hand ease. Her arm regained its usual fluid grace, its usual ease of movement, and once more became a thing under the dominion of her will.

Her hand came to rest on his cheek.

He didn't flinch. It was worth more than anything he could say and bridged the last barrier that remained between them.

She closed her eyes, leaned in, and kissed him. Her arm tingled. She felt his lips smile against hers before she felt his free hand settle on the small of her back. He pressed, and she welcomed the fold of his embrace.

Her arm quivered.

He rested his forehead against hers, took a breath, and returned the kiss. He held her tighter this time, and she felt the hidden strength she had once imagined in his shoulders. No one had ever touched her so; no one had ever held her so close, close enough that her breasts pressed against his chest.

A white flash seared her mind. Her arm quaked.

He kissed her cheek, kissed her neck as her read rolled back. He held her ever tighter. Her heart pounded. The room spun around her. Her nostrils flared until her mouth opened to draw in a tremulous breath.

He came back to her at once. She tasted his breath.

Her mind flashed. Within the white eruption she glimpsed an image, an image that clamped her heart and caused her arm to convulse. She tried to fight off the distraction. He stayed with her, his hand pulling her tightly to him in his excitement.

A third flash assaulted her senses. The image lingered a moment in shadow, as if she had stared at the sun for too long. She felt lightheaded. When she felt the tip of his tongue against hers, a wave of sweet delirium washed her mind of thoughts.

Another flash. In the clearing left by her passion, there was no denying the flash came from her arm.

There was also no denying what she saw in the image as it lingered in her mind's eye. Shape filled shadow, color filled shape, and the vision came, clear as day.

The memory was from the first night of her life. Her arm beheld the image as it clung to the window of the birthing room. It looked out into the night and focused on what light it could find. Nothing more than the glow of a lantern, it was nevertheless enough to illuminate what was happening by the kitchen basin of the Semenic home.

Her sight rocketed through time, through her memories, down the length of her arm, and back again to trample her with the overwhelming force of a stargrazer's massive hooves.

She saw her father. She saw Mena. She saw her father behind Mena.

Her father was in Mena.

She remembered, long ago, spying on Ivan as he watched two of their pigs rutting. He looked embarrassed when he spotted her and then told her it was just Nature's way.

It's what animals do.

She thought of her father.

He banished my mother . . . and all along, all along . . . no!

She bucked in horror. Her arm coiled and slammed into Kyle's chest to drive him away. He flailed for balance before falling to the floor. Angela fell at the same time. Her head thumped on the thick rug to further stun her. The image blazed through her once more and drove a hoarse shout from her throat. Her arm whipped around and opened its hand to let its one eye stare into her befuddled gaze. The sight of herself and her hand bounced between her and her arm until she screamed.

Kyle called to her as he grabbed the edge of his desk and struggled to right himself. The door to the office burst open. Sarah ran to Angela and dropped to her knees. Out of concern she took Angela's face in her hands. Angela's arm coiled and pounded into her shoulder, knocking Sarah off her knees and onto her side.

Angela rolled over, gained her feet, and clenched her fist. "No, no!"

Kyle and Sarah called to her. She ignored them as she flew out of the office, through the kitchen, and out the back door. Her clothes were hanging on a line under the warm sunshine. Without a thought she ran to the line, her arm dragging the nightshirt over her head and tossing it aside. Her arm wrapped its tail around the line and pulled the pants free and she all but hopped into them. Her shirt and poncho came next, followed by her hat. She didn't bother with her boots.

"Angela, wait!" Sarah called as she came running out the back door.

Angela ignored the plea. With the frantic strength of her arm, she grabbed her saddle, put a bare foot into a stirrup, and leapt atop her horse. She shook off her tears, traded her grief for rage, and raced off.

Kyle called to her.

She did not look back.

17

✝ ✝ ✝

Ivan was busy watching his daughters clean themselves in a stream when he heard the thumps of a horse running at speed. He glanced at Nathan, pointed for the girls to drop flat, and grabbed his repeating rifle. With a wave to Nathan, he flipped off the safety, ratcheted the lever grip to chamber a round, and looked down the length of the barrel.

Carl came into view against the afternoon sun, calling out so he wouldn't get shot. Ivan and Nathan rose to their feet and waved. Ivan looked over his shoulder and pointed for his daughters to stay put. The twins, still naked and caked with gore, their bellies distended to horrible distortion, their eyes still awash with red fury, made no effort to move.

Nathan lowered his rifle. "What are you doing out here?"

"Angela," Carl said in explanation as he came before Nathan. He leaned on the pommel of his saddle, took off his hat, and wiped his brow. "She rode out to our house late last night. She said Calliope was dead."

Nathan frowned. "Ivan buried her yesterday afternoon."

Ivan nodded and when Carl turned to him, he asked, "Is she all right? Angela? She was awful upset. Understandably so, bein' her ma died to keep her safe."

"She's fine," Carl assured him. He took a swig of water and pointed past Ivan to where Ruth and Rachel rested at the stream's edge. "Didn't either of you tell her what to expect?"

"The Rev told me seein' was worth more than any words could muster."

Carl turned on Nathan. "How could you take her out here and not warn her?"

"How did you find us?" Ignoring Carl, Nathan scanned the horizon.

"I followed Angela's trail," Carl said. "Did you forget I was a cavalry tracker before I married Sarah?" He threw his hands up. "Aren't you the least concerned about your daughter?"

Nathan took a breath. "She's Purdy stock. She'll be fine." He hesitated a moment before tipping his hat to Carl. "But I will thank you for taking her in. It was my belief that she raced back to my house."

"Did you put Calliope in the barn?" Carl demanded, his jaw set.

Nathan said nothing but Ivan's head dropped. There was no missing the glare of condemnation Nathan cast on Ivan for betraying the shameful truth.

"I can't believe you," Carl said, shaking his head and looking at Ivan. "You let him do that to her? You let him treat her like an animal?"

Ivan's gaze lingered on the ground. "It was the Rev's decree. Didn't like it none, but it was his decree, not mine."

"Then shame on you," Carl said, seething. He jabbed a finger at Nathan. "And you, who the hell do you think you are to do that? You have a lot of explaining to do to your daughter. That poor girl doesn't know which end is up anymore."

Nathan rolled his shoulders and took on his usual imperious stance. "She had to learn all our ways to be ready for Woolly Ben. The days are counting down to the deadline."

"What're you planning to do, kill the whole town?"

"That vengeance is not mine to work. We are merely the tools of Justice. It's a role we will fulfill with all the humility of our singular pride."

Carl stared at Nathan for a moment before tapping a finger to his temple. "You're just as crazy as Woolly Ben."

Nathan rested his rifle on his shoulder. "My daughter is needed at home," he said as Carl trotted around him. "And I wouldn't leave your son alone with her. She's grown to be quite an attractive young woman."

"Don't slander my son," Carl snapped. "He's an honorable young man."

Nathan grinned with amusement. "Honor is little more than a charade in contest to young passions. Keep your boy in check. I prefer my daughter remain chaste."

Carl clenched a fist. "You're the one recruiting her for mass murder."

"And you're the one who knows it has to happen. Don't make a fool of yourself, Carl. You know better than to mince words of moral piety with me."

"There's a special hell waiting for you, Nathan Purdy."

Ivan opened a hand. "Now, come on, Carl. That ain't fair."

Carl ignored him.

Nathan sighed. "Enough of this talk. We've been away from our houses for longer than I prefer. Carl, I want you to ride ahead to my house and check on things. I'll be joining you shortly. Ivan, you stay here to tend to your daughters."

Carl frowned, but after several moments he turned his horse. "I'll be waiting for you, Reverend," he said and rode away.

Nathan watched him go before turning to Ivan. "Pay him no heed. Cleanse your daughters."

Ivan looked back to Ruth and Rachel. They were in a wretched state, bloated and bewitched by their wild natures. Mena would be furious if he brought them back with even a smudge of gore or a hair out of place. She was always particular about her girls and took pains to maintain their appearance for Judah and Jonah. One day, Ivan knew, Nathan would inter-marry the twins, and their children would walk the Earth as creatures without precedent.

Ivan knew he was a simple man. Sometimes though, he had his doubts. Looking back at Ruth and Rachel, with the memory of burying poor Calliope and the impression of Angela's horror at the sisters' true manifestation still fresh in his mind, those doubts nagged him.

He wasn't worried. It wasn't the first time he had felt those doubts. He comforted himself with the notion that it wouldn't be the last time either.

Troubles were like seasons, he had once told Angela. They just come and go.

18

‡ ‡ ‡

Angela rode hard until her horse at last slowed to a halt not far from the site of the sisters' atrocity. It was evening, the blue sky above taking on the first violet tinges of night's easterly approach.

More out of necessity than pity, she dismounted, left the animal panting by a tree, and sprinted through the woods. As she neared the site, she slowed, taking care to pick her way from tree to tree so as not to be seen. When she was sure she was close, she let her arm go to scout the area ahead of her.

Her arm bounded forward, hand low but eye open, until the Outsider camp came into view. Her hand lifted, filled with a primal sense of caution, and scanned the area from behind the leaves of a low bush. The bodies of the Outsiders were gone, and the ground where they had lain for the sisters to devour had been swept clean with several evergreen boughs. In a similar way it was impossible to discern where Calliope had joined the earth, other than the position afforded by Angela's memory. The Outsiders' tents and gear were nowhere to be seen, the items undoubtedly either buried or pilfered for supply of the Range. As with the Outsiders, the bodies of their horses had disappeared without any visible trace.

Her father, the sisters, and Carl were missing.

What she did find was good old Ivan, wiping the sweat from his face as he stood by his shovel, the blade rammed into the soil. His rifle was on his back, the sling across his chest.

Angela sprinted forward, but she called out to him before revealing herself. Even so, he was taken aback, the rifle in his hands in a blink before he understood who she was. Angela walked toward him, her arm springing from its cover to land at her side. The hand waved before it spiraled up her leg and rejoined her shoulder.

It seemed to take a few moments before Ivan believed his eyes. "Why you here?"

"Where's my father?"

Ivan pointed behind him. "He rode off to the houses with Carl." Ivan slung his rifle, staring at her before he shook his head. "Carl said you was in a sorry state. Said you rode straight through the night to his house. You shouldn't do that. It's dangerous to ride like that, particular without your ma scoutin' ahead."

Angela didn't stop her approach until she was close enough to grab the strap of his rifle. "I've been lied to. That's why I came back."

Ivan glanced over his shoulder to the stream. "Look, I'm sorry 'bout you not knowin' the truth of what the sisters is. It's a right scary thing to see and harder yet to explain."

"I'm not talking about the sisters."

Ivan wiped his face. "I've loved them girls from when they was nothin'. Rev said he had a vision for their purpose, said we had to feed 'em raw meat soon as they could chew. 'Feed the purpose,' he said. Then we took 'em to the springs for the baptisms, and it made 'em what they are. Breaks my heart to see 'em when they get like that, but that's the way it is, and the way it has to be. That's what the Rev's been tellin' me since day one."

Angela tipped her head to catch Ivan's gaze. "It's my father, Ivan. He's lied to us."

"Now, I'll listen to a lot, but I can't listen to that," Ivan said with a shake of his head.

She yanked on his rifle sling. "I know you think what he did with my mother was wrong. You know it was wrong the way he treated her. After all the things he's said about who we are and our coming dominion, wasn't it wrong the way he treated her?"

"Don't be twistin' his words. That ain't right."

"I'm not twisting anything. Things are what they are." She stared into his eyes as they darted to her. "What am I saying that hasn't been done? Do you like what he has Ruth and Rachel do for him?"

"That ain't for him, that's for all us."

"By his claim!"

Ivan grabbed her hand and tugged it free from his rifle sling. He fell back a step, opening a hand before him. "Now you best stop. There ain't nothin' good where I think you're goin', not for any of us."

She stepped toward him. "I see the way Mena treats you."

He shook his head. "She's just particular is all. She's got standards."

"No, she's cruel." She watched as he froze, his eyes squeezing shut. "She's cruel, Ivan. She agrees with anything my father says. I see it all for what it is now. I see the truth of it now. You need to see the truth of it too."

"No, no, it ain't right . . ."

"They're not right!" She took another step to grab the collar of his shirt. "They keep all of us under their thumbs. He never says anything to cross her, and she backs every word out of his mouth. They're like a mirror and the reflection it holds."

"Don't be doin' this, not now," he said, his voice faltering with the plea. "I don't wanna hear none of this, don't wanna know it from nothin', and don't want it on my heart with Woolly Ben comin' down on us any day now."

"And who picked this fight with Woolly Ben?"

"Now, now, that goes way before you was around. You ain't got nothin' to say on that."

She shook him. "It's my life. It's your life. We have everything to say about it. Think about your daughters. Think what they've been made to do, and then think of your sons. Do you want them stained the same way?"

Ivan's eyes moistened. "I love you girl, so I'm beggin' you now to stop."

"He's going to end all of us. You have to see that! His prophecies call for blood and death, nothing more. This fight with Woolly Ben is nothing else but to fulfill his own nightmares."

Ivan shook his head. "You don't want to tangle with the townsfolk. You don't know them. You can't trust them no farther than you can throw them."

"Ivan! Are you ready to risk the lives of your children for my father's fancy?"

"You got my head turned 'round. You got me all confused."

Angela let go of his rifle sling and slapped his chest. "He told me where the twins came from. He told me they grew off Mena's body. Are they even yours?"

His eyes popped open. "Don't you say nothin' 'bout my twins!"

"Are they yours?"

"Don't you say nothin' 'bout them! Don't you . . . don't you take them away from me!"

"Ivan—"

He grabbed her throat with one big hand, forcing her back as he started marching with heavy steps, as if to trample her. "Stop!"

She croaked to draw a breath. "Ivan, are they yours . . . or his?"

He froze, glaring at her for a moment before throwing her to the ground.

She rubbed her throat and looked up at him. "You've known all along, haven't you?"

He clapped his hands atop his head, ground his teeth, and squeezed his eyes shut once more. "Shut your mouth, shut your mouth!"

"I saw them, Ivan. I saw them. My arm watched them."

"Shut your mouth!"

"The night I was born you were busy putting up the boards for the stargrazers, and they were together, rutting in your kitchen."

A shout of anguish burst from his throat. He stepped over, whipped the rifle from his shoulder, and leveled it on her forehead. "Take that back!" He sobbed, staring down the barrel at her bulging eyes. "You take that back. Take it back right now!"

She remained still even as her heart pounded that he might shoot her for the hurt of the truth. "I can't. It's there. It's been there since I've been born. Don't you see what they're doing? They forced my mother to the stable. Mena spends more time at my house than yours." She struggled to swallow, her throat dry with nerves. "What do you think will happen after he gets us to fight off Woolly Ben? If any of us are left, he'll turn on us, one by one."

"He's going to marry my twins. He told me again, just this day."

Her face fell in pity. "Ivan, think about it. We interbreed animals, not people."

He closed his eyes and gasped. Without a word he dropped his rifle and sank to his knees. "Then what's the point? What's the point of it all?"

"To serve him," she whispered. "He sees us as nothing more than things to serve him, to serve Mena. To serve them."

Defeated, Ivan put his hands over his face.

Angela rose to a crouch and pulled his head to her chest. It pained her to hurt him so, but she knew it had to be done. Her father was a liar, Mena was a liar, and there was nothing else to the matter. They were austere, hard people. She couldn't imagine the town's Outsiders being much worse. At least they were Outsiders, without cause or pretense of trust. Her father and Mena had inspired trust for the very purpose of concealing their deceptions.

She needed more people on whom she could rely. For the first time in her life, knowing only as many people as fingers on her hand seemed a problem.

The Eddingtons. I can trust them.

She blinked as she remembered the way she had fled their house, but it was only a moment of dismay. All she had to tell them was why she had left in such a rush.

Kyle would believe her. She pressed her lips together as the sensation of his kiss washed through her. Yes, he would trust her. He had to. If there was no trust between them, she would truly consider herself lost.

Ivan lifted his head. "What're we gonna do?"

Her arm trembled. Its primal instincts funneled through her as spoken words. "The problem is between my father and Woolly Ben. When the time comes, we'll leave him and let those two settle things on their own."

He stared at her in surprise. "You'd turn tail on your pa?"

She didn't flinch. "He's no more my father than Mena is your wife. Not after the things he's done. Understand?"

He put his hands over his face for a moment before dropping them into his lap. With a glance over his shoulder to the stream, he gave her a minute nod of ascension.

"We'll take the twins with us. We can follow one of Kyle's maps." She looked up to the sky. "There's got to be plenty of other places we can go. God can't have meant us to suffer and die for this one stretch of land."

Ivan took his rifle and stood. "Well, if nothin' else, your pa was right about one thing."

She took his offered hand and popped to her feet. "What's that?"

"There's no expectation of kindness in the life we been given." He frowned, took Angela's hand, and led her to the place where her mother had died. "But that don't mean we can't measure it out ourselves. She's right here, safe at rest, the way she deserves, and the way I know you'd like."

She gave his hand a squeeze and rested her head on his shoulder. "Ivan?"

"Yes, Miss Angela?"

"You're a good man, Ivan Semenic." She rose on the balls of her feet to kiss his cheek.

His eyes were moist, his face still drawn with the anguish of betrayal, but something had changed in him. He put an arm around her.

So they stood. Somewhere between the lies, between the hurt, between the loss, they found a measure of kindness.

‡ ‡ ‡

They camped that night in the woods, well aware that it was too late to ride back to the houses. Angela's horse was desperate for rest, so she brought it down to the stream, where she thought it would slurp up half the water before it was done. Ivan chuckled, watching as he got a little fire going and cooked a few thick strips of meat.

Angela left her mount and sat by the fire with Ivan. She looked to either side, feeling somewhat odd that they were enjoying a peaceful moment in the very spot where they had ambushed the Outsiders and her mother had met her death. It was only a moment of disquiet, dispelled when Ivan handed her a wad of meat on a tin plate.

"Found them plates when the Rev and I went through the catch," Ivan said with a wink. "Not as good as what we got back home, but then you get what you get when you're out here."

She took a bite and moaned with delight, unaware of her hunger until that very first taste of meat. It was a little tough. "Ivan, where did you get this?"

"Oh, from those horses we shot." He shrugged. "Seemed a damn waste not to make somethin' of them." He spat a bit of gristle into the fire. "Can I tell you a secret, bein' that we're layin' all the cards on the table?"

"What?"

He waved. "Sorry. Old saloon thing, from before we come out here." He leaned toward her. "This might be a bit off, bein' that we're eatin' horse, but it reminded me. You know our horses, and how the Rev said it ain't right to name 'em?"

"I know. Names are for people, not animals."

"Well, I named 'em all. Been 'round 'em too long not to name 'em. Besides, that's the way it's done anywhere else one might go." He pointed at his horse. "I call mine Haystack. Don't know why, but it just stuck in my head. Do you know what I call yours?" He grinned. "Buttercup."

Angela turned to look at her horse.

"Go ahead," Ivan whispered. "Call it to her. She'll come over, right friendly."

"Buttercup?"

Her horse raised its head and made its way to her. She stood, laughing as she nuzzled with her mount. It stomped a hoof, nudged her once more, and went back to the stream.

"See?" Ivan said. "Told you so."

She stared at the fire. "Thanks for telling me."

He took a deep breath and let it go. "I can't tell you how good it feels not to hide that anymore." He scratched his chin, debating with himself before clearing his throat. "I never liked that the Rev said no names for the animals. I got names for all the stargrazers, too." He gave her a furtive glance. "I can tell 'em to you, if you'd like."

She smiled. "I'd be honored."

His lips rose in an eager grin. "See, I named the gals after my sisters. Got five of 'em, you know, at least at the time when I left home to move out here with my uncle. They said it was best for me, bein' I was sick all the time and couldn't breathe right. Anyway, I don't even know anymore how long it's been, but I remember 'em just fine, bein' they was my family." He held up a hand and ticked off his fingers. "Let's see. There was Abigail, Emily, Clara Belle, Bessie, and Ella Mae. Now that Ella, she was the oldest, so she was like my second ma, but Bessie and me were the closest in age, so she was my favorite."

"Sounds like nice memories."

He stared at the extended fingers of his hand. "Yeah. I miss 'em terrible sometimes." He shrugged and looked at her. "But now I got my own, and I got you."

She slapped his shoulder with the back of her hand. "Well now, Ivan, thanks for including me," she said with a laugh.

He returned the slap, although with a mind to be gentle. "Pleasure's all mine."

As they shared their scant moment of merriment, she understood what he was doing. If the old life was going to pass away, it was time to make bonds for a new life. If that's the way it was going to be, she knew she had something to tell as well.

"Ivan?" She sobered from her humor. "I kissed Kyle. On the lips."

His eyebrows crept so far up his forehead she thought he might lose them in the coarse mass of his dark hair. He took a bite of meat, chewed it as best as he could, and spat the rest into the fire.

"Ivan?"

"Oh, I heard you, I heard you." He propped an elbow on his knee, glanced at the stars, and gave her a serious look. "Well, you mind if I ask how it felt?"

She shifted on her log, nervous for a moment. Without realizing, she followed his glance to the stars overhead. "It felt like I was up there," she said. "It felt like we were all alone, and nothing else in the world mattered to us, and nothing in the world could touch us." She looked back to Ivan. "I love him."

"Love?" he said with a low chuckle. "Well now, that's a big word for a lady young as yourself."

"I think I've earned my share of living these last few days." She waited until he conceded with a nod. "Do you know how I know I love him?"

"No, but I got a feelin' it's gonna be a good reason."

Her gaze sank to the fire. "I know I love him because what I feel for him is a world away from what I feel for my father." She let her gaze settle on Ivan. "It took a while to come to me, but I know it now for sure. I hate my father, Ivan. I hate him."

"That there's another big word," he said with a sigh. He tipped his head. "You best watch that, or it'll eat you up just the same as love can fill you up."

"It's because I hate him that I'll be able to hand him over to Woolly Ben. It's because I hate him that I'll be able to keep that plan secret. My father even told me about that one time. He said he and I had the strength to be just in our wickedness and wicked in our justice."

"The Rev told you that?" He scratched his jaw. "If you got the conviction that he's nothin' but a sack of lies, what makes you think he ain't just makin' a trap for you?"

She stared at him for a moment, speechless, until she realized her answer. "Because I feel it." She patted her chest. "I feel it, feel it just as true as the air I breathe."

Ivan frowned. "So let me get this straight. You're gonna lie for the sake of what you see as a greater truth."

She was about to speak when she realized where he was going.

"Yeah, that's the thing with hate." He took her chin in his big hand. "You best keep an eye on it, or you might end up same as the thing you hate. Damnation's a slippery road." He stood and kissed her head. "But don't you worry. You won't slip."

"Because I love Kyle?"

"Because I'll be holdin' onto you," Ivan said and lay down for the night.

She looked back to the fire. If only her arm's memory had come to her earlier, she might have been able to change things. She could've run off to the Eddingtons with Ivan. She could've brought her mother along. Together, they would've been strong enough to fight off her father and Mena. Ruth and Rachel, Judah and Jonah, she knew they'd be caught in the middle, but she figured they wouldn't last long without her and Ivan drawing most of the focus from her father and Mena.

The fire crackled. She wondered if Ivan had seen through her. Deep down, down in the depths of her arm's primal wisdom, she suspected there'd be no peace with Woolly Ben as long as her father lived. The hidden realities of her life had come to focus for her. The slaughter of the Outsiders, the hoarding of rifles and ammunition, the way her father and Mena had trained her since the day she left the Eddingtons those long months behind her, all those things drew one conclusion into sharp focus. They had trained her to be a hunter, to be a killer. There'd be no reason for that unless it was the only way for things to play out.

"Well then," she said beneath her breath. Her hand turned, her fingers opening to reveal the luminous green eye of her arm. "I guess he's right. Doom awaits us all."

19

‡ ‡ ‡

They rode hard, reaching their homes just before the sun reached the noon high. As they drew near, cracks of rifle fire sounded from the vicinity of the houses, and Angela exchanged a wary glance with Ivan before he shook it off as target practice. It didn't take much to guess that the twins were working their shot accuracy, now that the appointed day of Woolly Ben's reckoning was drawing near.

"Remember," Angela said as they trotted along, "I'll say I rode off because I was scared when I saw the sisters. That's true, and that's what I told the Eddingtons. I came to my senses the next morning and rode back out."

"You'll get a scoldin' for that," Ivan said.

"I know, but now I know better and can see it for what it is."

"Just keep in mind that can go both ways. Seein' through somethin' can make it a joke or make it bite all the deeper. No tellin' which 'til the moment comes up."

"Then I guess I'll find out soon enough." She took a breath. "I won't say anything about Kyle. I think that would be a big mistake."

"Oh, you can swear rain on that one."

"And I don't think Kyle will have said anything about it, so Sarah won't know. I can say that I flew out because I realized I rode off without telling anyone and I was afraid to create a stir."

Ivan glanced at her.

She pushed her hat back. "What's wrong?"

"It's what lyin' does to a soul," he said. "After the first it just gets easier and easier to tell more. Before you might know it, you can't even tell real from unreal from your own lips."

"Is that what you think of me, Ivan Semenic?" She looked away, somewhat offended. "You know I'm not like that. I don't like that you said that. It hurt."

"Well, now you learned somethin' else about lyin'," he said with a slow bob of his head. "It's like passin' a hot potato. You just spread the pain."

‡ ‡ ‡

Reverend Nathan Purdy was not a happy man, but he said nothing to Angela when she returned with Ivan. Instead, he stood still as stone as everyone awaited his response. Several excruciating moments of silence settled over the field behind the house before he looked away and studied the row of cans set up downrange from where Judah and Jonah were positioned prone in the grass, Carl beside them. Mena stood on the porch of the Purdy house, arms crossed over her chest.

Ivan waved to his wife. She glared at him, leaving him feeling like a fool, his hand in the air, as she settled her cold gaze on Angela.

Her father turned his back to her. "Continue," he said to Carl.

Carl looked at Angela, opened his hands, and went back to work training the twins how to target the rifles.

Mena remained on the porch, her typical dour expression failing to disguise the wrath in her eyes. She extended one arm, turned her hand, and pointed a finger to the ground before the porch.

Angela and Ivan exchanged a glance, dismounted, and led their horses toward her.

"How are the sisters?" Ivan asked as they drew near.

"Resting." Mena held her focus on Angela. "Young lady, you had no business riding off without telling anyone."

Angela lowered her head. "My mother was dead. I was upset."

"Do you think Woolly Ben will stop and let you weep?"

Angela pressed her fingers to her eyes. It was to hide her fury, but she realized it served just as well to appear as an effort to hold back her tears. "No. I'm sorry. I know it was wrong. But my mother died, and I've never seen Ruth and Rachel during the clean-up."

"Your father was very disappointed." Mena opened a hand to Carl. "If Carl hadn't ridden out, we'd have no idea where you were. That was very selfish of you."

"I'm sorry. It won't happen again."

"And you," Mena said, directing her disdain to Ivan. "How could you let the sisters eat so much?"

Ivan glanced at Nathan. "The Rev—"

"Don't dare pass the responsibility to our Reverend," Mena said, her eyes flashing with outrage. "You know the sisters can't control themselves. It will take two days for them to digest all that flesh, and when they pass it I'm not going to shovel out the mess. Put the horses in the stable and go see to my daughters."

Ivan responded with a dutiful nod and led the horses away.

Alone now, Angela didn't know what to say. When the rifles cracked, she jumped in surprise.

"Angela."

The sound of her father's voice pushed her a step forward. He had come up behind her without her knowing. Her arm coiled to her side.

He held his book to his chest as he paced around her, his head down beneath the rim of his black hat. His long coat hung from his shoulders. For the first time she realized he was very thin, almost frail. The only things that seemed to hold any weight beneath his coat were the revolver strapped to his leg and the chill in his heart.

"I'm sorry I rode off, Father. I was upset. I was scared. It won't happen again."

"I should hope not."

She looked up as he walked past her. "The Eddingtons were very nice to me. Please don't blame them. Carl rode out when I told them why I came unannounced."

"Yes, so he told me."

The rifles cracked. Her shoulders bunched up. Her father was behind her. She reached a simple conclusion. Coming back had been a big mistake.

Nathan circled her once more before stopping in front of her. He lingered there, standing in profile, his head down as he patted a thumb on his precious little book. "Did Ivan take good care of you?"

"Of course," she said with a nervous smile. "He always looks after me."

"Hmm. Indeed." He nodded. "I know you're very fond of him. Perhaps he can fill the void left by your mother's death, if you don't feel Mena can fill that place."

Her heart raced. *Does he know what I told Ivan? How could he know?*

Her father looked her square in the eyes. "Well? Is Mena not good enough to be your mother now, after all the things she's done for you?"

She looked at Mena. Acid bubbled in her stomach. "Aunt Mena's always been a mother to me," she said, her voice hoarse.

"Yes, yes she has, considering the condition of your birth mother. Now, apologize to your Aunt Mena for making her worry over your absence."

Angela closed her eyes to keep her calm. "I'm sorry, Aunt Mena."

"Look me in the eyes when you say it," Mena said.

Angela glared at her. "I'm sorry."

When the rifles let off another volley, she didn't jump a hair.

‡ ‡ ‡

She was banished to her room, without food, for the rest of the day. At dinnertime there was a single knock on her door that she chose to ignore, careless that it might put her in more trouble. The second knock was a sharp rap. Despite her bitterness, she knew it was foolish to continue a game from which she had nothing to gain.

She opened the door to find Mena standing in the hall with a pitcher of water. "Your father has decided that you will go without dinner. In his kindness, however, he has decided that you will not be denied water."

Angela reached for the pitcher. Mena stood resolute until Angela acquiesced. "Thank you for the water. I appreciate the kindness."

"Your father's punishment is to deny you dinner and that you stay in your room until tomorrow morning."

Angela put the pitcher on the floor by her bed. "I understand."

"But that is not the punishment you will receive from me. As your mother, it is my right to have a say in your behavior."

Angela stared at her, dumbfounded.

Mena glared at the curly locks of Angela's hair. "Tomorrow, I will cut your hair."

Without thinking, Angela's hand shot up to grasp her curls. "But it's only to my shoulders. It's not long. I like it this way."

"That's why it's going to be cut. The next time you get some foolish idea to run away, remember there is a price to be paid."

Angela stepped back. "I don't want my hair cut short."

Mena's eyes bulged. "Long hair is for whores."

Stung, Angela tensed. "Your hair is long."

Mena's hand whipped out in a flash, hitting Angela so hard it knocked her senseless. Her arm dropped from her shoulder as she stumbled back and fell on her bed. Before she could move, her arm sprang atop her, coiling to protect her, the fingers merged to a vicious point over its gleaming eye.

The threat held no sway on Mena. "A proper woman keeps her hair up. Tomorrow your hair will be cut and your arm will not interfere. Am I understood?"

Angela turned her face to her pillow. "Yes, you're understood."

The door closed.

She wept. Ashamed for the weakness of her hurt, she buried her face in her pillow to muffle the sound of her sobs. It took time, but the hurt hardened within her. She thought she knew about lies and betrayal, yet she was learning just how deep betrayal could sting. Although Mena was never one to show kindness, Angela understood there was a difference between discipline and violence. Aside from the one time Angela's father intervened when Mena was ready to lash out, Angela had been invested with the conviction that Mena would never hurt her by conscious intent.

It didn't matter what she remembered from her arm. She could be angry for the lies of her father, she could be furious for the betrayal he and Mena had inflicted upon Ivan and her mother, but the reality that the betrayal could manifest in her own physical vulnerability caught her unaware.

If Mena could hurt her, then she would hurt back.

It was late when her door opened. She looked up from her pillow to find her father in the doorway, a small lantern in his hand. She said nothing, instead sitting up and turning her face to show the welt on her cheek. She wondered if her father could understand the lesson of violence, given his own history of physicality.

She waited for a reaction.

His jaw clenched.

"She hit me," Angela whispered to drive the point. "Mena hit me."

He stared at her, the harsh angles of his face made more so in the yellow light and black shadows of the lantern. The muscles of his jaw clenched and released, clenched and released, as if he chewed on the direction of his will.

It seemed forever before he spoke. "Good," he said and closed the door.

Angela stared. If nothing else, he had given her a lesson she wouldn't soon forget.

He could still hurt her in ways greater than anything she might suffer from Mena's hand.

20

‡ ‡ ‡

Angela woke to a knock on her door. It was Mena.

"Those clothes are filthy. Did you wear them all night?"

Angela looked at her bed. "I didn't sleep under the quilt."

"People clean themselves and wear a nightshirt to bed. Animals don't."

Angela's head sank. "It won't happen again."

"Good." Mena stepped aside. "Now. Wash your face and those disgustingly dirty feet, eat your breakfast, and then I'll cut your hair."

Angela washed her face and scrubbed her feet with an old washcloth. When she was done she went downstairs for breakfast. She caught a glimpse of Ivan outside, working with Judah and Jonah to erase a set of hoof impacts left by passing stargrazers. There was no humor on Ivan's face. Ivan, who had once seemed a man of eternal happiness, looked miserable.

She stood by the walkway to the kitchen, her arm tightening.

Her father was already seated at one end of the table when Angela sat down for breakfast. Mena brought the food to the table, and when she sat in Calliope's chair, Angela ground her teeth. She looked at the two pieces of grain bread Mena put on her plate and slid before her. In the bile of her rising temper, she was possessed by a single thought.

I'd rather eat my foot than accept a morsel of food at this table.

Her father sat up straight. "We share our thanks."

"We share our thanks," Angela and Mena said together.

Angela looked at her father. "Did Carl go home?"

"Yes. He left shortly after you returned."

"I didn't get to apologize to him for having to ride out."

"I apologized for you."

Mena tapped a finger on Angela's plate. "Eat."

Angela stared at her plate for a moment. "I'm not hungry."

"Don't be foolish," her father said. "You must be hungry. Now eat. You have to be strong for our meeting with Woolly Ben."

"Soon," Mena said. "So soon before we sweep the heathens from the land."

Nathan lifted a hand to silence Mena then looked at his daughter. "Do you wish to ask me anything about the clean-up?"

Angela met his gaze. She decided to test him. "Have the twins been to Thetis Springs?"

"Yes. They were baptized, as were you." He set his book on the table and rested a hand on its leather cover. "I explained to you that it has a different effect for each one who enters. The twins, being twins, share the same gift."

Angela cringed. "Is what the sisters have a gift?"

"They perform a vital role. A needed role."

"And the boys?"

"We need strong hands. They have the gift of strength."

"When were they baptized?"

Her father stared at her for several moments before the corner of his mouth rose in a tiny grin. It wasn't humor—she knew he lacked that trait—but rather an expression of amusement, and she knew her father's only amusement was to watch someone flounder beneath his superior knowledge.

The grin told her all she needed to know. He didn't lie about taking the twins to the water when they were infants. Thetis Springs. She remembered the tale he had told her. The future and the past overlapped in her mind in the same way the echoes of his words overlapped, and her perception revealed a vision of its own. Her father took the twins down in the cave, held them in turn by their ankles to keep his hand dry, dipped them in the water, and told the water what he wanted of them. Their wishes were nothing of note, the choice of their lives taken from them, their future predetermined, and so the matter decided before they could conceive conscious thought.

He'd had a different plan for Angela. He had waited until she was older.

He had waited for her to be able to think on her own. There could be no greater justification of his doom-ridden prophecies than to have her play her part by conscious, if unwitting, collusion.

And there, nestled in the center of everything, resided her father. The water had indeed given him what he wanted: the ability to see himself as the center of his universe.

The water let him become his own god, and the only greater power a god could exercise on his world after its creation was its utter destruction. It was fulfillment through dissolution, absolution through apocalypse.

It was a splendid, if not horrifying, tapestry of deception and delusion.

It was a dreadful batch of thoughts to process over a stark breakfast. On the other hand, that coincidence also seemed anything but coincidence.

"Father, we all have our roles, don't we?" Angela said at last.

"Yes, we do."

There was nothing else to say. She ate the bread. Her father and Mena were right. She was going to need her strength.

‡ ‡ ‡

Breakfast was followed by a test of servitude. It was a matter of custom on the Range that no one left the table until Reverend Purdy called the meal's conclusion and excused those present. To leave beforehand or to leave without being excused were dire offenses.

Angela's father watched her chew every bite of her bread.

At one point Mena rested her hands on her thighs and looked at Nathan. "Reverend, my meal is done. May I be excused?"

"Of course, my dear Mena."

Angela kept her gaze on her plate. When she took her last bite, Mena reached past her and took the plate. The table stared back at her.

Nathan rested his hand on his book. After a few moments of silence, he did something quite unexpected. Without a word he slid the book across the table to where Angela's plate had sat and took his hand away.

She stared at the little volume. For the first time she was able to get a good look at this most-guarded possession. The brown leather was worn smooth, and there was a faint outline of his hand where the oils from his skin had discolored the old hide.

He turned in his seat to watch Mena as she worked at the basin. "I'll be riding out this morning with Ivan. I suspect there might be more Outsiders coming through. Will you take charge of my responsibilities while I'm gone?"

"My pleasure, Reverend," Mena said without turning.

Angela ground her teeth. The book screamed for her to take its little volume in hand and delve its secrets. At the same time, though, she was disgusted by the thought of touching the cruddy little thing. She was sure she had deduced its contents. She was sure the pages held nothing but her father's self-serving ramblings and his plan for manipulating the Range to suit his prophecy.

He stood.

"Father?"

"Yes?"

"Your book."

He went to Mena, seeming to ignore Angela, and whispered something in Mena's ear before returning. "Yes, my book," he said and took it from the table.

Angela held her head still, and she tracked him with her eyes as he went out of the house, calling for Ivan and Jonah. A few minutes later she heard the thumping of hooves as they rode off for the Outsiders' campsite.

Mena said nothing as she finished at the basin. Then she left the kitchen without providing the all-important permission for Angela to leave the table. There was nothing to prevent Angela from leaving her seat, but she figured getting herself into deeper trouble wouldn't accomplish anything productive.

So she sat, biding her time, and tried to keep her anxiety in check.

She prayed Ivan would be careful.

‡ ‡ ‡

Ivan kept watch as he followed Nathan through the woods to the Outsiders' campsite. Jonah was behind him. Ivan waited to catch the mute's attention, pointed to his own eyes, and then swept his hand down the barrel of his rifle. Jonah looked at his own gun, nodded, and tapped his temple. It was a simple exchange of primitive signing to make sure Jonah remembered to aim down the length of his weapon. Ivan had enough concerns about riding with Nathan, without worrying that Jonah might shoot him in the back by accident.

They came to the campsite and circled the area. Nothing had been disturbed.

Ivan shook his head. "Ain't nothin' here to report, Rev."

Nathan remained silent under the brim of his hat as he led his horse in a circle about the campsite. "Nothing obvious, no. I don't like it, though." He closed his eyes for a moment. "No, I foresee something quite different."

Ivan rubbed his forehead. "You havin' a vision?"

"Yes." Nathan looked into the distance, toward town. "Yes, there will be trouble. Soon." He turned his horse around. "Jonah. Ride back and get the sisters."

"Oh, I don't know 'bout that," Ivan said with a shake of his head. "Those girls are so full from the other day they're ready to pop."

"Duty doesn't afford us the luxury of comfort." Nathan pointed back to the Range. "Go, Jonah. Bring the sisters. Judah is to stay behind to watch over Mena and my daughter."

Jonah glanced at Ivan, who opened his hands in deference to Nathan. Full grown but slow witted, Jonah grunted, turned his horse, and rode away.

Ivan watched him go. He had always fancied himself a father to the sisters and brothers, but he knew now that was nothing but wishful thinking. Mena often told him he should be smarter, but even he knew he was a genius compared to Judah and Jonah. They could function, they could take orders, but there wasn't an original thought in their heads a single day of their life. Ruth and Rachel had their savage incarnations when the time came, yet they could function as anybody else might in day-to-day life.

He remembered when the twins hatched from Mena's shoulders. Doc Connors was there to make sure Mena would survive the delivery. The boys screamed, a dry wail that would not cease. Nathan suffered its noise for just a day before giving the order to Connors. After a swig of alcohol from his vest flask, Connors went ahead and did what he was told. First Jonah, and then Judah; he cut their vocal chords to keep them quiet.

Ivan made the maroon scarves to cover the jagged scars on their throats.

Thinking of it, he smiled. Maybe, he thought, he had been a father after all.

"I done the best I could," he said under his breath. "Yep, I done the best I could."

‡ ‡ ‡

Angela remained at the table. Her arm was restless, rising on its own to run her fingers through her loose curls of hair. She wondered what Kyle would think of her with her hair cut short, the way it was the first time he saw her. By the count of days, it was almost two years since that first visit, but her remarkable growth and physical maturation made such direct temporal measures seem like nothing more than vapor in the wind. It was no wonder he was confused. She left him looking like a girl and came back as a mature woman.

It was almost her fifth birthday. She decided then it was indeed for the better that she kept her age from Kyle. There was no point in trying to explain something she barely understood on her own.

At long last Mena stepped into the kitchen. "Come. Let's get this over with."

"Aunt Mena, you don't have to do this. I learned my lesson."

Mena crossed her arms over her chest. "A punishment unfulfilled sows the seeds for future wrongdoings. This was your making, not mine."

Angela rocked forward and let her head thump on the table.

"Delaying won't change things. Don't act like a spoiled child."

Angela didn't move.

Mena came to her, grabbed the collar of her shirt, and kicked the chair out from under her. The rapidity of the assault caught Angela by surprise . . . but not her arm. It spiraled around Mena's right arm and grabbed the collar of her black dress, scrunching it tight to choke her.

There they stood, locked, their faces turning purple as they glared at each other.

Mena's left fist shot up and cracked into Angela's jaw with the force of a hammer. Angela's chin split, blood spurting across Mena's knuckles. Stunned, Angela went limp in Mena's grasp. Her arm dropped from her shoulder. Mena cried out for Judah. He burst into the kitchen to find Mena with her hands clamped on Angela's shoulders to pin her to the table, while Angela's arm constricted Mena's throat. He grabbed Angela's arm. It was strong, yet it was no match for Judah's brute force. He wrestled it from Mena and ran outside as he grappled with its writhing coils.

All but defenseless, Angela wept as Mena kept her pinned. Mena grabbed Angela by her hair, yanked her head back, and forced her from the kitchen into the sitting room. A single chair was in the middle of the room. Mena thrust her into the seat and slapped her. The welt on Angela's cheek opened to seep blood.

Mena went to the mantle to fetch a pair of large scissors. "Is this what you learned from the Eddingtons, insolence and arrogance?" She walked around to stand behind Angela. "Or is it what you learned from that cripple son of theirs? Him and his books, they're so pathetic. I know more of the world in my pinky than that boy could ever know."

Angela winced as Mena grabbed the hair atop her head and yanked back, arching Angela's spine over the back of the chair. The next thing she felt was the pull of the scissors as Mena made a rough cut, lopping off a tangle of curly locks.

"Please! Stop!"

Mena was in one of her furies. "Shut up! You're spoiled. Do you have any idea what I knew before this life out here? You have no clue what cruelty is. How could you?"

Angela gasped as another lock of hair was cut from her head.

Mena held her hair tightly. "There's just me now, do you understand? Your mother is dead. The little princess act is over with your father. He told me to teach you, so now it's time you learn to be tough."

"I know how to be tough," Angela hissed between clenched teeth. "I killed the Outsiders."

Mena scoffed. "Killing is easy. It's quick. Quick doesn't make you tough." She leaned over to hiss in Angela's ear. "Suffering is what makes you tough. Suffering takes time. It endures to penetrate every corner of your being. Suffering teaches you about the world. What would you know? You've never had a man pull you by your hair, push your face in a pillow, and call you his bitch while he spends his lust in you."

Angela looked to her left. Mena was right there. So close and yet out of reach.

Her blood boiled.

Mena's eyes narrowed. "Or is that what Kyle did to you?"

Angela's rage burst in a rabid scream. She planted her feet and kicked with all the strength in her legs to smash her head into the side of Mena's face. The chair tipped and cracked on the wood floor as the scissors flew from Mena's hand. Angela tumbled over her shoulders. Mena staggered until her back slapped against the mantle.

Angela rolled over and planted her legs, ready to drive her shoulder into Mena's gut. Instead, she dropped at the sound of shattered glass, believing Judah had shot into the house. What she saw when she looked up was something much different. Mena shuffled forward, blood pouring down the front of her dress as saliva bubbled from what was left of her lips.

Angela's arm sped by, the fingers shaking off the strips of flesh it had ripped from Mena's face. In a heartbeat it coiled, readied itself, and launched once more. The narrowed point of its collected fingers hit Mena square on the cheek and tore into her face. Blood flew from her mouth as the arm looped around her head and then slapped its tail under her armpit to coil around her arm. Before Mena could recover from the trauma to her face, the arm sucked its two loops together in one brutal contraction.

The vertebrae in Mena's neck shattered like dried chicken bones.

Unstrung, she dropped to the floor.

For a moment Angela didn't move. She couldn't. The scene before her was unbelievable.

Her arm knew better. It raced across the room, attached to her shoulder, and brought her to her senses. With a shake of her head, Angela scurried from the room just as Judah kicked in the front door. She made it into the kitchen as Judah burst into the house. Seeing Mena's corpse, he stomped his foot. Although he was mute, he let out a hoarse groan of agony.

Angela ducked as she ran by the table. Her arm bounded from her shoulder toward the carving knives.

Judah came into the kitchen behind the barrel of his gun. He pulled the trigger the moment he saw Angela. Enraged, he shot wild, the bullet spraying wood chips in the air as it plowed into the thick slab of the table.

Her arm whipped around. A carving knife gleamed as it darted across the room and buried in Judah's shoulder. The gun fell to the floor as Judah's hand went numb. Angela dodged to the stove just in time for her arm to bounce to her shoulder, a rolling pin clutched in its hand. There was no thought, only reaction.

She swung with all her strength, smashing the heavy wooden roller atop Judah's head.

For all his strength, he nevertheless toppled to his side and crashed against the wall. Rising to his feet, he took a step, blinking away the blood pouring into his eyes. He grabbed the knife and yanked it from his shoulder. Angela was on him in an instant, coming on his blind side and whipping the pin in a vicious downward arc that buckled his knees. He dropped to a crouch, eyes bulging, his weight slamming down on the ruined joint before he flopped onto his side.

Angela knew better than to close on him. She darted to the kitchen and plopped on the floor by the rifle. Grabbing it with her feet, she cocked the lever action, sent a shell flying from the receiver, and brought home a fresh round. Her feet tossed the gun in the air. Her hand grabbed it as she hopped to a stance.

Judah managed to seize the leg of a chair. With little effort he threw it at Angela. She bounced to the side, leveled the gun, and fired.

The round plowed into Judah's head above his right eye. His brains exploded across the floor behind him in a messy red wash.

Angela stared at his motionless body until her rational mind accepted his death. Her knees wobbled, her hand set the rifle on the table, and she sank to the floor. Bewildered by the savage outbreak in her own home, she slumped against the stove and closed her eyes.

There wasn't a sound to be heard. It offered a harsh lesson.

For all the portents of fire and fury, it was silence that served as the true hallmark of Doom.

21

‡ ‡ ‡

Mena?

Nathan sat with Ivan at the Outsiders' campsite, the forest quiet and peaceful around them. After a simple lunch of bread and some jerked pork, they filled their waterskins from the stream, returned to the campsite, and continued to sit.

Now, in the midst of the solitude surrounding them, Nathan was seized by a most unsettling intuition.

My Mena is dead.

He fought to keep his veneer of ambivalence.

Yes, she's dead. After all we've been through. His eyes narrowed as the vision gained focus within his mind. *And who could do such a thing?*

He swallowed over a dry throat as a single face emerged. Of course. If it was going to be anyone, it had to be Angela. He couldn't suffer the thought of anyone else. As much as Mena's loss stabbed deep into his hardened heart, he drew solace that Angela had at last asserted her dominance. She was taking the seat of power.

"Rev?" Ivan waved his hand to get Nathan's attention. "Hey, you with me here?"

Nathan closed his eyes for a moment before looking at Ivan. "Yes. A vision came to me."

"That so?" Ivan sighed. "That vision of yours about other Outsiders got a time on it? Or you seein' somethin' else in the ether?"

Nathan stiffened. "Are you testing me?"

"No. Just wonderin,' is all. We been sittin' here a long time."

Nathan looked at the sky. "Then think of all the work in the stable you won't have to worry about today."

"Well, there is that." Ivan stretched, extending his arms to either side. "Say, Rev, when things settle down, you think my wife might be movin' back in with me, 'stead of spendin' all that time at your place?" He opened his hands. "Not that I mind none, but, well, she is my wife and all."

Nathan studied him for several moments. His suspicions spread like cracks in glass. Angela had ridden in the day before with Ivan. They'd had time to talk. They had each other's ear and shared a common sentiment. It was inconceivable that Ivan's line of questioning was mere coincidence to the vision lurking in Nathan's head.

They had made a plan. This dullard seeks to play me?

Nathan considered his thoughts in rapid succession before choosing his words with care. "I've meant to discuss this matter with you, Ivan. Angela took the loss of her mother very hard, despite Calliope's devolved nature."

"She's still a child that lost her ma."

"I understand that." Nathan glanced at his book where it rested on his thigh. It was time to put Ivan to task. "A young girl needs a mother. For now—for the foreseeable future—I think it might be best if Mena stays in my house to help raise Angela. She's become a precocious girl, but she needs Mena's steady rule to keep her in bounds."

Ivan dropped his hands with a yawn. "Now that you say that, I have to tell you my girls need their ma just as much."

"Ruth and Rachel are young women. They will do fine without Mena's full attention."

"And I got my two boys—"

"Ivan, please," Nathan interrupted with a shake of his head. "Must we play this game? After the twin-fold marriage, they will need a house for their lodging. I've discussed this with Mena. The only plan that makes sense is to have the twins share your house. Mena can stay with me to raise Angela."

Ivan scratched his chin. "So where might I lay my head?"

"In the stable." Nathan opened a hand. "I know it sounds harsh, but consider all the properties of our situation. The twins need their privacy if they are to bring forth new children. Angela needs Mena's guidance. Your duties revolve around the stable, its animals, and the fields, which also require the work of you and the animals."

Ivan leaned on his knee with an elbow. "Now, hold on a minute there, Rev. I don't get to live with the boys, the girls, or my wife?"

Nathan grew impatient. He could see Judah's body sprawled by the kitchen. There would be no marriage, no relocation, and no children. Doom was already drawing its dark veil around his world. Under such conditions it was difficult to pursue his little challenge of wits with Ivan. In fact Nathan found it quite irritating to be engaged in such a silly pursuit.

Until, that is, he remembered the deeper cause that had motivated his game in the first place.

Yes, my daughter needs to be taught a lesson. If she seeks to grab her power, then she must learn that power cannot be had without sacrifice.

Ivan's eyes narrowed. "Rev, I'm talkin' to you."

"Yes, yes, I heard you." Nathan scrambled for something to say. "You were asking about our lodging arrangements. You're not happy about the plan I've discussed with you."

Ivan shook his head. "I don't recall any discussion. I asked and you told. That ain't no discussion."

Nathan gasped. "Ivan, what would you have me do? Are you actually suggesting that I move out to the stable?"

"I could build somethin'. Somethin' small." Ivan grinned. "I could build it for you."

Nathan took a deep breath. He was tired of the game. Angela had hurt him; it was time to share the pain. If Doom was coming for them, if Angela had set the inexorable process of annihilation in motion, then there was no reason for him to hold back.

He rested a hand over his book before slipping it into the special pocket of his vest. Then he dropped his hand in a well-practiced motion that landed his grip on the shiny revolver strapped to his thigh.

He fired straight from the holster, the angle of his leg enough to send the round straight into Ivan's gut. The blast of the gun echoed in the woods, adding to the bug-eyed surprise on Ivan's face. Nathan stood, pulled his gun free, and fired the remaining five rounds of his revolver, striking the hammer with his left palm to discharge the gun as fast as possible.

Ivan wheezed where he dropped to the ground. He coughed up a wad of blood, his eyes burning as he looked up at Nathan. Instead of panic, instead of anger, he laughed. "You stupid son of a bitch. You can't keep me down with that pea-shooter."

Nathan knew his time was short. He ran the few steps to his horse, pulled the double-barrel shotgun from his saddle, and braced the stock tightly to his shoulder. The moment Ivan struggled to his feet Nathan unloaded with both barrels at once. He gasped, the recoil kicking his shoulder back as the vicious spray of its shells erupted from the barrels.

Ivan flopped onto his side, riddled with buckshot. Blood spurted from his wounds for a moment, then two, before slowing to a trickle. His face flushed as his body heated with its efforts to heal. Groaning against the pain of his wounds, he rolled over and crawled toward the log where his rifle waited.

Nathan dumped the shotgun to the ground and ran forward to snatch the rifle a moment before Ivan could get his hand on the stock. "Do you want to know my vision? Angela killed Mena and Judah."

"No. You're lyin'." Ivan groaned as the beads of buckshot moved about his body. "All you got in you is a pack of black lies."

"My daughter deceived you. She knows you're stupid. She played you."

Ivan's eyes bulged. "I ain't listenin' to that! I love that girl the way a daughter should be loved—like the way I tried to love my own."

Nathan glared down the length of the barrel.

"Did you finally run out of lies?" Ivan wheezed. "You ain't got enough bullets on all the Range to kill me."

Nathan fired, blowing off three fingers from Ivan's outstretched hand. "I don't need to kill you, Ivan. In fact, I'm not going to be the one who kills you."

"You pecker." Ivan stared up at him. "Rot in hell."

"There will be time enough for that, my old friend. Time enough for all of us."

They stared at each other. More than twenty years they had worked together.

Nathan planted his feet and jerked the lever to cycle a round. He fired—and kept firing—until the gun was empty.

22

‡ ‡ ‡

Angela hurried once she regained her wits. Leaving Mena and Judah in open view was nothing but an opportunity for trouble. There was no time to consider the repercussions or meaning of the killings. They attacked her; she defended herself. No right or wrong, no blame or trespass.

She had no problem dragging Mena out of the house, around back out of view from the Semenic home, and into the hay shed. It was faster than digging a hole and better than trying to stash her somewhere in the house. Even so, she did take the time to hack off Mena's hair. It was petty and spiteful, even as it burned with immense satisfaction.

With Mena buried under a pile of hay, she ran back to the house. Judah was much heavier. She wrapped his head in his maroon scarf to contain some of the mess of his exploded cranium and then rolled his mass onto a sheet. It made it much easier to drag him. After a good deal of huffing and puffing, and with her thighs humming from the effort, she had him in the shed and buried under another pile of hay.

When she closed the front door, she found the inside frame was damaged, but no one could see that unless they were entering the home.

The sitting room, kitchen, and hallway were a different matter. She realized there was no point even trying to conceal the mess. Instead, she straightened the furniture as best she could, threw another sheet over the kitchen table to cover the damage from the rifle shot, and repositioned the chair in the sitting room. No one would notice its cracked back unless they got close.

Finally, she washed her face and hand and dressed.

Judah's rifle had to be reloaded. She found the rounds in the storeroom, sat on the floor, and used her hand and feet. With that done she ran upstairs, put on her pair of spare boots, settled her hat on her head, and hopped down the steps to get the rifle.

She looked outside to see that Jonah was riding in on his horse.

For a moment she hesitated. The simplest thing to do would be to shoot him. But if Ruth and Rachel hadn't heard the two shots in the Purdy home, they would certainly hear shots outside. Besides, she hadn't wanted to kill Judah. He had left her no choice. She had always held a degree of tenderness for the boys. Those days were gone, though, and now the twins were nothing but dire threats. They followed her father without question and would sooner eat their hands than disobey him. No, she couldn't risk their wrath.

His wrath, she corrected. Only Jonah remained.

She decided simple was best, rested her rifle on her shoulder, and walked out to greet him.

He trotted toward her, his rifle resting across his saddle. His dull eyes darted toward the Semenic home. He held up his hands, forming the letter R twice and pointing over his shoulder to the distance.

Angela fought to keep her calm. "My father needs the sisters? Outsiders?"

He nodded, then pointed to his head and formed the letter M.

"Your mother is working in the kitchen. She sent me out to walk the perimeter. Your brother is helping her."

When he looked toward the Purdy house, Angela shifted to enter his view. Once she had his attention, she let him see the welt on her cheek and the split on her chin.

He frowned at her wounds.

"Jonah, you know she doesn't like to be bothered when she's working in the kitchen. I just got into trouble and now I have to walk the perimeter. I don't want to get into trouble with her again. Besides, if my father wants Ruth and Rachel, you better get them. If he knows you were late because we were talking, I'll be in more trouble."

He looked at her, smiled, and nudged her shoulder. With a nod he turned his horse, trotted to the Semenic house, and went inside. A little while later he came out with Ruth and Rachel, the girls struggling to walk, their swollen bellies bulging beneath their nightshirts. He helped them into the saddles of two horses, tied the reins to a single rope, mounted his horse, and rode away. The sisters looked over their shoulders in passing to stare at Angela with glazed eyes.

She waved them off. To make a good show of things, she strolled away to the east as they rode south, continuing on until they were out of sight.

Satisfied, she put her legs to work and ran at full speed back to the stable. She found her horse, pulled up into the saddle, and rested the rifle across her lap.

The horse didn't move. She rubbed its neck, leaned forward, and spoke in a soft voice.

"Come on, Buttercup, we need to ride."

The horse turned to look at her for a moment. She felt sorry to ask so much. Over the last days she knew she had all but ridden the poor animal to its death. To her relief Buttercup stomped a hoof, shifted on its feet, and trotted out of the barn.

"That's a good girl," Angela said. "Ivan might be in trouble."

23

‡ ‡ ‡

Nathan wiped the sweat from his face. Ivan was at his feet, naked; Nathan had stripped him of his clothes. Keeping the old fool down was taking more work than Nathan had expected, given the rate at which Ivan could regenerate. Nathan had gone so far as to smash his old friend's head with a rock—after covering him with his shirt so there'd be no blood spatter on Nathan's clothes—and still Ivan's body wouldn't quit. It wasn't that Nathan wanted to kill him; no, he had a plan for that end, but he couldn't suffer having Ivan recoup enough that he wandered off.

A faint wheeze sounded from Ivan's body. Two of his fingers twitched.

Nathan looked at the sky. Jonah would be on his way back with the sisters. It was time to tend to matters.

He crouched by Ivan, pulled his friend's head by the hair, and cut off his face.

‡ ‡ ‡

Jonah was tiring of the sisters' moans of discomfort as they rode out to the campsite. To his relief Reverend Purdy emerged from the woods on his mount and waved in greeting. The sisters said nothing. Jonah was incapable of saying anything, so he gave his mount a nudge and picked up the pace.

The Reverend rode out to meet them. "You're back in good time," he said with a nod. "We caught another Outsider scout. Your father is out searching for any others."

The sisters slumped in their saddles as their bellies wriggled.

"It's just one body," the Reverend said. "You can purge your stomachs at the river and see to this new task. Surely you can do this for us?"

Ruth and Rachel exchanged a glance. "Reverend," they said in unison.

"That's good. I'll take that rope," he said, pointing to the trailing lead of the horses.

Jonah handed it over. He patted his chest and pointed to the woods.

"No," the Reverend said at once. "Your father can take care of himself. Right now I want you back at our homes. Be ready, and be prepared."

Jonah rested a hand on his rifle.

"Yes, trouble is brewing." As Reverend Purdy trotted away with the sisters, he looked over his shoulder. "I have faith in you, Jonah Semenic."

Jonah smiled. He turned his horse. He had a duty, and he'd rather die than disappoint.

‡ ‡ ‡

Angela was pressed to ride as fast as she could, even though the intuition from her arm told her to keep a careful watch and not be reckless. Twice she was tempted to ride back and give Judah a decent burial; twice her instincts told her that act of decency would be her last earthly act.

She didn't think of Mena. The crows could have her as far as Angela was concerned.

Her route was lengthy. She knew Jonah couldn't move quickly with the sisters in their distended state, but she also knew it would be a disaster if he saw her riding after she lied that she was going to walk the perimeter. He might get suspicious, turn back, discover the scuffed earth leading to the barn, and find his mother and twin under the hay. There'd be no doubt then that Angela was responsible. Although she was sickened by the necessity of killing Judah, there was no disguising her luck in surviving his rage. To expect such luck a second time, beneath Jonah's doubled fury, was nothing less than ridiculous.

Buttercup was panting and Angela was forced to slow her pace. She eased to a trot and Buttercup bobbed her head in appreciation. If the horse dropped, Angela would be stranded. As fast as she could run, she wasn't her mother, and she could never cover the distance a horse could manage, much less try without collapsing from exhaustion.

The woods were close. There were only a few hills to cross, then the wide green plain, and she'd be on the eastern approach. With a little luck she could make it in time to help Ivan.

No sooner did the thought cross her mind than she spotted a cloud of dust rising from behind a hill. There was no mistaking such a sure sign of riders. She hopped from her saddle, scrambled up the backside of the hill, and dropped to crawl up to the rounded crest.

When she peered out from her height, sure enough, she saw them—sixteen riders making haste toward the houses. At their lead was a man who cut a distinctive outline. He was tall and thin like her father, but he had long dark hair that fell from under his black hat and swept across his shoulders. A sparse beard covered his jaw and a small horn glinted where it hung in his lap from a slender strap.

She only needed one guess to figure the man's identity.

It had to be Woolly Ben.

24

✝ ✝ ✝

Nathan fought to conceal his impatience as he brought the sisters to their work. It wasn't far from the stream where they had left their horses to drink.. He glanced over his shoulder to see Ruth and Rachel, their bellies distended from their last recent feast, waddling behind him with awkward, loping strides. The distraction was brief; he knew he had to get the sisters to Ivan. Every moment wasted was another moment for Ivan's body to heal and one more moment that his daughters might recognize him if his denuded face regenerated. Worse, Nathan knew the sisters wouldn't touch a feast if it showed any signs of life.

Entering the clearing where he and Ivan had camped, he saw the red mess of Ivan's naked form sprawled on his belly, just as he'd left it. The man hadn't moved since Nathan had skinned his skull. For safe measure, Nathan had also slit his throat, not only to drain a good deal of blood to slow Ivan's healing, but to sever his vocal chords.

A wet, ratcheting sound came from behind him. He stepped aside as he glanced back at the girls. Ruth and Rachel were purging, vomiting a good deal of soupy burden from their bellies to make room for their new feast. They were already devolving, their jaws hanging wide and slick globs of saliva dripping onto the rotund masses of their bellies between purges. Rather than help them disrobe, Nathan decided to back away and leave them to their task. They flung their clothes from their bodies as the hunger within woke.

"It's just one body," he said as their eyes washed red. "Enjoy."

They sank on all fours and scrambled to Ivan's body. Without pause they ripped into him, sinking their distended jaws into his shoulders to tear loose great slabs of tissue. Nathan's stomach bucked at the ferocity of their hunger and the ravenous work of their teeth. To his delight and immense relief, Ivan did not budge, other than an occasional twitch of his feet. The sisters failed to notice as they rolled him over, ripped open his belly, and slurped up his entrails. They purged and ate, ate and purged, pausing only to breathe.

Nathan sat on the log by the campfire. Black ashes were the only remnant of the once vibrant flames.

Before long, white bones licked clean of blood and sinew were the only remnant of Ivan's once vibrant body.

Nathan nodded. The sisters slumped on their backs, delirious after their feast.

All he had to do now was wait.

He didn't have to wait long.

Rachel was the first to emit a wince. Nathan watched her hands twitch, then her feet, before her belly undulated with a sickening wave of flesh. Ruth stirred beside her, and then both sisters arched their backs as their eyes, still red with cannibalistic delirium, bugged wide. Rachel clawed at the dirt while Ruth panted. Their bellies swelled, distending in different directions as something pushed outward from within. Panic filled their eyes. They kicked the dirt and thrashed to grab hold of anything nearby. It was a desperate, mindless effort. They rolled on their sides to vent eruptions of bloody vomit.

Nathan looked at his feet. He had found a large bottle of grain alcohol that the Outsiders had brought with them, filthy drunkards that they were.

"Father?" Ruth gasped.

Rachel sucked in a tight breath. "Father! Help us! Please!"

"Something . . ." Ruth's voice cut short in a spasm of agony. "Something's wrong!"

"No," Nathan said with a heavy sigh. "Everything is as it needs to be." He opened the bottle. "This is the passing of the old order, my dear daughters. Now you must pass too, like your father before you."

The sisters' mouths dropped. They exchanged a glance of horror before looking at their bellies.

It was too late.

Ruth's abdomen came apart with the sound of a wet tear as her bloated stomach burst wide. Rachel beheld her sister's evisceration for only a short moment before her own guts burst out her side. Pieces of Ivan spilled out between them, distorted extensions of malformed arms and legs where his tissue consumed the soupy remnants of the Outsiders lingering in the sisters' entrails. Unguided, unaware, Ivan's remnants grew wild, retaining no clue how to reassemble their original form.

Nathan stood. His practiced façade failed him in witness to the gruesome spectacle at his feet. Between Ivan's wriggling limbs, the sisters' shredded entrails, and the pools of blood and body fluids, it was impossible to tell what mess of flesh belonged to whom. Disgusted and yet satisfied with his plan, Nathan grabbed the dried branches and leaves he had piled behind the log and dumped them atop the trembling pile of twisted communal flesh. With the kindling in place, he grabbed the alcohol, doused a good deal over the dried leaves, soaked the sisters' nightshirts, and then stepped back.

"It's not that you have displeased me," he said as he pulled a book of matches from inside his coat. "It's only that the road I once saw for you has been lost. My apologies, for perhaps that road only existed within my desires."

He struck the match, lit the shirts, and threw them onto the kindling.

With a flash the fire caught and spread. He sat on the log and watched the smoke rise to the bright sky.

The sickening shrieks of the sisters' immolation found no purchase on his soul.

‡ ‡ ‡

Jonah rode back to the houses to find an unusual silence. The Reverend's flock was a small group, but there was always something that needed to be done and somebody outside busy to get it done before there was trouble. His mother was a strict taskmaster. Even if there was nothing to do, even when everything had been done to the Reverend's satisfaction, she would find something amiss.

Distressed at the lack of activity in the yard, he dismounted, led his horse to the Semenic house, and flipped the reins over the porch rail. He went inside and searched about, shook his head at the emptiness that awaited him, and decided to cross over to the Purdy house. His shoulders tightened the moment he grabbed the Purdys' front door. Close to the door, there was no mistaking the faint outline of a boot print by the latch. The door had been kicked open.

He ran back to his horse, grabbed his rifle, and stormed into the house. Bloodstains marked the wood-slat floor with rust-red splotches. Rifle raised, he turned and made his way to the kitchen. Streaks of blood stained the wall. A white sheet covered the table. He pulled it aside to see the broken edge.

Something bad had happened.

He remembered Angela. She had told him not to bother his mother. She would've been the last one to see his mother before . . .

His gaze settled out the kitchen window. It didn't take long for him to discern the drag marks leading from the back of the house to the barn. Slow as he might be, he had little trouble assembling evidence in open sight.

The call of a horn reached through the house.

Jonah glared over his shoulder. He knew what was coming. Reverend Purdy had been clear enough in his sermons over Sunday dinner. There might be a day when Woolly Ben struck first. And from what Jonah could see, strike he had.

Jonah knew the power in his limbs. His dim mind cleared to a single thought, a single conviction.

Vengeance.

25

‡ ‡ ‡

Angela hid behind the hill until Woolly Ben's party passed out of sight.
The wait was insufferable, the only comfort being that it gave Buttercup
a chance to catch her breath. It wasn't a long break by any means. Soon
enough Angela was back in her saddle and riding hard for the Outsiders'
campsite.

It was easy to find. She could see a thin trail of gray smoke rising from
the far edge of the woods. There was no doubt it was the right spot.

For all the anxiety embodied in the nervous tremor of her arm, she
slowed Buttercup to a trot through the woods and kept a ready grasp on her
rifle. When she was close to the campsite, she dismounted, whispered for
Buttercup to stay put, and made her way from tree to tree to stay in cover.
The memory of her mother's sacrifice was fresh in mind. With Calliope gone
there was no one left to keep watch for her, and she wouldn't be much help
to Ivan if another Outsider put a rifle round through her head.

Her throat went dry at the thought. If nothing else the fear of mortal
threat heightened her awareness. After all the time she had lived in the security of her home, it was still difficult to realize how fast a life could end. It
warmed her blood, tightened her mind and body, and sent her heart into
a heavy rhythm that reverberated through her limbs. Although part of her
gasped with the paralytic fear of mortal threat, that same fear fueled the rush
propelling her from its grasp.

Despite all her concerns, she was hit by a strange moment of revelation as she hid behind another tree. Fear had set her free. The horror of her mother's death, and witnessing Ruth and Rachel in their devolved states, had sent her into Kyle's arms. Killing Mena kicked her into action to rebel against her father.

She looked at the careless blue sky above, lit by the sun's blinding glare. Life, it seemed, burned brightest under the darkness of Death's shadow.

Ivan needed her. Kyle was waiting for her.

Her gaze sank to her arm. "Let's see just how bright we can burn."

‡ ‡ ‡

Jonah peered out from the window of Angela's bedroom. His father's voice whispered in his mind as he took count of Woolly Ben's party.

When it comes to shootin', try to get the height if you can. If your aim ain't nothin' special, then wait 'til things get close. It'll be easier to make your shots and move to your next targets.

Jonah would've given anything to have his brother and father at his side right then. Together, they'd wipe out Ben's party in the blink of an eye. On his own he knew he was in trouble. No matter. The Reverend was depending on him. His mother and twin were dead. He had the sisters and Angela to protect.

If he had to die, he'd make it count.

He slid the barrel of his rifle under the open sash of Angela's window, closed an eye, and took aim down the length of his gun. Woolly Ben was in the middle of his gang. Jonah hoped to get him with the first shot. If he shot wide, though, at least he'd still hit something.

He wasn't particular. He knew what his father would say. Dead was dead.

‡ ‡ ‡

Angela dodged among a few more trees before getting a view of the campsite. She caught a glimpse of a man seated on one of the logs and pressed her body against the protective mass of a tree. Her arm tightened its coils around the rifle's stock as her fingers clasped the trigger assembly.

She raised the gun and peered down its sights to take aim.

"You don't want to do that."

It was her father's voice. Her target turned to reveal his stolid gaze.

His prescience caught her off guard until her arm's instinct galvanized her resolve. She knew what she had to do. There was no point wasting any time. Her arm resumed its steady aim, a clear line straight for his chest.

"We both have crimes on our hands," he said, unfazed by the threat of her gun.

She held her silence. Her finger quivered against the trigger, her arm desperate to take the shot and be done with it, but her innards constricted with an impulse of suspicion.

He knew I would come. He knew I would aim. Why don't I shoot?

Her father sighed. "You won't shoot because you understand I wouldn't sit here defenseless unless I already knew you wouldn't shoot. You probably realize it as I say this, but the only reason to light a fire in the middle of the day was so you could find me by the rising smoke. And you only know this because you understand my complacency must be born of what I've foreseen."

More lies. She let her breath go. *Shoot him, shoot him, shoot him!*

"If you kill me here, your precious Kyle will die." He opened his hands to the certainty of his statement. "Now, lower your rifle so that you don't make a dreadful mistake."

"Where's Ivan?"

Her father turned to the smoldering pile of contorted, blackened flesh off to his other side. "I think you already know."

She quaked. "Did you kill the sisters?"

"I told you we've both committed crimes." He stood. "I know you killed Mena and Judah."

"Mena hurt me." She raised the rifle once more. "I didn't want to kill Judah."

"But you knew you had to."

"I . . ." She fumed. There was no need of foresight to know what he would say.

"Necessity possesses its own morality. Its Judgment is the matter of a moment, not of many moments. It has no care for hindsight and laughs in the face of foresight." He put his hands on his hips. "I won't ask for your forgiveness, and I have none to offer. Our present situation is a moral stalemate."

She glared at him.

He extended an arm, pointed to the gun, and waved his finger toward the ground. "You don't want to waste that bullet on me. You'll need every last one for Woolly Ben and his deputies."

She lifted her head from the rifle. "You've seen them?"

He slid his hand into the pocket of his coat, his stare holding on her. When his hand emerged, a cold gleam settled over his eyes. "I searched those four men we killed to confirm what my foresight has told me."

He opened his hand and let four shiny badges slip one by one from his palm.

She stepped out from behind the tree. The Outsiders they killed weren't prospectors. They were a scout party, a scout party for Woolly Ben.

"So now you see," her father said. "The End Time is upon us."

‡ ‡ ‡

Jonah settled into his shot the way his father and Carl had taught him. The crack of the rifle caused several horses to rear, others to spin, but the shot was wide nonetheless. Woolly Ben ducked in his saddle as the man beside him gasped, a spray of blood bursting from his chest as the rifle round blew through his body. Before he fell from the saddle, Jonah chambered and fired his second round, causing another man to yelp as the bullet tore through his thigh and into his horse's flank. The animal bucked, shook its head, and crashed on its side, crushing the man's wounded leg.

Jonah got off his third shot just before the element of surprise was lost. He aimed for Woolly Ben once more but misjudged the speed of the charging horses. His shot ripped through the empty air that Ben had occupied a heartbeat earlier and found a new home in the temple of another deputy. Red spray burst from the opposite side of the man's head, his hat flying free. In the next moment he tumbled from his saddle like a rag doll, only to trip up the mount of the man behind him. The horse slammed head first into the ground, throwing its rider forward to tumble across the earth in a tangle of broken limbs.

Woolly Ben led his party in a charge around the Purdy home, vacating Jonah's field of fire. Jonah ran from Angela's bedroom to follow the drumbeat of hooves racing from the back of the house to its front. Ignoring the rule against entering the Reverend's bedroom, he kicked open the door and hurried to the windows.

The glass exploded in a hail of rifle and revolver rounds, and Jonah threw himself backwards amid the flying shards of glass. He hit the floor hard, knocking the breath from his lungs. The shouts from outside failed to penetrate his daze until he heard the crack of rifle butts smashing open the front door.

"Torches!" a voice called out. "Burn that other house to the ground."

Rage brought Jonah back to his senses. The hidden strength in his limbs burst into his mind. He chambered a round, ran from the bedroom, hopped down the stairs, and surprised three men in the main room. They spun, revolvers drawn, but one of them collapsed with a shot from Jonah's rifle. He leapt forward, piling his shoulder into one of the remaining men, sending him flying across the room. A revolver shot whizzed over his head before he ducked and slammed a fist into the man's chest, cracking his ribs. The revolver fell from the man's numbed hand as Jonah grabbed the man's shoulders, hefted him up and then drove his limp body down on his own lifted knee. The man's spine shattered in a quick series of wet cracks.

Still holding firm to the man's shoulders, Jonah decided to use the man's body as a club to pummel the man he had tackled. Spurs scraped the ceiling as the man's crumpled body whipped around and slammed into the last deputy. Once, twice, and then a third time, Jonah swatted him before throwing the dead man through the front window.

The deputy who was sprawled on the floor, a rather large man, rolled onto his side and reached for his revolver. Jonah clamped a big hand on the man's head, jerked him upright, and bashed his face into the stone mantle over the fireplace. The deputy's skull collapsed with a sickening snap before Jonah threw him out the front window as well.

Shouts sounded from outside. Rifle rounds ripped through the broken windows. Jonah spun as a round tore across his shoulder. He ducked, charged into the kitchen, and searched for anything he could use. His rifle was on the floor of the main room. He knew he'd be shot to pieces if he went back to get the weapon. No, he needed something else . . .

He went to the iron stove and lifted the heavy door from its hinges. It wouldn't shield his entire body, but it would shield enough. No sooner did he turn than a revolver round panged off his improvised shield. Without looking, Jonah ran forward, trampling the man who dared shoot at him and stomping a boot on his head to squash his skull.

Jonah got a single glimpse of Woolly Ben sitting on his mount outside the front of the house. When Jonah looked out the side windows, he could see his own house ablaze.

Bullets rained upon him. A few buried themselves in the wall behind him, a few ricocheted from his door shield, but two found their marks, one ripping into his lower leg and the other punching into his belly. He slumped against the wall and clutched his gut as he peered over the top of his shield.

Woolly Ben sat still atop his mount. The look of disinterest on his face was oddly reminiscent of the Reverend's disaffected gaze during many a dinner sermon.

The house was surrounded. Jonah shook his head to rally his nerves.

He thought of the life now lost to him, the life promised to him from his first memories. Rachel was to go to Judah; Ruth was to be his. The bond they shared was innate, forged in the sweet gaze of Ruth's eyes when he looked up while suckling her breasts. She had coddled him, and he had intended to repay the favor by being a good provider and protector. Among the twilight shadows of his dim thoughts, he knew no other word or concept of what they shared other than to know it as love.

Love is a Temptress, the Reverend often said. Love whispers sweet delusions into the wanting ear for no other reason than to make sport of swooning fools.

Jonah had always wondered what the Reverend meant with those words.

He ducked as bullets tore through the house. He looked down at his belly where the warmth of his blood seeped between his fingers. Although he clutched the wound, the blood still found its way out. He was mute, but he didn't need words to understand the thought that possessed his mind.

If Doom had found him, he would make It proud.

He stormed out the front door like a wild bull, crouched behind his shield as his legs propelled him forward. Bullets ricocheted from the heavy, iron stove door. Horses whinnied at the speed of his charge. Men shouted.

At the full speed of his run, he popped his head up and hurled the stove door with all his strength. It tore through the deputies like a cannon ball, obliterating the first man it struck and bowling two more from their saddles before caving in the ribs of another man's horse. The damage was lost to Jonah as he leapt into the air, grabbed a deputy, and let the momentum of his body drag man and horse crashing to the ground. Keeping his grip on the hapless deputy, Jonah rolled over, planted his feet, and flung the man to take out another horse and rider.

The horse he had tackled bolted to its feet. He ducked behind its mass. The beast shuddered as a dozen or more bullets punched the breath from its mighty lungs. As it dropped dead Jonah hopped back to avoid getting caught under its weight. Had he the time to think things through he might have dropped for cover, but there wasn't time to think. It was his moment of righteous rage, and that rage refused to bow down.

He balled his fists. His sight filled with the red inferno consuming his home.

Gunfire erupted from all sides. His body burned with bullet impacts.

The Reverend was right. When the world ended, it would end in flames.

26

‡ ‡ ‡

Angela looked up to where her father pointed. A twisted trail of black smoke wound its way through the clear blue sky. There was no mistaking the direction of its source.

She stepped forward. "Jonah?"

Nathan closed his eyes for a moment. "If he's not already dead, he will be soon."

Angela spun toward him. "How can you be so calm?"

"How can you be so concerned?" He settled a caustic gaze upon her. "Don't be a fool, and don't be a hypocrite. Between you and me, we've killed more of our kind than Woolly Ben."

She found herself at a loss for a retort.

He nodded. "Yes, but even so, the outrage burns within you. I can see it because I know it. And do you know why it burns in you, as hypocritical as it might be after the things we've done?"

She knew where his thoughts went. As true as it was, it sickened her to admit the truth. "What we did was between our kind. Outsiders had no say in it."

"That's a good girl."

"Don't talk to me like you're still my father. That bond is as dead as everything else today."

"So you may think. Indeed, so you may think." He took off his hat, stared into its bowl for a moment, and then settled it back on his head. "Tell me this. With our homes burned and all but us dead, what target will be left for Woolly Ben to vent his purge?"

She blinked. "They're innocent!"

"No one is innocent," her father said with a hiss. "The Eddingtons will be the next to burn. And what shall we do about that?"

She didn't bother to answer. She was already running back to Buttercup.

‡ ‡ ‡

Jonah couldn't move. He was sitting up, his legs folded beneath him, blood dripping from the corners of his open mouth. By some miracle the volley of gunfire that had torn through him had failed to end his life. So he sat, helpless, hopeless, his knees shot out, his shoulders torn open, a dozen holes in his chest and gut.

The deputies were mocking him. One came by, spat in his face, and punched him. Strange, that these men who were once so frail beneath Jonah's strength now sought to bolster their egos by humiliating a man incapable of self-defense. If Jonah had been able to talk, he would have told them they seemed all the smaller.

A stern voice spoke through the blurred midst of deputies drifting by Jonah's glazed eyes. "Leave him be."

The deputy who had spat on him shoved Jonah's head.

"Hodges! I said leave him be."

The deputy glanced over his shoulder and hesitated.

Jonah wheezed.

Deputy Hodges bowed his head under Woolly Ben's glare and stepped aside. He shoved two of his fellows and pointed to the Purdy house.

Woolly Ben did nothing but stare at Jonah in silence. After several moments he crouched before him. "Young man, that was an impressive last stand. It's a good thing it was just you. Do you understand how I know it's only you?" He pushed his hat up and pointed a black-gloved hand toward the barn. "Your brother and mother are already dead."

Jonah gave away no sign of emotion.

Ben frowned. "That's right, dead and gone. But something tells me you already knew that, given that you fought like a man who knows he has nothing left to lose." Ben waited for a reaction before tipping his head back. "I guess there's no point waiting for you to say something, given that you're mute. So I'll ask, and you nod. Understand?"

Jonah nodded.

"That's a good boy." Ben waved off several of his men and pointed for them to wait before torching the Purdy house. "The Reverend. Is he alive? His daughter?"

Jonah tipped his head twice.

"Are they heading to the Eddingtons?"

Jonah stared. He gurgled, coughed, and a blob of bloody drool dribbled from his lower lip. His gaze sank as the tendril of muck stretched to the ground in a long, thick strand of gore. He had hoped to spit right in Ben's face.

Woolly Ben frowned. "I had a feeling this was a waste of time. We'll find whoever's left soon enough. In the meantime I'll put you out of your misery."

Jonah looked up as Woolly Ben stood. His eyes narrowed against the glare of the sun, Ben's form almost lost as a dark sliver against the light. Even so, there was no mistaking the feel of a cold circle against his forehead.

Jonah closed his eyes. The pressure of the gun on his skin changed as Ben's arm braced for the revolver's kick.

"Your kin will join you soon enough," Ben said and pulled the trigger.

‡ ‡ ‡

Kyle was sitting in his study, tending the balance books for the Range, when the rapid pound of hooves reached his ears. He grabbed his cane, pushed up to a stance, and made his way toward the kitchen. His gut told him something was seriously amiss, given Angela's unexpected arrival and her even more hasty departure.

It had been a strange moment when she had come to him and he had held her, stranger still when he had kissed her. He didn't know what to make of her age, what with her remarkable maturation. The numbers baffled him because none of them made sense. Too old to be a child, too proximal to a girl's age to be a grown woman. Her state was an opaque question made more confounding by his undeniable attraction and headlong desire to hold her. It was a welcome and eager departure from the monastic establishment of his life at the same time that it was a keg of dynamite to his perceptions of order in the world. Even more confounding was her sudden rejection of his embrace, a mystery locked shut beneath a figurative kick to the tender nerve of his male pride.

He didn't know what to make of anything that had happened. It was a strange state of confusion that had up-ended his little world.

But then life on the Range runs on different rules. Her arm tells me all that needs to be said on that matter.

Either way, in any way, he wanted—needed—answers. Something was indeed amiss, and the clear analytical lanes in his mind ached to have those answers.

His heart thumped with the rapidity of the nearing horses' hooves, as he knew full well the irony of the situation. She was at once the cause and cure of his curiosity, the wellspring of a desire he never expected to know in his life.

He ignored his mother as he hurried by and threw open the kitchen door to step outside.

To his delight it was indeed Angela.

To his dismay she was riding with her father. To his trepidation he could see the wild look of desperation in their eyes.

He turned and shouted for his father.

‡ ‡ ‡

Woolly Ben walked among the upstairs rooms of the Purdy house. The Semenic home was already crumbling into its own pyre, the smoke of its ruin curling high in the clear blue sky. A second tendril rose from the crackling flames of the barn. Soon the Purdy house would suffer the same fate as he continued his purge of the Range, but he wasn't quite ready to wipe the dwelling from the land.

He gazed into the front bedroom, the broken glass glittering where it was scattered across the floor. Ben frowned, his hand settling on his holstered revolver as he peered into what he knew was Nathan's bedroom. Ben had seen many things in his life, had participated in more backroom debauchery than he cared to remember, yet his imagination strained to summon a vision of Nathan and Calliope. For all the jaded cynicism born of a life of excess,

Ben had a limit, and bestiality was far past any line he was willing to cross. Although he could remember Calliope when she was still an innocent, sheltered, club-footed girl who would swoon at Nathan's sermons, he remembered her with greater ease in her equine transformation.

He spat on the floor of the bedroom and turned away. Aside from a closet with neat stacks of linens, there was only one other room, a spacious second bedroom with a single bed. He stepped in, anxious when he understood the room to be that of Angela's. It wasn't only that she was Nathan's child, it was the fact that of all his malformed children, she was the only one to live more than a day or two, and so the only one Connors didn't have to bury in some unmarked location. On those days, Connors would ride back, say nothing, get good and drunk, and disappear with the best whores Ben had in town.

Ben often wondered what it was that so rattled Connors. The man was an experienced surgeon from the army. He had cut off more limbs than a chicken farmer, or so he claimed. However, whatever had been off with those ill-fated offspring, everything seemed to be in order with Angela.

Ben looked about her room. There wasn't much to see. A shelf with some books which he skimmed and tossed aside when he saw Mena's neat block letters written over the ruled pages. As a man who had benefited from the finest private education his parents could buy, he found Mena's homespun texts a sorry state of institutionalized ignorance. He flipped over the mattress, felt through the meager stack of folded clothes on another shelf, and then stood in the middle of the room, hands on his hips.

His eyes narrowed as he looked back to the clothes. They were not sized for a child. They were sized for a grown woman.

Stumped, he turned, swung the door on its hinges, and stepped back.

A thick pencil had been left on the floor next to the wall. Low to the floor he found a series of hash marks, obviously made with the pencil. He crouched and counted them off to reach the number of his original guess.

"She knows her age," he said under his breath. He stood, hooked his thumbs in his belt, and stared at the markings. "A malformed arm, and a girl who grew too fast."

He made his way down the stairs to find three of his deputies feasting on a hearty loaf of Mena's grain bread. He waved for them to move as he went out the door and ordered Hodges to task his remaining men with torching

the house. Two parallel lines of disrupted turf denoted the scrape marks of
Jonah's boot heels as two of Ben's deputies dragged the young man's corpse
into the Purdy house to burn with the structure.

Ben settled into his saddle and looked over the desolation around him.
"All this emptiness," he thought aloud with a sorrowful shake of his head. "It
should have been a peaceful life."

‡ ‡ ‡

Sarah stood outside her kitchen door, her gentle features anything but
tranquil as she watched her husband hurry by. "So this is it? Everything we
worked for, it's just over?"

Carl avoided the heat of her stare as he tossed a belt of shotgun shells to
Nathan. "We always knew this day might come. It's too late now to worry
about it."

She pointed to the three gray threads of smoke snaking into the sky. "You
know what that is, don't you? Three fires. That's two houses and a barn."

Nathan's jaw clenched, but he said nothing as he flipped open his double-barrel shotgun.

Sarah stepped toward him. "That's your home, Nathan! Your home is
burning."

He snapped the shotgun closed and met her gaze. "And what would you
have me do?"

She threw her arms out. "Where's Ivan? Where are the boys? Where—"

"They're all dead," Nathan said, his stark monotone freezing Sarah in
place.

Just then Angela walked back from the little horse pen behind the house.
She had heard Sarah's shouts, so she wasn't surprised to find a scene, but her
father's honesty stopped her in her tracks.

Sarah fell back a step. It seemed a great effort for her to close her hanging mouth. Her head sank, her gaze darting about her feet as she smoothed
her white apron across her waist. The length of her flaxen braid hung like
a noose between her shoulders. She took a breath, her hands shaking a bit
until she lifted her head to stare at Angela. "Is it true?"

Angela pressed her lips together as her arm coiled against her side. She
replied with a single nod.

Sarah closed her eyes for a moment before looking back to Nathan. "We have to go."

"No," Nathan said at once. "We stay."

Carl shifted on his feet. "It's not a bad idea to go, Rev. We—"

"I said, we stay." Nathan's eyes narrowed

"Woolly Ben has twenty men!" Sarah's voice burst from her mouth, her face reddening as she pointed to the rising threads of smoke. "Twenty men. How are we supposed to fight them? Staying is suicide. We have to go."

"No, at most it's sixteen men, and I'm sure Jonah made it less." Nathan smiled. "And my dear Sarah, it's not suicide, it's fulfillment."

Carl rolled his eyes. Angela looked at Kyle, who stood silent in the kitchen doorway behind his mother.

Sarah's stare hardened to a pointed gleam to show all her Purdy stock. "Is this what it all comes to? Do we all have to burn for the sake of your prophecy? All the work, all the years, all the murder to secure this land, and nothing to show for it but our deaths?"

Nathan tipped his head back and squared his shoulders to take on his characteristic air of righteousness. "I think your question has answered itself. All dues need their pay."

Sarah's hands balled to fists. Tears of fury seeped from the corners of her eyes. "Then what was the point? Tell me! What was the point of this, of any of this?"

"Her," Nathan said with a tip of his head to Angela.

All eyes went to Angela.

Her throat went dry. Her arm tightened.

Sarah turned on her cousin. "Do you want her to die? Is that what you want?"

"She will not die. She will triumph."

"She'll die like the rest of us." Sarah shook her fists. "Nathan!"

"No, she will triumph, and a new kingdom will rise—"

"Nathan!"

"A new kingdom will rise in glory!" he declared, his face almost purple with the indomitable rage of conviction.

Sarah spun to Angela. "You don't have to listen to him."

Angela fought to find her voice.

Sarah threw her arms out to spur a response. "Angela! You don't have to listen to him."

Nathan's smile returned. "No, you don't have to listen to me."

Angela felt her resolve solidify. She wouldn't listen. She would defy him.

Her father waved to the distance. "Go ahead. Give the order. Ride out."

Angela opened her mouth, ready to answer his challenge. He was insane. He wanted them to die. She could choose a new plan. A plan to live.

All they had to do was ride out. The momentum of the urge all but choked the air.

Clop.

Angela looked at Kyle. He had stepped back—sunk back—into the shadows of the kitchen. The truth of a single stark memory vomited to the forefront of her awareness.

Kyle can't ride.

Her blood thickened to tar.

Kyle would have to stay behind.

Her mind shot toward an awful, inevitable conclusion.

Kyle would have to die.

The horror of it all but strangled her voice in her throat. "No," she said, her arm ready to spring from her side to guard Kyle where he stood. "No, no, I can't leave you—we can't ride . . ."

"Angela, please." Sarah stepped toward her, for a moment too lost in her desperation to understand the cruel realization that had hit Angela until she noted the drift of Angela's eyes. Sarah went rigid, her face paling, her mouth dropping in a silent cry of anguish as she turned to her son.

Kyle kept his head down. "Go," he said. He wiped his eyes before looking up. "Go. I'll do what I can to buy time."

Carl's rifle fell from his numb hands. Sarah trembled, sobbed, and sank to the ground as her knees gave out.

Kyle shook his head as he looked at his parents. "Go," he said, the desperation clear in his voice. "I don't want you to die because of me."

Carl went to Sarah. He crouched to hold her in his arms, but his eyes were on his son. "We can't leave you." He shook his head. "We won't leave you."

Angela stared at them before looking at Kyle. For the first time she saw a look of shame on his face. It pained her, pained her in a way she had never felt before, stabbed her in a way at once so different and so similar to the way her mother's death had stabbed her.

She had been impaled with the grief of losing her mother in a moment she had not foreseen. With Kyle it was plain as day what would happen to him. There was no need for foresight. And anyway, foresight was not her gift. No, that gift belonged to someone else.

She glared at her father.

His smile lingered. Whether it was an expression of joy from self-satisfaction or doom realized was impossible to tell.

Perhaps, she decided, it was better not to know. In that moment it made little difference, for the past, present and future collapsed upon her, upon all of them, as they stood in a welcoming home under a bright sun on a day of such pleasant weather. She remembered the day her father had taken her to Thetis Springs, the way his voice had echoed and resonated, tonal vibrations overlapping to merge moments into one impression of timelessness, the very source of his prophetic gift.

She understood then what she could no longer resist to perceive. He had brought her to the Eddingtons after Thetis Springs. It was all part of his foresight. Meeting Kyle, their mutual affection and attraction, the wondrous notion of an intimate companion to contrast a dire life subjugated beneath Mena's tyranny, all of it was to produce a moment—the one moment she now occupied—this one moment in which she stood, so that she could fulfill its demands in the only way she could, in the only way possible, in the only way her short existence would allow.

And so she would stay.

They would make their stand.

Her father and Woolly Ben would have their day of reckoning.

Her arm begged to fly out and strike her father down. She ached to let it go, but she knew better through the clarity of his foresight. If there were to be any chance, they would need him in the fight. He said if he died Kyle would also die. In all the convoluted twists of his black heart, she knew he had never lied about his foresight.

He had her trapped. There was no decision to make because her decision was already made, had been made from the day she was born. There had never been a choice, only a charade.

She despised him, cursed him, spat on the notion of his very existence, the temper of her scorn made all the hotter by the fact that she was powerless before him. Only then did she remember the pledge he had sworn when he stood over her down in the cavern with its miraculous water: that she would hate him before their time was done.

Hate him she did, with every fiber of her body, with every sinew and striation of her flesh, with all the fire and fury of every emotion she possessed. It hardened her to her deepest core, driving out any remaining notions of childish innocence that cowered in the secluded corners of her mind, until she came to one final conclusion, one last way to rebel.

I will hate you until you breathe your last breath.

27

‡ ‡ ‡

Woolly Ben glanced to either side as he rode toward the last hill before the Eddington house. Only six deputies from his original posse of twenty remained, riding three to his right and three to his left. He had lost four men in the advance scouting party he had sent out, the disappearance of which had spurred him to ride out in force in the first place. Another eight had died at the hands of the wild mute, along with a pair too injured to ride anywhere but back to town.

Thinking of it all, Ben understood why Nathan had grown so bold. If he had all his flock in place, they could fend off a hundred deputies. It was a startling conclusion, made all the more tantalizing by the fact that the flock had turned on itself.

No matter. It would ease the last act, so to speak. After seeing what Jonah could do, Ben was no longer interested in gold. He wanted the secret, the precious secret Nathan had guarded, the secret as to how his flock had grown into freaks.

And splendid freaks they were.

If Ben could possess the secret, he wouldn't need gold. No, people would pile gold at his feet for just a taste of such extraordinary abilities.

He waved for his men to slow to a trot and drew them in line as they crested the hill. If it had to be bloody, then it would be bloody. On the other hand, Ben considered himself a businessman, and businessmen always sought resolution through negotiation.

The plan was simple enough.

Ben lifted his little horn, gave it a blow, and decided on the business of murder.

‡ ‡ ‡

The report of Ben's horn found its way into the kitchen of the Eddington house, where everyone was seated around the table, cleaning and loading a stockpile of arms and munitions. As one they stopped short among the clicks and clacks of weapons and shared a communal stare before scrambling to the living room. Kyle followed in their wake, head hanging in shame for the liability he was inflicting on his parents.

Angela glanced back at him as she moved to a living room window. Her arm tightened its grasp of her rifle. She hoped to encourage him with a smile.

"Eyes forward," Carl said to her as he leaned against a window frame. He braced the deadly length of a bolt-action hunting rifle to his shoulder and looked out the window. Sarah mirrored his pose with a lever-action rifle on the other side of the doorway.

Nathan rested his rifle across his chest and strolled out the front door to stand on the porch. "Why, if it isn't my old friend Ben Wu Li."

Woolly Ben sat still atop his mount, just at the peak of a hill. Two deputies milled about on their mounts, passing back and forth before him. It was enough of a random screen to make a long shot almost impossible.

Nothing stood between the Eddington house and Ben's position other than a wide expanse of turf glowing beneath the buttery afternoon light.

Ben tipped his hat in greeting. "Good to see you, Nathan. I was worried about you."

"Not too worried," Nathan said and pointed to the distant tendrils of smoke.

"That's all quiet now." Ben waved it off. "And it's all behind us, you could say."

"I still have time on the prospect."

Ben shook his head. "We both know you never put one day into prospecting. But that's behind us as well. I'm not interested in gold anymore. I'm interested in something else you've been hiding out here, something I've left to you all these years out of misplaced generosity. That measure has run out. I've come to collect."

Nathan stood defiant. "That was never part of our arrangement."

Ben straightened in his saddle and opened his hands. "Let me cut to the heart of the matter. You have a secret. I want it. We can be gentlemen, settle it today, and remain neighbors, or the men I sent back to town can be out here in two days with fifty gunmen." He rested his hands on the pommel of his saddle. "Your mute boy killed deputies, Nathan. Can't have men of the law laid low without repercussions."

Nathan lowered his head for a moment before meeting Ben's waiting gaze. "This sounds more like a threat than a proposal."

"It's the only deal that's left. Call it whatever you want, but you best think it over."

Nathan said nothing.

At Angela's side, Carl was sweating. Sarah had planted her shoulders against the wall, closed her eyes, and was looking at the ceiling as she muttered a silent prayer. It was no mystery that they were tormented by the terrible proposition of an impossible, inescapable situation. They couldn't run because they couldn't abandon Kyle. They wouldn't submit to Woolly Ben, and they wouldn't defy Nathan. There was no mystery to those thoughts either.

They were simple thoughts.

They were obvious thoughts.

Angela looked over her shoulder. Without a word, Kyle had retreated to the kitchen. He was a good man. A good man devoted to his parents. Just as they were willing to lay down their lives for him, he would understand that he might have to lay down his life for them. It was a matter of one loss rather than two, math that could be counted on just one hand.

Her fingers popped open. Her arm coiled and sprang from her side before her rifle hit the floor. Kyle looked at her as he put the barrel of a revolver to the side of his head. His mouth dropped as his thumb pulled back the hammer. Her arm punched him square in the face, knocking him out cold with the force of the blow. The gun flew from his hand as he toppled backward and hit the floor.

Sarah dropped her weapon and ran for her son the moment she understood what had happened, but Carl lingered a moment before pointing to Nathan. "Make the goddamn deal," he said before hurrying to his family.

Nathan glared over his shoulder at the Eddingtons. He closed his eyes, only to open them on Angela as her arm coiled around her leg to resume its place at her shoulder. She met her father's stare, unsure what to say. For the first time she was possessed by the horrible suspicion that their situation was hopeless. She knew her father would never give up the secret of Thetis Springs. Likewise, they couldn't fight off Ben's regiment of deputies. Once the deputies killed them, it was only a matter of time before Ben discovered the location of the cave. Either way—any way—all was lost.

Nathan took a breath before turning back to Woolly Ben.

Angela's heart quaked as her suspicions darkened. Her father had the gift of foresight. Had he seen such a moment? And if he had, what would a man of apocalyptic conviction surmise from such a vision?

Nathan cleared his throat. "May I have a minute or two?"

Ben stared at him. After a heavy silence he smiled. "I thought you might want to talk it over. Make it quick."

"It won't be long," Nathan said. He turned, opened the door, and stepped into the house. The feathery weight of the screened door closed against his shoulders. He leaned his rifle against the wall before taking his hat from his head to stare into its bowl. His finger traced around the black satin of the hat's inner liner. "Do you love him?" he whispered.

Angela froze. Her arm's primal instincts whispered doom on any answer she gave even as she knew there was only one answer she possessed.

Her voice came as a faint rasp. "Yes."

He squeezed his eyes shut. "Then remember that his life rests in my hands."

How do you fight a man who has the gift of foresight?

"Daddy . . ."

He threw his hat toward her face. Startled, her vision obscured, she sank back, disrupting her arm's trajectory as it launched from her side. With its fingers narrowed to a vicious point, it shot out, tore through the crest of his hat, and found nothing but empty air and the oak doorjamb to welcome its strike.

Nathan had dropped to the floor the moment he tossed his hat. Now he whipped his revolver free and slapped the hammer with his left palm as he fired in rapid succession. Sarah turned, her eyes going blank as the first round hit her square in the forehead. Her lovely flaxen braid came apart in a blossoming fountain of gore as her brains blew out the back of her head. Carl was mid-turn from Kyle's still form when the second round slammed into his shoulder, knocking his torso around to leave him exposed in full. The next three rounds tore through his chest, their impacts kicking him back bit by bit until the sixth and final round found its mark square on his left cheek. His jaw shattered, several teeth flying free to hit the floor past the sinking body of his wife. His right ear mushroomed as the bullet tunneled through his head and failed to return to the light of day.

First Sarah and now Carl dropped dead on either side of Kyle.

At the same time, Angela's arm cracked into the doorjamb. Angela's knees wobbled with the numbing impact, leaving her to slump into the corner by the window.

Her arm fell beside Nathan, struck senseless.

Nathan doffed his long black coat in the blink of an eye, bundled it around her arm, and used the sleeves to tie it tightly like a sack, then he sat on the floor with a sigh. With a practiced flip of his wrist, he released the drum of his revolver, shook the weapon by his shoulder to dump the still-smoking shells, and replaced them with six fresh rounds. After a quick look at the ruin of the Eddington family, he set his hat on his head, slid his revolver into its holster and stood.

Angela could do nothing but watch.

He put his hands on his hips and with his back to her he said, "In answer to your unspoken question, you are powerless to fight a man with the gift of foresight." He turned to face her. "You, and everyone else, are powerless against me. My life ends on my call, and my call alone."

She craned her neck to peer over the windowsill as he went out the door, hands raised and open at his shoulders. Her gaze darted to the hill to find the dull sheen of seven rifle barrels spaced along its crest.

"It's all over," Nathan called out. "There's no need to be excited."

Ben rose in the saddle, his rifle fixed on Nathan. "Reverend?"

"It's just us now, Ben. It's just us." Nathan lowered his hands. "I'll show you my secret."

‡ ‡ ‡

Angela scurried to where the Eddingtons lay on the kitchen floor. She rolled Sarah and Carl away from Kyle so he wouldn't have to look into the dead, distorted faces of his parents. It was bad enough he was sprayed with their gore. With their bodies rolled so their backs were to their son, Angela dropped to the floor, her knees to either side of Kyle's face. For lack of any other way to dignify him she leaned over, licked the bitter blood and gore from his face, and spat it to the side. Some of the blood, she realized, was from his nose, left from where her arm had struck him to stop his sacrificial suicide.

When she licked his eyelids, he at last blinked and regained consciousness.

The charge of hooves sounded outside the house.

Her father stood on the front porch, arms crossed over his chest, showing no more sign of worry than if he were watching the grass grow.

Kyle blinked. "Angela?"

The moment she heard his voice her eyes welled up. "Kyle!" She dropped her head to kiss his forehead, his cheeks, and last his lips. "I'm sorry, I'm so sorry."

He took her face in his hands and eased her back. With her kneeling by his head, they saw each other upside down. It was an odd view, made all the more strange when her tears dripped on his cheeks.

His stare locked on her eyes. "Why'd you stop me?"

She sucked in a breath, trembling in the hold of his hands. "I, I couldn't let you . . ."

His gaze filled with horror. "I wanted to save you. I wanted to save my parents."

She closed her eyes and rested her forehead against his. "There's no saving any of us," she whispered with a shake of her head.

Her father's voice reached her. "Don't hurt them, Ben. Don't hurt them, and I'll show you everything."

Angela shot up straight, her eyes kindled with fury.

It was a defiant moment, but no more than a moment. One of Ben's deputies slammed the butt of his rifle into her forehead and knocked her senseless.

28

‡ ‡ ‡

Angela woke to the rhythmic jostle of a horse's trot. Crusted blood fell from her eyelids as she forced them open. A short length of rope was looped around her torso and neck and tied to the horn of her saddle so that she wouldn't topple from her horse. She couldn't sit up, though, and she missed her arm.

A cry of agony reached her ears. Her gaze darted about and drove a nauseating dizzy spell through her gut until she found the horse beside her. Kyle was draped over the horse's flanks, his hands tied at the wrists and his legs dangling loose. The sight of him sharpened her wits in a heartbeat.

His face worked through contortions of pain until it burst from his mouth, only for the cycle to repeat.

She struggled against her binding. It was no use.

Her father came up on her other side, his body framed against the darkening sky. "Stop," he said as a single, simple command. "Don't fight it. You'll hurt yourself."

She summoned a wad of saliva and spat at him.

He looked down at his vest before nodding to her. "That's it," he said under his breath. "Hold onto that. You'll need it soon enough."

She watched as he trotted ahead of her to ride next to Woolly Ben. "She's awake."

Ben glanced back at her before looking at Nathan. "Her eyes burn with righteous rage. Without a doubt, she's your daughter."

Nathan met Ben's gaze. "You gave me your word not to hurt her. Or Kyle."

"Indeed, I did," Ben said with a nod. "You keep your end and show me the secret, and I'll keep my end."

Kyle groaned.

"You're hurting him," Angela said. "Let him down."

Ben turned to her. "That's not possible, Miss Purdy. He's the only one here who really isn't a threat. Naturally, he's both the best insurance and assurance I have to keep you and your father in check." He pointed past the deputy with Kyle slung over his horse to another man carrying the bundled sack of her father's coat. "And if that weird arm of yours decides to have a mind of its own, I won't hesitate to have it hacked to pieces. Do you understand?"

Angela bared her teeth as she strained against the binding. Her neck and face all but purpled with the effort until she gave up. Her arm thrashed inside the coat-sack until the deputy carrying Kyle leaned over and punched the sack several times. Angela grunted as if the punches had hit straight in her gut. It took effort against the beating, but she managed to still her arm's rage. She looked at Ben. "You better pray we don't get loose, you heathen bastard."

"Such insolent language." Ben waited to slap Angela until Nathan turned away. When her gaze burned on him all the brighter, he slapped her again. "Nathan, your daughter has discipline issues."

Nathan lowered his head. "She's a Purdy. She follows no authority but her own."

"Then perhaps she'll learn a lesson today in seeing where such arrogance has landed her father," Ben said with a sigh.

They rode in silence for several moments before Nathan pointed ahead.

"There," he said. "There's the cave. We'll have to dismount."

"Good." Ben patted Nathan's shoulder. "It's nice to see that after all these years you've finally learned to be a gracious loser."

‡ ‡ ‡

The stars were bright over their heads, little glimmers in a night sky marked by a bright, waxing moon. Woolly Ben and Nathan dismounted before Ben signaled his men to fetch Angela and Kyle. Hodges cut the rope by Angela's neck and knocked her from her saddle. She hit the rocky ground with a wheeze, causing Buttercup to whinny and circle around her until a deputy seized her reins and dragged her away. Hodges laughed as he went to Kyle, grabbed the waistband of his pants, and jerked him from the back of the horse. Kyle screamed as his bad leg collapsed beneath his weight.

Hodges mocked his scream before slapping him, grabbing his suspenders, and dragging him along the ground.

Nathan turned to Ben. "Is that necessary?"

"No, not in the least," Ben said with a chuckle. "That's what makes it so entertaining."

The deputies laughed at their boss' lack of empathy. Rough hands seized Angela and yanked her to her feet. Only then did she realize she was barefoot. It wasn't much, but it was something.

Hodges returned to ball up the collar of her poncho to keep it tight around her neck. "You're a sweet lookin' thing, even if you ain't got no arms," he said with a grin.

A second deputy prodded his shoulder. "Perfect marryin' kind for you, Hodges. She won't be able to slap you around none when you come home from whorin'."

"And you won't have to worry about this lame-leg chasin' you down," another deputy said and kicked Kyle's bad hip.

Hodges watched Kyle writhe in agony before spitting on him.

"That's enough," Ben said with a glare. "Two of you take the cripple's arms across your shoulders. He's no good to us if he's half dead from being dragged over these rocks." He turned to Nathan. "Down the cave?"

Nathan set his hands on his hips. His holster was empty, the bright silver mass of his revolver tucked into Hodges' gun belt. "There's a pool of water at the bottom."

Ben smiled as he leaned toward Nathan. "And what else?"

"Two rules."

Ben's eyes narrowed. "Let me guess. You'd sooner take those rules, the cripple, and your daughter to the grave than tell me right here and now."

Nathan rested his hand over the special pocket of his vest that held his book. "I'll tell you at the water or not at all."

Ben waved the party forward and they made their way down the length of the tunnel, some of the deputies tripping and staggering over the broken rocks along the floor. Twice the men carrying Kyle toppled over, causing Kyle to scream in pain. Hodges lost his patience the second time and knocked Kyle out with a single vicious punch. Angela fought against the deputy holding her until her father shouted for her to stop. Ben shook his head in frustration as he snapped at his men to hoist Kyle's now limp mass and carry him the rest of the way.

It seemed a lifetime to Angela since she had walked the length of the tunnel with her father. If her life had changed with that first descent, she knew her whole world, her very existence, was changing with every step of this second descent. Whether or not her life would come to its final end in the ghostly twilight of the pool was of little concern to her.

She was too angry to care. The only question in her mind was how she could kill Ben and his deputies before her own life was forfeit. Given her situation, it seemed insane to think she could inflict so much as a single cut, but her hate burned bright in the cauldron of irony fueled by one simple, twisted fact.

Her father had betrayed her in every conceivable way. At the same time, she refused to believe her father would turn over Thetis Springs to Ben and his ilk. The only choice, then, was to trust her father, trust his foresight, and trust that he had some last, hidden plan.

Then and only then she could kill him, too.

‡ ‡ ‡

"What's with that light?" one of the deputies said, pointing to the pool.

Ben lowered the man's arm and stared at Nathan. "Now. Tell me these two rules."

Nathan held up his hand and raised a finger. "Don't stay in the water but for a few moments." He raised a second finger. "Never return to the water once you've left."

Ben set a wary gaze on Nathan. "How long were you in the water?"

Nathan looked up at the faint echoes surrounding them. "A few moments."

Ben stroked his beard. "How long was Calliope in the water?"

"Longer than any of us."

"I'll take that as explanation enough." His gaze settled on the water. "Now tell me what happens if you go back for a second baptism."

"It's best if I show you." Nathan pointed to the coat-sack. "I can't go in. Neither can my daughter. To prove the veracity of the rule, however, there is the matter of her arm. If you let me remove it, I can show you what you need to see, so that you never suffer the temptation to return to the water, and so that you never suffer the seduction of thinking I've somehow duped you to cheat you of further potential."

Ben hesitated several moments before nodding. "Hodges. Give him the sack."

Nathan took the coat-sack. He shot a quick glance at Angela as he turned to the edge of the pool. The deputies shifted on their feet, but Nathan smiled at them. "There's no need to fear. Her arm will be quite tame this close to the water. Isn't that true, Angela?"

Everyone turned to her. She frowned before acquiescing with a nod of defeat.

Ben tipped his head. "Go on then, Reverend."

Nathan crouched by the edge of the pool. With care he undid the knot of his coat sleeves and folded back the crumpled mass of the coat until the arm was revealed. He fixed a quick grasp on the wrist as if he were snatching up a serpent and took its tail in his other hand. With theatrical flair, he held it up to show the deputies before turning toward the pool. The arm tightened in his grasp as his hands neared the water. He shushed its sinewy length.

Angela took a breath. The two deputies carrying Kyle dumped him to the floor. Still unconscious, he made no sound. The deputy who kept Angela throttled drove her to her knees so that he could rest a hand on his sidearm.

She closed her eyes to focus on her arm.

The hand opened, the one green eye nestled in its palm staring back at Nathan. He nudged his chin to his hand where he held the far end of her arm. The hand turned around in his grasp to see his hand open and stiffen against the toe of his boot.

It was an ideal launching platform.

Ben took a step. "What are you doing there? Get on with it."

Nathan looked over his shoulder to Ben. "As you wish." He leaned toward the water. The arm coiled in his hands. When he could compress it no more, he let his right hand snap open beneath its wrist.

The arm shot free, flying past Ben as he ducked aside. Angela threw her weight back to tip the deputy throttling her. Her hand opened, latched onto the throat of one of the other deputies, and tore out the flesh. She thrust her foot in a vicious kick to buckle her deputy's knees. The man went down with a shout. Nathan dove for the nearest deputy and wrestled for the man's sidearm.

Angela's arm sprang forward once more as the deputies opened fire in the shadowy twilight. Gun blasts reverberated in the cavern as her arm speared into a man's side, wrapped its length around his arm for leverage, and then tore its hand free with a spurting mess of entrails in its grasp.

The deputy Angela had crippled reached for his gun. Free of his hold she rolled over, slapped her legs around his neck, and threw her hips in a violent heave to snap his neck. Nathan got hold of the sidearm of the man he had tackled, twisted the gun into the man's gut, and fired to still the man's resistance.

Ben got to his feet and staggered back, shooting wildly amid the dizzying flashes and befuddling, deafening echoes of gunfire. He ran behind Hodges, dropping with a gasp as Angela's arm slapped itself around Hodges' neck and ripped his face from his skull. Shocked to his senses, Ben stuck his arm out toward Nathan and fired blindly as he made a dash toward Kyle's prone form. Nathan rose to a crouch by the deputy he had killed, only to gasp as one of Ben's rounds hit him and knocked him back.

Angela beat her heels into the man she killed to get free of his body. Her arm quaked as Hodges made a last desperate attempt to save his life. His arm snapped up and fired. The round grazed her arm before punching into his skull. A red geyser burst from the top of his head as he dropped to his knees and flopped dead to the floor of the cave.

The last deputy turned to run. Nathan lifted his arm and shot once, hitting the man square between the shoulders, causing him to stagger and wheeze. Angela rolled to her feet, charged the deputy, and threw her shoulder into him to knock him on his side. No sooner was he down than she planted her shoulder to the floor, rose up on one knee, and thrust her other knee forward to crush the deputy's windpipe. He convulsed against her as she ground her knee into his neck. After several thrashes he went limp beneath her weight.

Kyle gasped as Ben splashed into the pool. Ben shouted, his wordless cry bouncing about the cavern as he dragged Kyle out to the depths. Kyle struggled against Ben's clutch of his shirt collar, coughing against the water that flooded his mouth.

Angela gained her feet and ran to the edge of the pool. Her arm unwound from Hodges' neck, coiled up her leg, and joined her shoulder. The wave of solace to once again be whole was dispelled as she watched Ben paddle away.

She clenched her fist. "Bring him back!"

Nathan rolled over and clutched the wound on his side. He pulled back the hammer of his stolen revolver and took aim.

Ben's eyes were wide and wild. "Shoot me and the cripple drowns!"

Angela spun to her father.

Nathan staggered to the edge of the pool, his arm leveled at Ben, before he sank to his knees. After a moment his arm sank as well. He spat a wad of blood to his side. "Ben! You'll die if you stay in too long."

"Then the cripple dies with me," Ben said, fighting to stay afloat with the ragged weight of Kyle's body.

Angela looked down at her arm. She forced it to coil against her side. When she turned to let it loose, it shrank against her chest. Aghast at a seeming treachery she had never foreseen, her gaze dropped to her arm. The hand turned and opened, the single green eye glaring back at her.

"It's too far," her father wheezed. "It'll never make it."

She glared into her palm. "You have to try. You have to try!"

Ben thrust his legs to get his head clear for a breath. "Back off! Leave the cave and I'll bring the cripple out."

Her arm shrank against her chest. It wouldn't budge. She turned to her father, her eyes filled with expectation.

He stared at her. "You know we can't let Ben out of here." He tossed aside the stolen revolver and fetched his trusted sidearm from Hodges' belt. "You know he has to die."

She trembled. "Kyle will drown!"

Ben raised his gun from the water. The trigger clicked, but the soaked weapon refused to fire. Frustrated, he threw it aside as useless weight.

Her father stared at her. "Kyle doesn't have to drown."

She shrank from him. The moment had come, the moment he had foretold with such terrible portent, the horrible apocalyptic moment when she would have to throw her indignation aside, cast off her vengeance, and ask the one thing she swore she would never ask.

She needed his help. She needed his help or Kyle would die. She remembered her father's fateful words.

His life rests in my hands.

The prophecy reverberated in her with the ferocity of hammer blows between the echoes of splashing water. She remembered the wall behind her bedroom door where she kept the hash marks made with her thick pencil, the pencil Ivan had made for her so she could keep track of time. Now she felt the rub of the pencil on the wall, felt it move with agonizing slowness as seconds plowed past her, plowed through her, pressing her, compressing her, squeezing her until two words burst through her hate and resentment like puss from an abscess.

Every fiber in her body quivered in revolt to utter those two words. Even so, it was hard to believe as the world silenced about her to let her delicate whisper deafen her with the ferocity of a thunderclap.

"Daddy, please?"

Nathan stood. He took aim. Ben's face drew into a state of bewilderment as Nathan fired. The bullet sliced open Kyle's right ear before shattering Ben's face. He sank beneath the water, Kyle disappearing with him. Angela moved, only to recoil as her toe hit the water. A bolt of pain rocketed up her leg to almost knock her off her feet.

Her father dove into the pool. She stumbled back before charging to the water's edge. He surfaced, gasping and gurgling as blood spurted from his mouth, but on he went until he dove once more to retrieve Kyle's sinking form. A moment later he surfaced, paddling like a madman toward the shore. Blood seeped from under his clothes, leaving an ever-darkening red wake as he pressed forward.

Angela grabbed Hodges, dragged him to the water's edge, and used his corpse as an extension of dry ground to grab Kyle's collar and pull him onto the rocks. Her father came out, struggling on his hands and knees, even as his flesh bubbled and erupted in bloody sores. She pulled Kyle away, desperate to keep him from her father's ruin.

Nathan croaked, retched, and arced upward on his knees as his body contorted. Red vomit burst from his mouth in a violent spray. His shirt bulged before coming free of his pants, his entrails toppling from his body in a steaming red slosh of tissue. He held for a moment, swaying on his knees, before his femurs popped loose of his dissolving pelvis. The bones tore out from his ragged flesh as his body collapsed on itself and left him a contorted mess held together by nothing more than his clothes.

It was impossible for Angela to look away. Horrible as it was to watch her father's demise, she was nevertheless frozen in the grandiose agony of his doom. His arms contracted to his chest as his ribs let out sickening snaps and pops. In the last moment before his body flattened to a pool of steaming red fluids, his right arm shot out to his side.

A wet breath rattled in his chest. Somehow, some way, the spark of life still clung to what remained of his body. His bloodshot eyes rolled over to fix on her. "Saved him," he rasped. "For you."

She stared at him. For a moment she forgot his sins before the glaring triumph of his incomprehensible agony. She had once sworn that she would hate him to his last moment. Like so many things, though, the anticipation of a moment and its fulfillment can be alien worlds separated by an unimaginable gulf.

She had his death, but only for Kyle's life. The joy of retribution rang hollow in balance to an eternal gratitude she could not forsake. Her stomach knotted until she heard the unavoidable, inescapable words slip from her mouth, a reply so subtle it seemed more like a thought until it echoed back to her.

Thank you.

She squeezed her eyes shut.

Thank you.

Something like a single, small laugh gurgled in his throat.

Thank you.

Between the echoes of her fateful words she discerned the weak rasp of his voice. "Finish it," he whispered. "Finish it."

She forced her eyes open to behold him one last time. His head lolled so that his blank gaze was fixed on the roof of the cavern. Darkness filled his sight as his life drained away. Bit by bit his eyelids drooped until they at last closed. Two trails of blood, loose and diluted with tears, seeped from under his eyelids to sear the raw angles of his denuded cheeks.

Such was the passing of Reverend Nathan Purdy. From the water his foresight had come and to the water it returned, thus closing the circle of his life.

His fingers fell free of his hand to reveal the wet mass of his precious book.

For some time Angela found herself incapable of anything other than a hypnotic stare at her father's remains. The cave was quiet but for the gentle rustle of Kyle's breaths between her tight gasps. By force of will she moved, reaching past Kyle to grab the leather-bound volume. It was slick with her father's dissolution, but such disgust was lost to her as she held that last secret in her hand, the secret he had thrust toward her with his final measure of life.

Her hand shook as she opened the old leather cover. The pages were yellowed, stained with blood and translucent from their soaking in the pool, but what they held was of greater impact to her than the pain lancing her fingers from contacting the wet paper.

After all the years, after all the mystery, her father's most treasured possession held but one message for her to discover. It was no more than a single word.

Not just any word, though, but one particular word; and not just one particular word, but a name.

Angela.

Over and over he had written her name to fill every page.

She sank to her side and wept.

29

‡ ‡ ‡

It wasn't long before Angela found herself staring at the roof of the cavern. Kyle was still unconscious. She knew he would slumber as the water worked on him. All of night's long, shapeless hours might pass before he stirred.

Her arm was restless. It left her shoulder to slink about the cavern, each time staring toward the world outside before returning to her. And each time it returned, her hand opened for the single eye to stare back at her, an unblinking stare as expectation seeped into her body and transformed to trepidation. Perhaps, she wondered, it was the source of her lassitude. Deep down, though, she knew there was no denying what waited to be done.

Finish it.

It was a simple thought to be laden with such horrible portent.

Finish it.

There was no choice in the matter. She knew what had to be done, regardless of whether she felt conviction or trepidation. What beckoned to her was far bigger than she was, yet at the same time, she realized it was dependent on her alone to fulfill.

She rolled over, blessed Kyle with a gentle kiss on his forehead, and left the cave.

‡ ‡ ‡

She sped through the night, prodding Buttercup to run with everything the horse's legs could offer. Regular glances to the stars and moon served as a guide, and Angela's familiarity with the land allowed her to guide Buttercup away from anything that might hurt her in the darkness. Soon enough she rounded a grove of trees, crested a hill, and came to a stop.

The stargrazers lifted their heads and looked at her. In turn she let her arm go and watched it race across the turf until it came to the water's edge and rested its green-eyed gaze upon the beasts. The wide rims of their nostrils fluttered as they blew out a collective breath.

Angela gave Buttercup a gentle tap of her heels to nudge her forward. The horse was hesitant, perhaps intimidated with the proximity of the stargrazers' might, and would only go half the distance to the resting lake before making a determined stop and shaking her head.

Still, the stargrazers did not move.

Angela cleared her throat. "Hey," she called through the still night. "Abigail. Clara Belle. Emily. Ella Mae." She stopped to remember the fifth name. When it hit her, she recalled it was Ivan's favorite of his sisters, and she was struck with sadness for the loss of her dear friend. She cleared her throat to find her voice. "Bessie."

Her arm looked at her. It turned to the stargrazers and darted back and forth along the shore. One by one the animals began to follow the dance of her arm. When it had their attention, it coiled and sprang back to Angela in three vaults to rejoin her shoulder.

Angela sat in her saddle. The wait was insufferable. "Hey!"

One of the animals shook its head. It shifted, rose to a stance, and nudged its fellows. Together, they plodded from the water, shaking the ground as they neared to stand before Angela.

"Good," she said with a nod. Her hand grabbed the reins. Together, they led Buttercup around.

There was only one direction to go. She rode due east, with the stargrazers in tow.

Somewhere ahead, Deepwick sat, unaware of what drew near.

‡ ‡ ‡

She wasn't sure how close she was until the stargrazers began to grunt with agitation and pick up their pace. Without warning they let out blasts of air from their mighty lungs, lowered their heads, and drew abreast for a charge. The impact of their hooves almost knocked Angela from Buttercup's back, and the poor horse all but flew to get clear of the stampede. Angela wrestled with the reins to keep the horse under control, drawing far aside from the stargrazers as they stormed past her. She gave them some distance before Buttercup would consent to keeping chase.

The stargrazers were lost ahead of her, disappearing over one of the innumerable folds of the rolling landscape. Angela kept on until her arm tugged at the reins to bring Buttercup to a halt.

Frustrated, she glared at her arm. The hand turned to her, the eye popping open before the hand turned once more to jab a pointed finger to the distance. There was no hiding what she had hoped to instigate. She remembered what Kyle had said of the townspeople, about the way they lived and, of greater importance, what they ate for sustenance. They butcher anything on four legs. She remembered as well what Ivan told her the day they had worked in the milking basket, that there was only one thing that riled the stargrazers—the smell of beef, the scent of their sisters under the butcher's blade.

The water of Thetis Springs had made the stargrazers mighty in their primitive inclination to see size as security. Perhaps, somewhere in the luminous depths of the water, an agenda had been at work too sublime for even her father's foresight to discover. Then again, maybe what was about to happen was a precise fulfillment of what he had foreseen. Once again, the past echoed through the present to the near future as the future looped back to the past.

The enormity of it numbed her mind.

She looked up. The darkness trembled with the heavy drumbeat of the stargrazers' charge. Something different came to her then, a different set of sounds rising up between the thunderous roll of hoof impacts reverberating through the soil. It took a moment before she could decipher what she heard. When she understood, though, her arm coiled against her side.

It was the sound of timbers shattering. In between there was another sound, a horrible sound; a sound that echoed back from her arm's first memory after her birth.

It was the sound of screams, of terrified, panic-laden screams.

She looked at her hand. "For all his lies, he was right," she whispered. "The land can't suffer two kinds of people."

Her hand closed and nuzzled to her chest.

It was a choice between her and Kyle or the townspeople. It didn't take foresight to know that choice had but one outcome. She sat, listening to the destruction. One by one the screams quieted, some of them cut short with the stomp of a massive hoof. Soon enough all was quiet but for the intermittent pops and cracks of burning wood.

I have the strength to be just in my wickedness and wicked in my justice.

The stargrazers marched past her, their massive bodies backlit by the yellowish glow of the town's immolation. The creatures looked at her and bobbed their heads as they returned to the night. Glowing embers drifted like fireflies on the gentle breeze.

Alone, she sat in the dark before a scene of apocalyptic devastation.

She couldn't help but know herself as anything other than her father's daughter.

‡ ‡ ‡

Dawn was yet to take purchase on the Range when she returned to the cavern. Exhausted, she staggered down to the water, curled up beside Kyle, and fell fast asleep.

"Angela."

She struggled to open her eyes. It took a moment to remember where she lay until the discomfort of the rocks beneath her summoned her senses.

The cave. The water. Daddy . . .

She lifted her head. Kyle was crouched before her, his head down. His shirt was loose, draped over his shoulders like a blanket. A single, silvery bead of water clung to the end of his nose.

"Kyle?" She pushed up with her arm to sit before him. "Are you . . ."

He held up a finger to silence her. "Angela," he whispered. "I don't know who I am."

"You're Kyle," she said, wary of his failure to meet her gaze. "You're my Kyle. You're all I have left."

"Am I?" His body swelled with a deep breath. "I'm not what I was."

She stared at him, unsure what to say. His hand rose to pull the shirt from his shoulders and toss it aside. Only then did she realize he had shed the rest of his clothes. Her gaze snapped back to him. "Kyle, look at me. Please?"

"No. First look at me, and tell me if I'm still me."

His shoulders flexed as he splayed his hands and planted them on the cavern floor. With his head still down he took a breath, tensed, and straightened his legs. His body unfurled from his crouch to a full stance before her, his skin glistening in the twilight glow of the cave. Bare before her, he kept his head down until he stood straight. After a moment he lifted his chin and opened his eyes upon her. "Now tell me, who do you see?"

She stared at him, struck dumb by his transformation. Her throat clucked as she struggled to swallow and find her voice.

"You're my Kyle," she said again.

"Am I?" He looked down at his body. "I've known myself like this in my dreams, but I never dreamed it could be." His gaze returned to her. "Who am I?"

She stood, staring into his eyes as she rose before him. His face filled with trepidation as she studied him, his gaze sinking as her hand settled on his chest. The moment she felt the warmth of his skin, she pressed her hand flat against him.

The beat of his heart rose through her arm.

She looked up to meet his waiting stare. "You're my Kyle," she said, pronouncing it for the third time with authority. The proclamation echoed back, wrapping around and through them as they both felt its reverberation moving between their bodies to enmesh them in the same collapsing moment of her father's prophetic vision realized in full.

She remembered the question that had struck her at the Eddington house.

How do you fight a man who possesses foresight?

Her mind cleared to perceive the answer.

You don't have to.

The future, present, and past merged in the soft echoes of water dripping from the roof of the cavern. Ripples of sound, ripples of water, ripples of fate; they were all circles moving through each other. There was no need to fight her father's foresight. He saw only what his ego desired to see, despite ambitions born of any higher aspects of his personality.

A sight of fate or a fateful sight? It was a simple play of words, an echo of its own thought, an inversion of its own nature.

There was, she realized, a word for such a thing. A word she could use to answer Kyle and put his insecurity to rest once and for all, even as it followed its own ironic inversion to ground his humility for the rest of his days.

"Angela?" His eyes took on a plaintive cast. "How can you be so certain?"

"I know it's you because you've become what I always believed you to be."

"What's that?"

She smiled. "Perfect."

30

‡ ‡ ‡

It was evening and Angela Eddington rested in one of the chairs on the front porch of her house. Kyle sat in the chair beside her, holding her hand as they waited for the stars to reveal themselves.

Life had grown comfortable in the years since those chaotic days of her old life. As her father's sole heir, the Range was hers, no questions asked. Not that anyone asked questions, because there was no one in all the lands around them. If any townspeople had survived the stargrazers' charge, it was certain they never ventured back to rebuild Deepwick. Towns came and went on the land. The vanishing of one little town wilting on the tree of progress wouldn't draw any attention. No, the Outsiders would move on, move away, and find some other place to desecrate.

In the meantime the Range was free of their filth.

Angela and Kyle didn't see their lives as lonely. Their childhoods had been fostered in parallel seclusion, so the emptiness of the Range was something very different to them, inhabited by something they decided to call the serenity of solitude. When they hungered for adventure, they rode across the Range's expanse for days at a time. When they hungered for something more, they went to Kyle's books. There were more worlds of wonder waiting for them in his thick volumes than they could ever venture to explore on their own.

They felt no urge to leave the Range.

There was no need, after all. Angela knew that for all her father's madness, for all his crimes, she had come to understand the truth he had sought to summon, the truth he had sacrificed his life to bring into reality, that had formed the conviction that had burned him with such white-hot intensity.

He had once told her the land could not suffer the stains of the impure. Purged of all but Kyle and Angela, singular creatures constituted in ways like no others that roamed the Earth, the land no longer suffered. The bitter irony of her father's fateful foresight was his own enclosure in its doom. Sometimes, at night, she wondered if he had been so blinded by his ego that he had failed to see his own pending doom, or if he had been so enamored with the power of his vision that he had sought to bleach his own sins from the land through a demise of epic proportions. She knew such a prospect would have found a happy home in the black pit of his vanity. If he had to die to bring forth his vision—to vindicate his vision—then he would suffer nothing less than a death of epic proportion.

Either way, they were thoughts of only passing interest to her, lost in those half-numbed moments of darkness before sleep stole her away and banished such idle concerns to the shapeless shadows of night.

Big things are best left to themselves.

She had reached a simple conclusion, a conclusion that set her free of everything but the lingering loss she felt for her mother and Ivan.

The seasons change . . . and will change yet again.

Kyle and Angela looked at each other. The notion of the change floated over their tidal resolve of serenity without a single trace of its passing. Like the waters hidden in their secret cave, they too were imbued with an eternal, mirror-like calm. And like the water that unified their existence, when the season of change came to visit, they would stay pure, hidden behind the world's reflection.

In the meantime a plate of tea cakes beckoned from the warmth of their home.

###

A note from the author...

I would like to take a moment to thank you, the reader of this book, for taking the time to follow Angela's story. I hope it brought as much enjoyment to you as it brought me in its writing.

For those of you familiar with my other books, you've noticed I like to do something a little different with every story I write. With *Angela's Arm* I went to a realm I've always wanted to portray, although in Angela's story it was seen through the tight lens of her experiences on the Range. The setting therefore served a two-fold purpose, to anchor the book in a certain time period and to provide isolation for Nathan Purdy's ambitions.

As you know by now this is not a gentle story; indeed, this was not a gentle period of history. The backdrop of Indian massacres, slave labor and exploitation of Chinese immigrants, and the various vices of the 1870's midwest are more than convenient window draping. Rather, they were worked into the narrative for the specific purpose of contrast to the life Nathan tried to create and yet show the hidden moral rot that is part of the human condition, as evidenced by Nathan's misdeeds and moral hypocrisy.

For more insight on the creation of *Angela's Arm*, visit my website at www.rolandallnach.com.

In the meantime, authors rely on the enthusiasm of their readers, so a kind review or simple social message about a book can go a long way toward a book's success. I will say in advance that you have my sincere gratitude.

Thanks for reading... Roland Allnach

About the Author

After more than twenty years of hospital night shifts, Roland Allnach has witnessed life from a slightly different angle. He's been working to develop his writing career, drawing creatively from literary classics, history, and mythology.

His short stories, one of which was nominated for the Pushcart Prize, have appeared in many publications. His first anthology, *Remnant*, blending science fiction and speculative fiction, saw publication in 2010. In 2012 he followed with *Oddities & Entities*, a collection spanning the supernatural, paranormal, horror and speculative genres. His third book, *Prism*, published in 2014, follows a winding road through diverse genres and narrative forms. In 2015 he saw publication of two more books, the dystopian science fiction novel *The Digital Now* and the his first foray into nonfiction with *The Writer's Primer: A Practical Guide for Aspiring Authors Seeking Publication*. In 2016 he returned to stranger realms with *Oddities & Entities 2: Vessels*.

Roland's books have received unanimous critical praise and have been honored with more than a dozen national book awards, including honors from National Indie Excellence, Foreword Reviews, Readers' Favorite, Feathered Quill Reviews, Pacific Book Review and Book Excellence Awards

Roland is an active member of his local literary community on Long Island, New York. He serves as president of Long Island Authors Group, representing more than 70 Long Island authors. He also implemented and manages the Group's Traveling Bookstore, which tours local town fairs and has appeared the last two years at the prestigious Brooklyn Book Festival. This effort placed the Group's books and authors in front of 100,000 people in the first year alone. Roland has also been on national and local television, terrestrial and internet radio, and has conducted presentations on publishing at local libraries and art venues.

When not immersed in his imagination, Roland can be found at his website, rolandallnach.com, along with a wealth of information about his stories and experiences as an author. Writing aside, his joy in life is the time he spends with his family.